With thanks to Bec and Rob

CHAPTER
one

The silver bell above the door chimed, a soft sound that complemented the singing coming from the café's small kitchen.

I looked down from my perch on a ladder across the other side of the dining room, where I was hanging fairy lights. The woman who entered was tall, brown-haired, and wrapped in a vivid red coat so bulky it hid the shape of her body. Her complexion was pale, her face angular and, aside from the color of her coat, she looked no different to the half dozen other women who'd entered the café since we'd opened yesterday.

But the psychic bit of me—the bit that had caused so much damn heartache in the past—began to stir.

This woman was trouble. The sort of trouble I'd been running from for the past twelve years.

Her gaze swept the room, no doubt taking in the mismatched furniture, the bright prints and old plates that covered the walls, and the small teapots of flowers that decorated each table.

What she thought of it all, I couldn't say, because when her gaze finally met mine, all I could see was her fear and anguish. The force of it was so strong, it wrapped a fist around my heart and squeezed tight.

I don't need this, I thought. *Not now, not again.*

I hardly think this woman's problems are going to be that bad, Lizzie. The comment ran through my mind so clearly it might well have been said out loud. *It surely can't hurt to at least hear what she has to say.*

Isabelle—the singer in the kitchen and my closest friend—was not only a spirit talker gifted with telepathy, but also my familiar, and *that* meant we had constant access to each other's thoughts. Not all witches had familiars, of course—only those of us born to blueblood families. I had no idea why that was, but I suspected it had something to do with the greater power most bluebloods could call on. Familiars were usually of the animal or spirit kind, but I was at best a less than average blueblood witch, so of course my familiar was always destined to be something so far south of the norm it was yet another disappointment to my family.

I had a very long history of letting my family down— one that had started with my birth.

You say that with such surety, I replied, mental tone dry. *Anyone would think precognition was one of your gifts.*

Her sharp snort echoed through my brain. *It doesn't take precognition to make a statement like that. I was with you twelve years ago, remember? Nothing could ever be as bad as that. Nothing.*

The woman took several tentative steps forward and then stopped. "I'm looking for Elizabeth Grace."

Her voice was as uncertain as her steps. I hooked the unstrung portion of fairy lights onto the ladder and then climbed down. "Please, just call me Lizzie. What can I do for you, Mrs.—?"

"Banks. Marjorie Banks. And I'm sorry to come here so late, but I saw your light on and I just thought—" She paused, and then continued in a desperate sort of rush, "I just thought you might be able to help me find my daughter."

A runaway, Belle said. *That's hardly dangerous.*

Maybe.

Well, if you wanted to avoid any chance of the past repeating itself, we should be running an ordinary café rather than playing about with psychometry, dabbling in readings, and selling charms.

Psychometry isn't magic. And it wasn't as if the charms we were selling did anything more than grant the wearer a greater chance of collecting good fortune rather than bad.

But those charms still contain real magic, even if we don't advertise it, Belle said. *And it's a sad fact that those without psi skills often align them to magic. Besides, it's not like psychometry or charm making are your only skills.*

No, but it wasn't like I was much more than the sum of those two, either. Hell, my lack of magical strength was one of the reasons behind my estrangement from my family.

That, and my sister's death.

Cat's death, Belle stated, mental tone tart, *was hardly your fault.*

But it *was*, if only because I'd tried to save her myself rather than informing my parents.

Your parents would not have listened.

But I could have at least tried. If we'd both insisted, Mom might have investigated—

My input wouldn't have made any difference. I'm your familiar, and one of the lowly Sarr witches besides.

Unfortunately, there was a bitter edge of truth in that statement. There were six lines of witches—three of whom were considered "royalty," and three who were rather disparagingly described as "commoners."

Like most of those from the lower witch houses, Belle hadn't always viewed my family in such a dour light. In fact, she'd held the so-called bluebloods of witchery on something of a pedestal. That had all changed in the aftermath of Cat's death.

I stepped clear of the ladder and brushed some dust from my hands. "How old is your daughter, Mrs. Banks?"

"Please, call me Marjorie. And she's sixteen. She went out with friends last night, but she hasn't come home and I know—" She paused again, and swallowed heavily. "Something has happened to her. I can feel it."

The certainty in her tone had my gaze narrowing. Underneath the pall of misery that hung around her body like a heavy cloak were flashes of hazy purple, and *that* was usually the sign of an untrained talent. Of course, her certainty could also be nothing more than the deep connection of a mother to her daughter.

Either way, this really *wasn't* something I should be getting involved in. "Mrs. Banks, you really need to report this to the rangers—"

"I *have*," she said. "And they're looking, but it's not enough. I know it's not enough—"

She broke off, obviously battling tears. I hesitated, then walked over and tentatively put an arm around her shoulders. She stiffened briefly, and then her body sagged and she started sobbing. I didn't say anything; there was little that *could* be said other than the usual useless platitudes, and she'd undoubtedly already heard those from the rangers.

After a while, she pulled back and dug a tissue out of her purse. "I'm sorry. That was very ill-mannered of me."

"But totally understandable." I kept my voice soft. I had a bad feeling a full breakdown was only one harsh word away. "How about I make us pot of tea, and then you can tell me about your daughter?"

Hope flared in her brown eyes. "Then you'll help me?"

I hesitated. "I don't know if I can." Which was an honest enough answer, but not something she wanted to hear right now. As her face began to crumple again, I quickly added, "But I'll try."

Do you want me out there? Belle said. *Or are you going to use the reading room?*

I hesitated again. When we'd decided to offer psychic readings as well as the usual café fare in an effort to establish a point of difference from all the other cafés in Castle Rock, we'd set up a small rear room strictly designed for that purpose. As such, it was not only a soothing space to be in, but also one that was magically well protected.

But most of those spells had been specifically designed to counter arcane forces, and wouldn't actually repel the dark, desperate energy Marjorie was emitting. It was the sort of energy that could draw even darker emotions to it, and I really didn't want to risk infecting the warm, safe environment we'd created in the reading room.

I think it might be wise if you are, Belle, just in case things go ass up. Out loud, I added, "Mrs. Banks, do you mind if I call my friend in to help me when I attempt it?"

Marjorie frowned. "Is it necessary? I really don't want

the whole town knowing I've come to you for help. It would be… inconvenient."

"Belle is co-owner of the café," I said, "and the soul of discretion."

Your parents wouldn't agree with that.

My parents didn't agree with a lot of things, especially when it came to the two of us. They hated Belle almost as much as they hated the fact they'd bred a daughter so low down on the scale of magical ability that I might as well have been born to one of the more common lines.

"If you really think it's necessary—"

"It *is* if you want a better chance of the reading being successful."

"Then I agree."

"Thank you." I cupped a hand under her elbow and escorted her across to a table. "How do you like your tea? And would like something to eat? Belle's just baked a fresh batch of rather decadent red velvet cookies."

She wiped a tear from the corner of her left eye. "That would be lovely, thank you."

"Cookies for three please, Belle," I said, and made my way behind the counter to make a large pot of tea. When that was done, I wasted several more minutes studying the multitude of cheery china cups and saucers, trying to decide which ones to use. Like most of the items in the café, we'd salvaged them from various secondhand stores, and they all had a history and a presence the sensitive could feel. While most people would scoff at the thought of something as simple as a cup making any sort of difference to a person's mood, I knew from experience that the *wrong* choice could have an unsettling effect in this sort of situation. Even though the holiday season was still over a month away, I eventually selected cheery Christmas ones for Belle and me, and a more ornate white and gold cup for Marjorie.

"Right," I said, as I placed the full tray on the table between us. "Tell me what you know."

"That's just it," Marjorie said. "I don't know much. No one does. And no one will believe me when I say she's—"

She stopped, her gaze going past me and widening just a fraction. I knew without looking that Belle had just entered, because by anyone's standards, she was a sight to behold. At just over six foot and with an athlete's physique, she was something of an Amazon. She was also stunningly beautiful, with ebony skin, long, silky black hair, and eyes that were a gray so pale they shone silver in even the dullest of light.

That eye color was the one feature all six witch families had in common, and I couldn't even get *that* right. Mine were emerald green, the same as my grandmother's.

"Mrs. Banks?" I prompted when she didn't immediately continue.

Belle placed a small plate of red cookies on the tray and then began pouring our drinks. Hints of lemon and passionflower teased the air; it wasn't strong enough to overpower the taste of the English Breakfast tea, but it would, hopefully, help soothe the older woman's jangled nerves.

Marjorie cleared her throat and said, "They don't believe she's in trouble. They just think she's run off again."

"So she's run away before?" I asked.

"It was a regular event when her father and I first separated, but it had stopped until about two months ago."

"What happened to set her off again?"

"I wouldn't let her go out with her boyfriend." She accepted the cup of tea with a tremulous smile. "My mother had a set like this. She used to bring it out when we were having a 'proper' English afternoon tea."

Which was why I'd chosen it. While this particular cup hadn't belonged to Marjorie's mother's set, as far as I was aware, something about its resonance had suggested it would raise happier memories—and Marjorie very much needed those.

I offered the older woman the milk jug, then, when she shook her head, poured some into my own tea. Two teaspoons of sugar followed rather than the usual one, as I suspected I was going to need the energy boost to get through the night. "Is there a chance she's simply run off with the boyfriend?"

Marjorie shook her head even before I'd finished the question. "The first thing I did was ring and check with his mom. Jason is home, and hasn't heard from Karen in over a week."

"Is that usual?" Belle asked.

Marjorie shrugged. "Who can say? They're teenagers. One day they can't keep their hands off each other, the next they're not talking."

"What about her friends? She did go out with them, didn't she?" I said.

"Yes, but they said she got a call about nine and claimed it was from me. That I said she had to go home." Tears filled Marjorie's eyes and she rapidly blinked them away. "It wasn't me, of course, and that's the last time anyone saw her."

Which sounded suspiciously like Karen was meeting someone she either didn't want her friends to know about, or that she knew they wouldn't approve of. If I'd been a cop, the first thing I would have done was get hold of the kid's phone records. But I wasn't, and I had no idea if the rangers here had that sort of power. Castle Rock was the capital of the Faelan Reservation, which was one of only seven werewolf reservations here in Australia. Rangers—who were always werewolves nominated by the council elders rather than those who lived within the reservation—had full police powers when it came to dealing with their own kind, but were somewhat more restricted when it came to the humans living within the reservation. Which was rather archaic, given humans now accounted for nearly 40 percent of Castle Rock's regular population—and that figure increased dramatically over the summer months, thanks to the mineral springs located in the nearby town of Argyle.

Of course, archaic pretty much described the world in general. There might have been huge leaps in technology and medicine, but magic and tradition still ruled in many ways.

And what *that* all meant was, if something bad *had* happened to Karen, then the rangers would be forced to call in the Interspecies Investigations Team. And *that* wouldn't go down well with either the rangers *or* the pack elders.

And unhappy elders generally meant an unhappy town.

I took a sip of tea and winced a little over its sweetness. "Are the rangers searching for her?"

"Yes. I asked them to send some trackers into the scrub."

Meaning Marjorie had some pull in this town. But given the hills surrounding Castle Rock were heavily forested, a werewolf's keen nose probably *was* Karen's best hope if she was lost out there somewhere. "Then I suggest your next move should be to go home and wait for their call—"

"No! I can't. I *won't*." Marjorie's expression was a mix of desperation and determination. "Surely you can understand that? Surely, if you were in my place, you'd be doing everything you can to find your child?"

Old pain rose, and I briefly closed my eyes. I *had* been in the same position, even if the life in question had been that of a sister rather than a daughter.

The past is never a good place to dwell, Belle said gently. *Especially when there's nothing you can do to change it.*

I knew that, but knowing never stopped the guilt. Never stopped the nightmares that still plagued me. I took a somewhat shuddery breath and said, "I do understand, Marjorie, believe me. It's just that—"

"*Please*," she said, her voice soft. Beseeching. "You're Karen's only hope. I just know it."

I leaned back and rubbed my arms. Every instinct I had was screaming *any* search—be it mine, or the rangers'—was going to end badly. Was it selfish of me to *not* want to confront all that again? Probably. But the real question was—could I live with the guilt and the what-ifs if I *did* walk away?

Probably not.

Besides, the moment I'd allowed Marjorie to step through the door and tell me her story, I'd basically forsaken any hope of refusal. Hard-hearted, I was not.

"No matter how certain you might be," I said slowly, "there's no guarantee that I'll be able to find her. Psychometry—or any other psi talent, for that matter— isn't always as reliable as true magic. Maybe you'd be better to seek the help of the local witch—"

"There *is* no witch in Castle Rock," she cut in. "The elders declared the reservation a witch-free zone just over a year ago."

I shared a surprise glance with Belle. *That* was something we hadn't been aware of when we'd come here, and it made me wonder why they'd approved our permit for the café. Granted, it was now an accepted fact that psi skills were totally unrelated to mainstream magic, but—as Belle had noted—there were still many who thought otherwise.

How could the elders even pass such a rule, let alone want to? It was a government requirement that a witch be present on all reservations. Aside from providing magical assistance when needed, they were also the government's mouthpieces and rule enforcers. But it was the magic aspect of the situation that made the decision even more surprising. Castle Rock was filled with wild magic, and it was very dangerous to leave such a force unguarded for too long. While wild magic in and of itself was neither good nor bad, without a witch to protect and channel it, it *would* be a draw to the darker forces of the world.

Maybe that's why you felt called here, Belle said. *Maybe you're meant to take up that position.*

Even if wild magic had the will to do such a thing, I said, mental tones heavy with sarcasm, *it could certainly do a whole lot better than me."*

No one fully understands the wild places of this world. Don't be so certain such magic has no sentience.

Which only reinforces my point. I took another sip of tea. "Why would they ban witches? What happened here?"

Marjorie shrugged. "No one really knows. The elders don't always communicate the reason behind their rulings, and it's not like we humans are invited to council meetings."

Because all werewolf reservations were self-governing—up to a point, anyway— any humans who chose to live in them had to accept that they would never have a say in any decisions made.

"Please help me," Marjorie added softly. "You *must*."

I blew out a breath and crossed mental fingers that my intuition was wrong—that this search *wouldn't* end as I suspected it might. "I'll try. Just… don't get your hopes up. As I've said, there's never any guarantee when it comes to this sort of search."

Marjorie leaned forward and clasped my hand. The move caught me by surprise and images surged; *a pigtailed little girl, laughing in delight as her father swung her around in a circle. That same girl—older, angrier—screaming at Marjorie that she was the reason her dad had left and that she never wanted to see her again.* Recent history, not past, at least in the case of that last vision.

"You're trying," Marjorie said. "That's all I want. All Karen needs."

I blinked and the images shattered, leaving behind little more than childish echoes of anger and hurt. I gently pulled my hand from hers. I'd been well enough trained that touching people generally posed no threat; the only time my talents broke free of their leash was when I either desired it, or at times like this, when I was caught by surprise.

"I need something of hers. Something she has a lot of contact with."

"*That* would be her phone," Marjorie said. "And she has it with her, even if she's not answering."

I half smiled. "I mean something more personal;

something she wore close to her skin."

"Ah." Marjorie frowned. "Would jewelry do? She has a locket her father gave her—"

"That," I interrupted, "would be perfect."

"I'll go get it now." She rose swiftly and then hesitated. "You will search for her tonight, won't you?"

"Yes," I said heavily. "I will."

"Good." Marjorie spun and marched for the door, her steps far more determined and hopeful than they had been when she first arrived.

The small bell chimed at her departure. I wearily rubbed my eyes. "I hope I'm not doing the wrong thing."

Belle leaned forward and placed her hand over mine. The strength that flowed from it infused my body with a sense of calm. "You can't go back on your word now. That choice, as you've noted, left as soon as you allowed her entry."

"I know. I just—" I stopped and shrugged. "I was hoping I could stick to finding things that *don't* matter. You know, car keys, jewelry, etcetera."

"Then we shouldn't have used the 'Coffee Served, Futures Told, and Things Found' slogan when we opened this place." Amusement touched Belle's voice. "The truth of the matter is, you're finally tired of running, and we both know it."

Yes, I was. But it wasn't like I'd ever had much choice, and we both knew that, too.

"Cat's death was twelve years ago, Lizzie. Many things can change in that time—maybe even the attitude of your parents."

I snorted. "Yeah. And next year, the prime minister and his party will renounce its reliance on the council of advisors, and the three royal families of magic will suddenly find themselves out of favor."

Belle laughed. The sound was so warm and carefree it brought a smile to my lips.

"That," she said, "is something I'd love to see. Your father's expression alone would be worth the chaos that would undoubtedly unfold."

"Yes, it would." Hell, he considered it enough of an affront that he'd sired a daughter blessed with so little in the way of magic; the shock of being tossed out of power would probably kill him.

Not that *that* was something I wanted, no matter how badly he'd treated Belle or me.

I picked up a still warm biscuit and munched on it contemplatively. It didn't do a lot to calm the growing sense of trepidation, but it tasted as delicious as it smelled and certainly made my stomach happy. And *that* was better than no happiness at all.

The door chimed again as Marjorie returned. Either she lived close by, or she'd had something of Karen's in the car, just in case. The older woman didn't say anything, just sat down opposite me and held out her hand. In her palm sat a heart-shaped locket on a fine gold chain.

I brushed the crumbs from my fingertips then reached out for—but didn't quite touch—the locket. The last time I'd tried searching for some*one* rather than some*thing*, that person had died.

I briefly closed my eyes and shoved the thought away. This situation was different—and if my psychometry *did* find Karen, Belle could call the rangers while I headed out. If Cat's death had taught me anything, it was the fact that there were some situations neither magic *nor* psychic power could salvage.

Heat began to burn across my fingertips, a sure sign

that the connection between the locket and Karen was strong and active. Which meant, as of this moment, the teenager was still alive.

But I wasn't about to offer that hope to Marjorie. Not when hope could be killed as easily as a life taken.

And I certainly didn't want to examine the reason behind *that* particular thought.

I took another of those deep breaths that didn't do a whole lot to calm the butterflies. Then, before I could think about it too much more, I picked up the locket and pressed it into my palm.

For several seconds, nothing happened. Then the locket began to burn against my skin, its heat initially clean and bright, but gradually becoming darker. I shuddered, suddenly uneasy.

I'm here, Lizzie, Belle said. *I'll pull you back if need be.*

I knew that, but it didn't stop the growing tide of reluctance. But I'd said I'd do this. I couldn't back out now.

Not allowing myself any more time to think—or fear—I closed my eyes again and reached down to that place deep inside where my second sight lay leashed and waiting.

The minute I set it free, pictures flowed, but they were fragile things, little more than a reel of bright flickers. I let them slip by unheeded, waiting until I drew closer to a more recent memory before I slowed that reel down.

And what I saw chilled me: *a laptop, a chat room, an older man who made her laugh and who promised to help her escape her mother's iron fist. A clock, chiming at midnight. Climbing through her window to meet the man with dark hair and darker eyes. Warmth and laughter and exploratory passion.*

The only thing that hinted at danger in those images

was the fact that Karen was meeting a much older man, and that really wasn't surprising if she was looking for someone to replace her father's absence in her life. But there was no hint as to where she was now, and that meant I had to go deeper into her memories if I wanted any hope of uncovering that information.

I'm here, Belle repeated, her voice distant but filled with reassurance. *I won't let you get lost in there.*

I tightened my grip on the locket, pressing it more forcefully into my skin. But instead of growing stronger, the images momentarily fled and an oddly dark force rose to resist me. I fought on, determined to get into the more recent store of memories.

Then, without warning, a connection formed and I was *with* Karen, seeing what she was seeing, feeling what she was feeling….

…and oh God, it felt glorious. He touched her, caressed her, made her feel, burn, in a way that Jason never had.

"Stroke me," he whispered, his voice a low rumble that vibrated through every part of her.

Karen glanced down. His erection seemed huge and oddly pale in the light of the campfire and fear momentarily filled her. She'd never taken this final step….

He took her hand and placed it on his cock. "Be not afraid. It will never hurt you."

Karen swallowed her fear and let her fingers play up and down his skin. He was hot, hard, and somehow very different to Jason. But then, Jason was a boy, not a man like Tomme. When he groaned, a smile tugged her lips and she became bolder. He took off the rest of her clothes and touched her, teased her, and soon she couldn't breathe, it felt so good. And when he finally thrust inside of her, it hurt, but he kissed away her pain and began to move, and an avalanche of unfamiliar but amazing sensations flooded her body.

As his movements became faster, his lips returned to hers. He kissed her cheeks, her chin, her neck....

Lizzie, a distant voice screamed. *Pull the connection.*

His teeth scraped her neck, the sensation unpleasant. But before she could say anything, he kissed the sore spot and brushed his tongue across her ear. She moaned in pleasure. He chuckled softly and bit her again. This time, his teeth pierced her skin. Pain bloomed, and she tried to jerk away from him. But his left hand gripped the other side of her neck and held her motionless. She cried out, begging him to stop, but he didn't. She struggled, hit him, doing all that she could in an effort to get out from under him, but he didn't stop fucking her and he didn't stop biting her, and there was warmth on her neck and she couldn't breathe....

Water—*hot* water—hit my face and the connection snapped. For several seconds, I didn't move. *Couldn't* move. My heart raced, my stomach turned, and my body burned with the echo of the teenager's desire. And the warm water that dribbled down my neck felt an awful lot like blood....

"Excuse me for a minute," I muttered, and stood up so suddenly my chair crashed to the floor.

I dropped the locket onto the table, then, without looking at Marjorie, turned and bolted for the bathroom. Once there, I lost everything I'd eaten over day.

Belle followed me in. "How the hell did you form such an intimate connection? That's *never* happened before."

"Not to that extent, no." I took a deep, shuddery breath, then flushed the toilet and walked over to the hand basin. My reflection was flushed with heat and my irises wide with a mix of fear and desire, but my skin was paler than usual, and it made the smattering of golden freckles across my nose and cheeks stand out sharply. Never, ever, had I expected *anything* like that.

I flicked on the cold tap, cupped my hands under the water, and splashed my face. And wished I could do the same to both my memories and the unwanted burn.

"Is she dead?" Belle asked softly.

I glanced past my reflection and met Belle's silvery gaze. "You didn't catch it?"

"No. But there's nothing unusual in that."

Because, as my familiar, it wasn't her job to follow me down the rabbit hole, but rather to monitor me, ensuring my vital functions were not being so completely taxed by whatever I was seeing or doing that it could lead to my death. She was my security *and* my strength.

I reached for a towel and patted my face dry. "She's currently alive, but I don't think she's going to remain that way for long."

There'd been far too much blood running down her neck for life to continue on without swift intervention.

"You can't tell Marjorie that."

"No, but I can't give her false hope, either."

Belle grimaced. "It's a bitch of a situation. Maybe we *should* have said we couldn't help her."

"More than likely." But then a teenager would be out in there in that forest, all alone and without hope. At least if I tried to find her, there was the tiniest of chances that I could help her. Save her.

Even if that inner part of me was saying otherwise.

I took a deep, calming breath, then squeezed past Belle and headed back into the main café space.

Marjorie's expression was a mix of anxiety and fear. "Did you find my daughter? Is she okay?"

I hesitated. "She's in the woods somewhere. There was a campfire and a man."

"Who? A friend?"

"I don't know."

"But she's alive? She's okay?"

Again I hesitated. I certainly couldn't tell the truth, but I couldn't risk an outright lie, either. Not when the warm pulse of blood down my neck was still so fresh in my memory.

"She was when I saw her. If you'll lend me the locket, I'll go out now and try to find her."

"Please, hurry." Marjorie swept the locket off the table and held it out to me. "Because something is very wrong."

Yes, it was. I stared at the shining, dangling locket, and saw the shadows gathering around it. Those shadows were death. And for too many seconds, I simply couldn't force my hand to grasp the damn thing.

The minute I did—the minute it touched my skin— the images surged: *lethargy, the sensation of floating, light, bright light, light that wasn't calling her but rather pushing her toward the growing darkness....*

I clamped the leash on my abilities and ruthlessly shoved the images away. I didn't have the time for the fear and questions they raised... and neither did Karen.

"I need to go now, Mrs. Banks. Give me your phone number, and then go home."

"But I want to help—"

"No," I cut in. "You can't. I'm sorry, but for this section of the search, anyone too close can interfere with my ability to find whatever—whoever—is missing."

Her expression suggested she wasn't happy, but she pulled a business card from her purse and handed it to me. *Marjorie Banks*, it said, *Attorney at Law.*

I shoved the card into my back pocket and tried not

to think about the havoc a grieving lawyer could cause to the woman who failed to find her daughter alive.

Even before Marjorie was out of the shop, we were gathering everything I needed: a first aid kit—which also included herbal remedies like yarrow and agrimony to stop both internal and external bleeding—a couple of potions to ward off evil, a knife made of silver, and finally, my warding stones. I had no idea who that man with Karen was, no idea whether he was just a human sicko or something else entirely, but I fully intended to be as fight-ready as I could.

Even if the last time I'd gone running to the rescue similarly prepared had ended in utter disaster.

"Better grab the flashlight," Belle said, as I slung the backpack over my shoulder. "It's as dark as Hades out in the scrub."

"A flashlight will warn that man of my presence way sooner than I might want. I'll call a wisp if I'm having trouble seeing." And at least calling a will-o'-the-wisp—or ghost candles, as they were more commonly known around these parts—to help me wasn't beyond the range of my meager magic skills.

"Be careful out there." Belle hugged me briefly. "You dying will play utter havoc with my lifespan."

I smiled, despite the tension riding me. "You and I are destined to live very long lives."

"Says the woman who has never seen *anything*—good or bad—relating to us in her dreams."

"I don't have to. Not when I'm hell-bent on remaining alive just so I can become the bane of my father's existence."

"He has to care that you're actually alive for that to work." She pushed me lightly to the door. "Go. I'll ring the rangers and tell them what's going on."

She would also, I knew, keep track of my whereabouts via our connection, and come running to the rescue if my own abilities were somehow overwhelmed. Although in this case, that might be too little, too late, given I'd be deep in the forest's heart.

I zipped up my jacket as I exited the café and headed up Lyttleton Street, the burn in the locket guiding my steps. All too soon I'd entered the thickly treed Kalimna Park, and the darkness grew heavier as the trees closed in around me. I followed the road for half a mile or so before the locket pulled me left, into the deeper darkness. My steps slowed, and then stopped. It was so damn black that I could barely see my hand when I stuck it in front of my face, let alone anything else. But the fear pounding through my veins had little to do with the thought of falling over and breaking a limb, but rather the darkness staining the locket. It had grown so heavy it was a dead weight in my hand. Death's talons had reached the teenager, and that meant I only had a small window left. While it *was* possible to keep a soul from moving on if its body was still alive, not even my parents—who were not only witch royalty, but two of a only a handful of witches who were considered the most powerful in Australia—had the power to call a soul back once it had begun its journey. I had to hurry.

But to go faster, I needed light.

I quickly kicked off my shoes and socks, and then dug my toes into the dirt. It felt warm against my skin, and filled me with an odd sense of energy. That meant there was wild magic near, which was strange, given how close I still was to town. Usually it kept to the wilder places of the world.

But I thrust concern aside, wriggled my toes a little deeper into the soil to ensure I was well grounded, and then began the summoning incantation. It wasn't exactly a smart thing to do this close to wild magic, but I didn't have time to go elsewhere—and neither did Karen.

After several minutes, warmth caressed my skin. When I opened my eyes, I discovered a wisp hovering a meter or so away from my face. It was orb shaped, and the glow of its being caressed the nearby tree trunks with a cool blue light. Wisps weren't ghosts despite their nickname; they were spirits, and very fragile by nature. Wind could tear them away, rain could wash them out, and they couldn't stand the touch of sunshine. Sometimes they were helpful, and other times they weren't. The myths of them leading travelers astray were very much based on truth. This one was older, if its size and glow were anything to go by, and that generally meant it'd be more inclined to help.

I bowed slightly. "Thank you for answering my call."

The wisp spun in response, its light briefly pulsing. Wisps undoubtedly had their own language, but it was one most witches didn't understand.

"I'm here to find a teenager—a girl who is in deep trouble. Could you light my path through the trees?"

The wisp seemed to consider me for a moment, then its light flickered. When it didn't disappear, I took it as acceptance.

"Thank you," I said, and bowed again. Though I really hadn't had a lot of experience dealing with spirits—that was more Belle's forte—and had no idea if they actually cared about politeness, I'd always worked on the theory that it cost me nothing.

The wisp moved closer and settled about half a meter

above my head. Its cool blue light fanned across the darkness, lightly touching the tree trunks around us and providing just enough light for me to make my way through the thick scrub. I shoved my feet back into my shoes, then grabbed my socks and ran.

The pulse of life in the locket was dying.

I crashed my way through the scrub, the noise echoing across the night. Branches whipped across my face and tore at my clothes, but I ignored it and kept on going. Time—and the teenager—was slipping away.

Deeper and deeper into the trees I ran, until the thick canopy above me blocked the stars and even the distant sounds rising from Castle Rock faded. The only noise to be heard—aside from the racket I was making—was the occasional hoot of an owl, and even that halted as I drew close to it.

The locket's pulse stilled, and the warmth and connection began to fade. I cursed and ran on. There was still a chance I could save the teenager, still a chance I could bring her back to life if she hadn't bled out. The soul didn't leave the body straight away, and while it was still present, there was always hope.

The smell of smoke began to taint the crisp, eucalyptus-scented air. The memory of the campfire rose and I ran on, my speed close to reckless in scrub this thick. A branch snagged my jacket and ripped my sleeve; I pulled free, leaped over a log, and ran on. The ground began to rise and, up ahead, the trees seemed to be thinning. Hope flared, and I pushed on.

When I reached the top of the hill, I paused despite the urgency riding me. The clearing was small and half filled with leaf and tree litter. The teenager lay in the middle; there was no life in her, just as there was no life in the locket. Her spirit had fled.

"Goddammit, no!" The words were wrenched from me. I'd been so close—so damn *close*. But once again, close enough simply wasn't good enough. A thick sense of uselessness washed over me and, for a second, all I wanted to do was drop to the ground and let the tears flow. Not just for this teenager, but also for the sister I'd failed to save so many years ago.

But tears had never helped anyone. Not then, and certainly not now.

So I shoved my emotions back in their box and studied the clearing. The embers still glowing in the fire pit provided little in the way of light, but it was enough to see Karen's clothes were missing. Maybe the man she'd been with—the man she'd called Tomme—had taken them. Maybe he'd wanted a memento of his sick crime.

The wisp shot forward unasked, its light trailing behind it like a comet as it ran along the length of the teenager's body, not only highlighting her nakedness but the dark dampness matting her blonde hair. The memory of Tomme biting her neck rose. Had it been a fetish, or something worse?

Something like a vampire, perhaps?

Even thinking the word had me shuddering. Vampires existed, everyone knew that, but they certainly weren't the accepted part of society that werewolves had become. Vampires were not only loners, they were also hunters, in a way that werewolves had never been. The simple fact was, vamps needed human blood to survive and went mad if they didn't get it. All the rot Hollywood and fiction had everyone believing about them being able to survive on animal blood was just that—fiction. They could certainly drink it—and often did—but it wouldn't sustain them long-term.

Of course, few vampires risked killing their human prey these days, but that didn't alter the fact they were an unwelcome addition to most towns and cities. So unwelcome, in fact, that few announced their presence and they generally hunted well away from home ground.

Was that what had happened here?

Until I saw the wound, I wouldn't know for sure. I shoved the now dead locket into my pocket and continued on. The wisp's brightness had muted, until the only thing it highlighted was Karen's face. The cool light gave the teenager's skin a frosty, bluish tinge, and yet her lips seemed to glow a rich, ruby red, which was decidedly odd.

I stopped and stared down at her for several seconds. Despite the flush of heat still in her lips, her face was drawn and her expression one of terror. Whoever said a vampire's bite was orgasmic either had rocks in their head or had clearly never been bitten.

I squatted down beside her and reached to sweep her bloodied hair away from her neck. But as I did, the wisp's light went out.

Then, from behind me, a deep voice growled, "Don't you *dare* touch her, witch."

CHAPTER
two

I froze, momentarily unsure if it was the killer or someone totally different behind me.

"Now get up, and step away from her," he continued.

The voice was deeper than that of the man who'd killed the teenager, and filled with a whole world of anger. It might not be the killer, but it *was* someone who was very ready to kill.

I frowned at the strange insight and carefully obeyed, not even daring to look over my shoulder to see who was speaking. It wasn't someone I'd met in town over the past few months, that was for sure.

"I didn't kill her," I said. "I've only just arrived."

"When I said step away, I meant completely." His words remained clipped, vibrating with an odd sort of violence.

I retreated a dozen more steps. A man stepped into view; he was tall and rangy, with darkish blond hair that was streaked with silver in the moonlight. He was wearing baggy track pants, a sweat-stained T-shirt, and a shoulder holster. The gun that should have been in that holster was aimed directly at my face.

And *that* meant he was both a werewolf *and* a ranger. They were the only ones allowed to carry weapons within the reservation.

"Do you often take your gun for a run in the forest?" I asked, and almost instantly regretted it.

His gaze met mine, and all I saw was death. My death, if I wasn't very careful. Not because he believed I was responsible for Karen's murder, but because his hatred for witches ran so deep—was so intense—that his body practically hummed with it.

And the fact I was gaining such an insight about this man without even touching him scared me a whole lot more than the gun still pointed at my face.

"Take that backpack off then place your hands behind you and turn around."

"Please, just look at her neck and you'll see—"

"Do as I goddamn say, witch, or I *will* make you."

"I'm *not* a witch, Ranger." Not one with any sort of power, anyway. I took off my pack, placed my hands behind my back, and then turned around as ordered. "And the man who killed the teenager is getting away while you hassle *me*."

"The trouble with *that* statement," he snapped, "is the fact there're only two scents evident in this clearing—yours and Karen's."

"That's *not* possible. He was here. I saw—" I cut the rest of the sentence off. I suspected reminding him I had *any* sort of ability—magical or not—wasn't a great idea right now.

The ranger wrapped what felt like a cable tie around my wrists. Obviously, the gun wasn't the only thing he took out for a run.

"Now, stay there and don't move," he growled.

"Or what?" Fear might still be riding high, but frustration was starting to overwhelm it. "You'll let your hatred override whatever speck of common sense you have and shoot me? Because *that* would be a really stupid move when I'm the only link you have to Karen's killer."

"We'll let the coroner be the judge of that."

I swung around to face him. His eyes, I noted, were a deep blue rather than the usual amber of a werewolf. "Then damn well get the coroner out here!"

"She's already on her way." He retreated several steps and picked up the backpack. "Is there anything dangerous in here?

"For you, yes—there's an unsheathed silver knife."

"And why would you have that? You have to be aware it's against the law for *any* citizen to carry such a weapon within a reservation."

"Yes, but silver is a ward against evil as much as a defense against werewolves, and I wasn't sure what I'd find up here."

He opened the bag and peered inside. The knife had been tied to the back of the pack and posed no immediate threat to him unless he was stupid enough to touch it. But the fear of silver was so ingrained in werewolves that few would. Some reservations had even gone as far as banning *anything* made of silver—even something as innocuous as a neck chain.

"What are in the vials?" he asked

I shrugged. "Nothing dangerous."

His blue eyes sparked dangerously. "Just answer the

question."

"They're potions. Protection potions."

"I thought you said you weren't a witch?"

"I'm not—"

"No, because everyday citizens regularly carry potions and silver knives around in their backpacks." His voice was a little more regulated. He was obviously regaining some control over his emotions.

Or rather, his memories.

And I *really* wished I could stop getting these insights. I didn't need to understand the man. I just needed to get out of this clearing and stop— I thrust the rest of that thought away. I didn't need to be thinking along *those* lines, either.

He put the pack down. "Don't move, and don't try to spell me."

I snorted. "If you knew me better, Ranger, you'd know just how ridiculous that statement is."

"Trust me, I have *no* desire to know you or any other witch better. Just do as you're told and remain still."

He took out his phone then walked across to the teenager and began taking photos. I watched, frustration growing. Why wouldn't he believe me? And why couldn't he smell anyone else in the clearing but Karen and myself? Tomme *had* been here, with the teenager, introducing her to the glory of sex before taking her on to the emptiness of death.

"If you move her hair, you'll see the wound on her neck."

"I can't touch the body until the coroner gets here."

"Why? Did you forget to pick up gloves when you packed the gun and the ties?"

His gaze rose, and just for an instant, amusement

gleamed. But the hatred quickly smothered it again.

"I can smell the blood," he said. "But there's not enough of it on either the ground or in her hair to be the cause of death."

"That's because the man she was with drained her—"

"There are *no* vampires on this reservation," he cut in.

"I didn't *say* he was a vampire, but are you really sure of that?"

"Yes."

He glanced around as a woman stepped into the clearing. She was tall and rangy, with blonde hair and a sharp but pretty face. His sister, instinct whispered.

"It's about fucking time, Ciara."

"It's my night off, remember. You're damn lucky I got here as quickly as I did." Her gaze scanned me, judged me. Whatever conclusion she came to wasn't showing in her expression. "This our killer?"

"She was leaning over the body when I got here."

"I didn't kill her." I was beginning to feel like a CD stuck on replay.

"There's no other scents in the clearing," Ciara said. Whether to me or to her brother, I had no idea. She swung the pack from her shoulder and unzipped it. "Tala's on her way."

"Good. She can take over control of the crime scene while I escort our witch to the station for questioning."

"I'm not a witch," I said. "And I do have a name."

"Most of us do." He wasn't even looking at me when he said that. His attention was on his sister. "Be careful out here. And give me the autopsy results as soon as possible."

"I will, but just don't expect miracles when it comes to DNA." She hesitated. "You're going to have to call the

IIT."

"Just as long as we have something to go on before they get here, I'll be happy."

"But I'm betting *they* won't be if you start interfering with their investigations again," she replied. "Not after last time."

"That last time is the reason we *will* continue investigating," he snapped. Then he thrust a hand through his short hair. "Sorry."

Ciara shrugged. "I understand, Aiden, but we need to step lightly on this one."

"I know."

His gaze came to mine, and a chill ran through me. He might have been warned to step lightly, but I had a feeling that didn't exactly apply when it came to me.

"Move," he said. "Back to town."

"Here," Ciara said, and handed him a flashlight. "I wouldn't want her falling over and breaking something. That might just raise IIT's ire."

His expression suggested he really didn't care what the IIT might think, but he nevertheless flicked on the flashlight and motioned me on ahead of him.

I went without comment, but I couldn't help wondering what had happened in this wolf's past. If the darkness that almost consumed his aura was anything to go by, it had been something bad. Something that had plunged this normally vital and creative man—if the golden orange of his remaining aura was anything to go by—into deep and unending sorrow.

That something had obviously involved a witch. All his words and actions practically screamed that point. Given what Marjorie had said about the elders banning witches, it wasn't such a huge jump to figure his sorrow and that banning were connected.

Karen's murder had obviously dredged up those bad memories, and I just had to hope he'd treat me reasonably—professionally—and not mix past hurt with the current investigation.

The ranger station was located near the corner of Hargraves and Templeton Streets. It was a beautiful two-story stone building that had obviously been built during the gold rush days, as it possessed that old colonial look that many of the buildings from that era had.

The ranger unlocked the front door, switched on the lights, and then guided me past the reception and through a secure door into the main office area. Though his grip on my arm was light, the heat of it radiated through my body and had the threads of unquenched—and unwanted—desire flicking through my veins. Which wasn't good when he was a werewolf and well able pick up the scent of arousal. I frowned and tried to concentrate on my surroundings rather than the man walking by my side.

There were half a dozen desks in the rather large room, but only three seemed to be in use. There was also a huge whiteboard along one wall and, beside it, a roster, which currently held only four names—which was surprising given the size of the reservation.

He didn't stop there, however, but marched me through another door into a long corridor. Six rooms ran off this, several of which were obviously cells. Thankfully, he didn't take me into one of those, but dumped my backpack on the counter of what looked like a storeroom, then guided me into a nearby room. It was large and square, and had little more than a table, four chairs, and a rather pristine-looking media hub on the wall.

I was rather unceremoniously thrust into one of the

seats.

"Don't move," he all but growled.

I did as bid. There was no point in saying anything, because while he might want answers, the ones I could give him weren't the ones he wanted to hear.

He walked across to the media unit, his strides long and loose-limbed. Though he was, like most wolves, rangy rather than muscular in build, his shoulders were nicely wide and his arms had just the right amount of muscle. My gaze slipped down his back to his butt. If he looked this good in baggy sweats, he'd look more than fine in a pair of jeans.

Hello, Belle said. *This all sounds rather interesting.*

Not when I'm tied up and about to be interrogated, it's not.

From the thoughts I've heard, it sounds as if being tied up by that man might well be worth it.

You're supposed to be concerned about my welfare, not having inappropriate thoughts about our ranger.

I'm not the one checking out his butt, Belle said. *And that alone tells me you're doing just fine right now.*

Belle, rack off.

Her laughter spun through my thoughts and tugged a smile from my lips.

The ranger finished his fiddling and swung around to face me again. His blue eyes were icy, and his expression like stone.

He did his obligatory spiel about my rights, told me everything was being recorded, and then added, "State your name and address for the record, please."

"Elizabeth Grace, currently living at fifty-eight Mostyn Street."

Disbelief flickered across his strong features. "You're living here? In town?"

"I believe that's what I said, Ranger." I paused, but couldn't help adding, "And isn't it mandatory when interrogating a suspect that you also state your name and rank?"

Annoyance momentarily overran the stoniness in his expression. "Aiden O'Connor, head ranger Faelan Reservation, currently interviewing Ms. Grace about the death of Karen Banks."

So I was not only being interviewed by the boss of this whole shebang, but by one of the O'Connors—the original occupiers of this area before some long-ago government decided the three Victorian packs held too much land—and therefore power—between them, and had forcibly moved the other two into *this* territory. Of course, they hadn't gone easily, and the resulting turmoil was the reason werewolves today were basically self-governing. In the end, it had been the only way to make both sides happy and avoid an all-out war. It had been witches who'd brokered that deal, which was perhaps why many packs to this day remained unhappy about the presence of witches on their land.

Being an O'Connor also explained his unusual hair coloring, as they were gray wolves who tended to run the entire gauntlet of that color rather than being the usual brown, black, or even red.

"Now," he added, "tell me why you were in that forest."

He pulled out the chair and sat down opposite. The thick veil of sorrow and anger that all but smothered his aura washed over me again, and it was so damn strong that for several seconds I couldn't even breathe.

I leaned away even as I swallowed the desire to ask what the hell had happened to him. Doing so would only be a waste of words, as he didn't look the type to share that sort of information with those he was close to, let alone a stranger. A *witch*.

"There's little point in me answering your questions," I said. "Because I really can't answer them in the way you want me to."

"I just want honesty."

"And yet you won't believe me if I *am* honest."

His narrowed eyes glittered dangerously. "What makes you think that?"

"Because you hate witches and you desperately want to believe I'm guilty of this crime so that everything is tied up in a nice neat little bow."

Though his expression didn't change, I had a feeling I'd scored a point. "Actually, I don't believe you're responsible for Karen's death, as you didn't have the time to kill her before I arrived on the scene. I do, however, believe you know more than what you've already said. So tell me, for the record, why you were up there."

"Mrs. Banks came into my café earlier this evening and asked me to find her daughter—"

"And your café's name?" he cut in.

"The Psychic Café. And before you ask, yes, I have elder approval for both the café and my use of psychometry."

"But not magic, which is what you were using up in Kalimna Park."

"Summoning a wisp is only very minor magic, and that's all—"

"*All* magic is banned in this reservation, minor or not."

"Something I *wasn't* aware of, Ranger." Which wasn't a lie, because no one had mentioned witches being banned before tonight. "And surely I could be given a pass in this situation given I only summoned the wisp to make my passage through the park faster?"

His expression suggested the reason *didn't* matter, and once again I wondered what the hell had gone on in this place that had led to witches and magic being banned. They surely *had* to be aware of the danger they were placing everyone in by not having a resident witch on the reservation?

"For the record," he said, "explain what psychometry is."

"It's the ability to catch thoughts and feeling from objects via touch," I dutifully stated. "And sometimes, if the connection is strong enough, you can go deeper, gaining a location as well as idea of what might they might be doing."

"And this is what happened with Karen?"

I nodded. "Marjorie gave me one of Karen's lockets to use. The results were... unexpected."

One eyebrow rose. "In what way?"

Heat invaded my cheeks. Which was stupid, really. He was a werewolf *and* a ranger. He'd probably seen and done more than I could ever imagine. "They, uh, were making love."

Amusement briefly touched his lips and it transformed his face, lifting the stoniness and shifting his features from merely pleasant to striking.

"I see."

"Trust me, it wasn't something *I* wanted to see." Or feel.

That touch of amusement grew, making me suspect he was all too aware of exactly *how* that connection had affected me.

Well, as you've already noted, he's a werewolf, Belle said. *And they're big on the whole scent thing. Makes them as horny as hell.*

You're not helping matters, you know.

Wonder if he's at all tempted—

Belle, shut the fuck up.

She laughed again but otherwise did as bid.

"So, it was this connection that told you they were in the park?" he said.

"Well, no. I only caught glimpses. I had to use a locket to guide me up there. We also left a message on your answering machine." I paused, and silently added, *Belle, you did make that call to the rangers, didn't you?*

Hello, didn't you just tell me to shut the fuck up?

About him, dimwit.

Her warm laughter ran through my mind, tugging a smile to my lips. *Yes, I rang and left a message. I didn't ring the emergency number, though.*

"We?" Aiden prompted.

"I mean Isabelle—she co-owns the café with me."

"And she's another witch?"

"We're *not* witches—"

His gaze lifted to my hair. "That color is *not* out of a bottle."

Well, no, because try as they might, no company had ever been able to perfect the sheer richness of the crimson hair coloring that was the one true sign of a royal witch. "But my eyes aren't silver. There may be witch in my background, Ranger, but that doesn't make me one of them."

There was a decided lack of expression on his face, and I had absolutely no idea as to what he might be thinking. Belle could have told me had she been here, but

43

she couldn't read anyone but me from such a distance.

"And your friend's full name?" he asked eventually.

"Isabelle Kent. And she's a psychic rather than a witch." I hesitated, and then added, "You can check my story with Mrs. Banks, if you'd like."

"Oh, I intend to."

"I'm hardly likely to lie about something like that."

He raised that eyebrow again. It was amazing just how much disbelief one small movement could imply. "Did you see anything that might give us some clue as to the identity of the man with Karen?"

I told him everything I'd seen then added, "None of which is overly helpful, I know."

"No." He tapped his fingers lightly on the table, a soft beat that matched the rhythm of my heart. I wondered if he was aware he was doing it. While only vampires could hear the pulse of blood through veins, a wolf with sharp enough hearing could certainly hear a heartbeat at close range. "And you have no idea who that man in the clearing was, or why he left no scent?"

"None at all."

"So why didn't you call the emergency number? Why run up there yourself, especially when you thought this Tomme might have been a vampire?"

"I never claimed he was a vampire, just that he was drinking her blood." I hesitated. *Belle, why didn't you call the emergency number?*

Because making the call to the general number covered our backsides, but anything else risked exposing us as witches, given you were going to use the wisps. She paused. *Which I guess is what has now happened anyway.*

It's only exposed me. Unless they know a lot about the witch houses, they won't suspect you. Out loud, I added, "I ran up there because I knew Karen didn't have much time left."

"It would have only taken a minute, if that, to make the additional call—"

"Why are you making such a big deal of it? The first call obviously worked, given you arrived up there not long after me."

"Yes, but only because I happened to be at the station and saw the answering machine's blinking light." He thrust to his feet and walked around the table. The sheer power of both his aura and his presence wrapped around my senses like a thick, warm blanket, and it was all I could do to remain still—though whether I would have leaned away from him or *into* him, I wasn't entirely sure.

There was a soft click and then the ties binding my wrists fell away. He shoved the knife back into his pocket as he walked across to the media unit. "Interview suspended at—" He glanced at his watch. "—ten fifty-three."

I blinked. "Meaning I'm free to go?"

He punched a button then picked up a small plastic pack of tissues and tossed them to me. "The scratch on your cheek is still bleeding. And not until I confirm your story with Marjorie."

And with that, he departed. The door slammed behind him and the sound echoed.

I tugged one of the tissues free and held it up against my cheek. I'd no doubt received the cut during my mad dash through the trees, but now that he'd mentioned it, it started hurting like blazes. And my head had decided to join in on the fun. While psychometry might not be magic, there was still a price to pay if you went too deep, and for me, it was blistering headaches at best, and *that* along with projectile vomiting at worst. If the ranger didn't motivate himself, he might just find himself with a mess to clean up.

I got up and began to pace. It didn't help the head much but neither would sitting still. Only resting in utter darkness for a couple of hours would provide any sort of relief.

The ranger had said there were only two scents in that clearing, but how could that be? The only way to hide your presence so fully was via a spell, and it was very rare for a vampire to also be capable of magic. Or, at least, the type of magic *I'd* grown up with. But there *was* another type of magic—one that was born from either the blood of the practitioner or from a sacrifice. While most witches considered it an unclean and unsafe magic, history was littered with those who'd nevertheless risked it, with varying degrees of success.

Was that what we were dealing with here? A vampire capable of using blood magic? It would certainly explain the absence of his scent in the clearing. And it would also, I thought with a sudden chill, explain why I'd seen so little of him when I was connected with Karen. While I'd sensed no magic, he might have been using a glamour to fudge his looks whenever he was with her.

God, the last thing this place needed was a vampire capable of using the darker arts. With wild magic loose and unprotected, it would be very easy for the vampire's actions to taint it, and *that* could have disastrous consequences for Castle Rock. Once evil found a hold in a place like this, its stain grew until the whole area became unlivable to all but those who followed darker paths.

This place needed a witch, and it had to be someone far more capable than me. Only the truly powerful could protect and guide wild magic, and as my parents had been wont to tell me on numerous occasions, I was seriously lacking in that department.

But if the ranger's reaction to *me* was anything to go by, then the one thing that this place desperately needed was the one thing it wasn't about to get.

So where did that leave us?

Up that well-known creek without a paddle, Belle said cheerfully. *Which is not a situation we're unfamiliar with.*

It certainly wasn't. We might have lived life more or less on the run for the last twelve years, but as much as we'd tried to avoid any sort of situation that would draw attention to ourselves, we seemed to have an uncanny knack for doing the exact opposite.

Perhaps this is fate's way of telling us enough is enough, she mused. *It's not as if changing our surnames would really have stopped your family from finding you if they'd been truly determined.*

That was an undeniable truth—and one that still caused me pain in the deepest part of the night.

The door opened as the ranger returned. His gaze swept the room before coming to rest on mine. There was little evidence of emotion in either his expression or his eyes, but I nevertheless felt the impact of it like a blow to the gut.

And I wasn't entirely sure if it was the unhappiness staining his aura, or something else.

Something like an unneeded, unwanted, attraction to the damn man.

Because really, how stupid would that be?

It's hardly stupid to be attracted to a good-looking man, Belle said.

Yes, but this one hates witches.

Hatred has little hope against lust, she said. *And I'm speaking from experience here.*

There's no indication of lust, let alone attraction on his part, I replied. *Besides, I've sworn off men and relationships after that mess in Birdwood, remember?*

As I've repeatedly said, Kyle was a sack of shit who proved himself unworthy of your emotions.

A fact that doesn't alter my determination to avoid relationships of any kind for the foreseeable future.

I'm not talking about relationships, but rather sex. A hot, heavy fling will do your soul a world of good.

Belle, just drop it.

Seriously, she continued blithely, *there's a very fine line between love and hate. Once he gets to know you a little better, he could slip over that ledge and good things could happen.*

Knowing *any* answer would only encourage her musings further, I ignored her and crossed my arms—which was a thoroughly defensive gesture, though against what I wasn't entirely sure. "Anything wrong, Ranger?"

"Marjorie confirmed your story."

"And that's a problem?"

"No. You're free to go. Just don't leave Castle Rock, as we'll probably need to speak to you again." He stepped to one side and made a sweeping motion toward the door. "And I've confiscated both your knife and your potions."

Meaning it was just as well I hadn't decided to take my athame with me. I walked toward him. "I've been thinking about the situation and Tomme, and I believe—"

"You are *not* to involve yourself in this investigation in any way, shape, or form," he said, voice sharp. "Is that clear?"

I nodded. "But—"

"But *nothing*," he practically growled. "If I discover *any* interference on your part, I'll throw your butt in jail so fast your head will spin."

I took a deep breath and slowly released it, but once

again it failed to ease the annoyance. At least I'd *tried* to warn him. Not that *that* would help if the situation escalated, and I had a bad feeling it would.

"Fine." *On your head be it.* "But if anything strange happens, anything that might involve magic—"

"That," he cut in brusquely, "is unlikely, given the only person capable of magic in this territory appears to be you."

"This whole goddamn territory is filled with magic, Ranger, and if you and the elders aren't aware of that, then you deserve the shit that's coming your way."

"Is that a *threat*?"

His low tone sent a shiver down my spine; the only trouble was I wasn't entirely sure it was fear, given his voice was decidedly sexy when it took on that timbre.

"No, it's merely a truth. You shouldn't be afraid of the small amount I'm capable of when the wild magic is absolutely everywhere in this place, and there isn't a proper witch here to protect it."

He snorted softly and gestured me to follow him as he led the way back through the building. Either he didn't believe in wild magic or didn't believe it could be dangerous.

My backpack was still on the counter where he'd dumped it, and I paused. "Can I take the pack with me?"

"Yes." He keyed open the door into the office area. "As I said, I've already confiscated the illicit items."

I grabbed the pack and slung it over my shoulder. "You might want to keep the potions rather than pouring them down the drain. They'll keep you safe when few other things will."

His brief smile held very little in the way of humor. "Trust me, vampires—and there's no evidence so far this

Tomme is one—hold few fears for a werewolf."

"Then let's just hope a vampire is *all* you're dealing with here."

His gaze narrowed. "Meaning what, exactly, Ms. Grace?"

"Nothing more than what I said. I've told you everything I know, Ranger, and you don't want to hear what I suspect."

"I listened to the words of a witch once before. Hell will freeze over before I make the same mistake again." He opened the external door and waved me out.

I gave him a thin, tight smile. "I'd like to say it's been a pleasure meeting you, but that, I'm afraid, would be a lie. Good night."

And with that, I left. But his gaze continued to burn a hole in between my shoulder blades, and as I turned into Mostyn Street, I glanced over my shoulder. Though I couldn't see him, I knew he was still there. Still watching me.

It was a realization that made my pulse dance for a beat or two. Apparently, my hormones hadn't gotten the memo about no more men.

I was about thirty feet away from the café's front door when a wave of grief hit me so hard that I actually staggered back several steps. I sucked in air and quickly shut down the sensory input as my gaze ran across the nearby shadows and parked cars.

A figure detached itself from the nearby building and walked toward me.

Marjorie Banks.

But her expression wasn't grief-stricken. It was one of utter fury.

CHAPTER
three

"Mrs. Banks," I said, doing my best to keep any sort of inflection out of my voice. "I'm so sorry for your loss. I tried, but—"

Her mouth flattened into a thin line. "I want you to find him."

Of the many things I'd thought she might say, *that* hadn't been one of them. "I *can't*. I'm not a ranger or even a private investigator. The rangers will—"

"If the fucking *rangers* had listened to my fears earlier," she cut in, "then Karen might now be alive."

Her brown eyes glistened with tears, but guilt sparked in the deeper depths. She wasn't only angry with the rangers for not acting sooner, but also herself.

"You can't be sure of that," I said. "No one can. Not until the coroner hands in her report, at least."

"We both know what that report will show," she said, her fists clenched. "We both know she was still alive when

I came to you. You did what they did not, and now I want your help to catch this bastard."

"Mrs. Banks—"

"Marjorie," she said. "And you cannot—*will* not—say no."

I stared at her for a minute, a deep sense of unease filling me. "Marjorie, the rangers have emphatically warned me away from any further action regarding your daughter's murder. I *cannot* help you."

"Oh, you can and you *will*, or I'll make your life so damn miserable in this town that you'll have no choice but to leave."

And that right there was the sucker punch I'd been waiting for. So much for Belle's theory that fate might want us to settle in this place.

Fate works in mysterious ways, Belle said. *But it does appear the same old shit is hitting us yet again.*

Well, not exactly the same shit. This was the first time we'd been threatened for *not* using our abilities.

I rubbed my head and then said, "If the rangers have the slightest suspicion I'm helping you, my ass will be thrown into jail so damn fast—"

"And I'll get it out just as fast, believe me." She reached out and grabbed my hand, but this time I was prepared for her. No images surged; all I saw, all I felt, was bleak sorrow and utter devastation. Her demands were born of a need to do something to help ease her guilt and heartache, I knew that, but it didn't help *me*. "Please, Elizabeth. You have to do this. You must."

Which was almost an exact echo of her earlier plea, and one that would undoubtedly get me into even more trouble.

I gently pulled my hand from hers. "If you give me

your address, I'll come to your place and examine Karen's room. We'll see where we go from there."

She frowned. "How will that help?"

I hesitated. I didn't want to give her false hope, not when the man behind Karen's death had gone to such lengths to conceal his presence. "I might be able to find something that has the man's resonance on it. It might give us some clue as to who he is or where he is staying."

"Then come with me now—"

"No." I held up a hand, cutting off her protest before she could utter it. "I'm just about dead on my feet, Mrs. Banks. I couldn't sense anything now even if I wanted to. Tomorrow is the best I can do."

Her expression was less than pleased, but there was little point in pushing the issue, and she knew it. She gave me her address and then added, "Nine tomorrow morning, then?"

I hesitated and then nodded. "But it's possible the rangers will want to do their own search, so please warn me beforehand if they're there."

The last thing I needed was to be going against O'Connor's orders so soon after they'd been given. She nodded, and after a slight hesitation, spun around and walked back to her car. I waited until she'd left and then headed into the café.

Belle met me near the door and handed me one of her concoctions. It was thick, green, and rather odorous, but I knew from experience that the worse they smelled, the better they worked.

I held my nose and quickly swallowed it, but a shiver of distaste still ran through me. "Seriously, can you not add a little sugar or something to make these things a little bit more palatable?"

"Sugar is bad for you." She plucked the glass from my hand. "Unless, of course, it's consumed in the form of cake, biscuits, or chocolate."

I snorted, and almost instantly regretted it when pain shot through my brain.

"You," Belle said, voice severe, "had best get upstairs quick smart. I'll finish up in the kitchen and check on you later."

I nodded, squeezed her arm in appreciation, and then headed for the small set of stairs at the rear of the café that led up to the first floor and our accommodation. There wasn't all that much floor space up there, but we each had our own bedroom and there was a separate toilet and bathroom. The living room was tiny, but had enough room for a kitchenette, an under-bench refrigerator, a small coffee machine to save us heading downstairs all the time, and a microwave, as well as a two-person sofa and a TV. It might have been stifling had it not been for the balcony that extended out over the sidewalk, providing us with enough space for a table and four chairs while giving those in the café who wished to have their coffee and cake in the fresh air some weather protection.

My door creaked as I opened it, and the sound echoed nastily through my brain. I winced and made a mental note to oil it in the morning. I didn't bother turning on the light—it would have hurt too much. I simply stripped off my clothes, climbed in under the blankets, and let it all go. All the tension, all the hurt, and all the fear—most of which *wasn't* mine. It might well come back to me in the morning or even in my dreams, but I'd worry about that if and when it happened.

I closed my eyes and, within seconds, was asleep.

It was a distant but insistent ringing that woke me. I felt around until I found my phone and then forced one eye open to see what the time was. Ten past nine.

Oh shit....

I flung off the blankets and scrambled out of bed. Mrs. Banks was not going to be happy.

"I rang her earlier and told her you were unavoidably delayed," Belle said, as she carried a tray into my room. "So get your ass back into bed and eat your breakfast first."

I grabbed a fresh T-shirt and pulled it on as I obeyed. "Then who was on the phone?"

"Someone wanting to know if we did birthday cakes."

"And do we?" I asked, amusement touching my lips.

"We do if she doesn't want anything too fancy."

She waited a moment until I was fully settled and then placed the tray on my knees. It not only held bacon and avocado croissants and a mug of tea, but also another of her green concoctions. This time it at least smelled like banana rather than something left out in the sun too long.

"We're a little light on cash at the moment," she added, "so every little bit helps."

It did indeed. "Was there any gossip at the produce market this morning about last night's events?"

"No, but the spirit world is rather uneasy. They're not liking the situation."

"Are they saying what, exactly, they're not liking? Or are they just being their usual unhelpful selves?" I picked up one of the croissants and bit into it. Delicious didn't even begin to describe it.

Belle smiled as she sat on the edge of my bed.

"They're not liking the fact the wild magic is unprotected. They're saying you should go out there and find its source."

I frowned. "To what damn purpose? It's not like I can commune with the stuff."

"You are still a Marlowe, even if a lower powered one. That alone gives you the right to at least try."

I wrinkled my nose. "Mom was almost lost to such magic the one time she was asked to intervene and redirect it. If that could happen to her, what chance would I have?"

"Arguments I also made, but the spirits are nevertheless insistent." She shrugged. "At the very least, we could try placing some form of protection spell around the wellspring."

"That's not going to stop it getting stained by darkness."

"No, but it will at least prevent whoever is responsible for Karen's death from tapping into it, especially if we *are* dealing with a vampire capable of powerful magic."

"*We* aren't supposed to be dealing with this situation at all."

"I know, but since when has that ever stopped us?"

"Good point." I finished off the croissant and then picked up her concoction. "Did Mrs. Banks mention whether the rangers had been there yet?"

"They were there earlier this morning, apparently. They took away several items, including a laptop."

Given Karen had been using the laptop to communicate with her killer, it would hopefully lead them to his location and capture, and we'd be free of having to deal with the whole situation any further.

"Since when has it *ever* been that easy?" Belle said. "I've called in Penny to help me in the café just in case there's a morning rush, so you can take your time at Marjorie's."

"And what constitutes a morning rush?" I asked, amused. "More than the half dozen people we had yesterday?"

"Hey, that's infinitely better than no people."

And there'd certainly been other times and other cafés when that was exactly what we'd gotten. Witches were a competitive lot, especially those who came from the lower houses—like those of the Fitzgerald line who'd all but run us out of the last town we'd set up in. They might have been little more than carnival fortune-tellers and tricksters of no real power, but they'd been well-known and liked in the small town. Gossip and innuendo had killed our business before it had truly gotten off the ground.

"And I still think you should have put a hex on the bastards." Belle pushed to her feet. "Or at least allowed me to order up a haunting or two to liven up their days and spoil their profiteering."

"Would a little rat infestation suffice instead?" I asked mildly.

She blinked, and then a slow smile stretched her lips. "Tell me you did it. *Please.*"

"Well, it's totally possible I might have thrown a small incantation their way as we were leaving."

"You're getting sneaky in your old age. I didn't even sense you doing it." Amusement crinkled the corners of her eyes. "How bad a rat infestation are we talking about? Enough to put a serious dent in their fortune-telling scam?"

"Let's just say I doubt many of their patrons will be willing to sit still and listen to a reading when there are rats running all around the room."

She laughed in delight. "Oh, you are *brilliant*."

"I do sometimes have my moments."

"Indeed." She glanced down at my tray. "Make sure you finish all that."

She meant the potion more than the croissants, and I nodded dutifully. As much as I bitched about them, her potions were the one reason common incantations didn't affect me as badly as they did other witches. There were benefits to having a human familiar aside from the whole friendship angle.

I listened to the clatter and voices drifting up from downstairs as I finished my breakfast. If that noise was anything to go by, we'd at least doubled our number of patrons from yesterday. If we kept that up, we might just start making a profit from this place inside of a year.

If we lasted a year, that was. I wouldn't put it past our head ranger to drive us out of town, just as the Fitzgeralds had. His reasons might be born of hate rather than professional jealousy and fear of exposure, but the result would be the same—another hit to our savings. One I wasn't entirely sure we could easily recover from. As Belle had noted, our financial situation was rather precarious at the moment.

I thrust the worry aside; there was no point thinking about it until it actually happened. I finished the rest of the potion then slid the tray onto the bedside table and headed for the shower. Once I was clean and dressed, I went back to my dressing table and studied the array of pretty charms that were hanging from their stand. I ran my fingers across each one, letting the stones speak to me, and eventually settled on one designed to keep those with malevolent natures at a distance. It wasn't strong enough to actually stop anyone attacking me—none of these charms were—but it would at least make anyone intending ill think twice about approaching me, even if they had no idea why. I slipped it around my neck, pocketed Karen's necklace, then grabbed the tray and headed back downstairs.

Belle gave me a smile but her gaze swept me critically. "You're still looking a little ragged around the edges. Don't overdo it at Mrs. Banks's."

"I won't." I dumped the tray in the empty kitchen, gave Mike—our chef—a cheery hello, and then added, "Wasn't Frank rostered on at ten thirty?"

Frank Rueben was our fifty-nine-year-old kitchen hand and the only person who'd actually answered the ad for the position. Apparently there wasn't only a decided lack of youngsters interested in menial jobs in this reservation, but—from what Frank had said—also very few employers willing to take on someone so close to retirement. His age certainly hadn't worried us, although Belle did check both his references and the spirits' thoughts. Apparently, omens were good for his employment.

As usual, they didn't deign to explain that particular statement.

"His car broke down on the way here," Belle said. "He'll be twenty minutes late, but said he'll make it up at the end of shift."

"Ah, cool." I stepped aside as a middle-aged woman with long brown hair and merry blue eyes approached. "Morning, Penny."

"Lizzie," she said, "hope you're feeling a little better now."

"I am, thank you." Once she'd squeezed past, I glanced back at Belle and said, "You need anything while I'm out?"

Belle shook her head. "Just take it easy." Silently, she added, *And just in case you decide to go in search of the wild magic's source, I've readied the backpack.*

The spirits are that insistent?

You have no idea.

I'm not up to spelling today.

Which is why I've only included warding stones rather than anything more potent.

Ah. Thanks.

Her smile flashed. *Anticipating your needs is the reason I exist.*

I snorted softly and scooped up the pack as I headed out. The morning was gray and rather cold, but there were small patches of blue visible that gave me hope it would get warmer as the day wore on. While it might have been winter when we'd first arrived in Castle Rock, we were now zooming toward Christmas and that was supposed to mean summer here in Australia. But maybe the weather gods had forgotten to read that particular memo this year.

Mrs. Banks lived on Kennedy Street, only a block away from the train station. Her place was not what I'd been expecting—a worse-for-wear white weatherboard house on a slightly elevated block, rather than one of the grand old Victorian homes that could be found everywhere in Castle Rock. The metal gate scraped across concrete that had seen better days, and the wooden steps up to the front porch were decidedly spongy. I kept a hand on the rail as a precaution, and then walked over to the front door and pressed the bell. After a few seconds, the sharp tattoo of footsteps approached.

"Who is it?" she said, without opening the door.

"It's Lizzie Grace." As the door opened, I added, "Sorry for not coming earlier, but my recovery took a bit longer than expected."

She nodded and stepped to one side. I didn't immediately enter, instead reaching into my pocket to retrieve Karen's locket.

"I thought you might want this back," I said softly.

Her fingers were trembling as she took it from mine, and grief replaced the slight edge of annoyance in her expression. She didn't say anything for several seconds, and then she took a deep breath and said, "Karen's bedroom is the second door on the left."

The inside of her house was everything the outside was not. The long, pristine hallway was decorated with rich tapestries and ornately framed paintings, the mahogany timber flooring looked freshly varnished, and there wasn't a speck of dust evident—a hard thing to achieve in flooring like that, I knew—and the coat stand to my right was a gorgeous old antique. Maybe Marjorie was concentrating on getting the inside right before she bothered with the outside.

I entered Karen's bedroom and was confronted by chaos. There were clothes, books, and God knows what else all over the floor. The bed was unmade and sheets looked as if they hadn't seen the inside of a washing machine for months. I glanced around. "I take it the rangers didn't do this?"

Marjorie snorted. "They're responsible for the white dust, but everything else is pure Karen. I gave up trying to get her to tidy up, and simply shut the door."

"Teenagers, huh?" Which made me sound decidedly older than I was, but then, I'd also been forced to grow up and look after myself a whole lot faster than most teenagers. I stepped carefully around a pile of clothes and take-out containers. "Did the rangers have anything to say this morning?"

"No." She crossed her arms and leaned against the doorframe. The wave of grief that washed over me suggested she very much needed that support to keep her upright. "They took her laptop and a couple of other bits and bobs, but I have no idea if they're any closer to catching the bastard. All they're saying is that it's too soon to know what killed her."

"Which it is," I said gently. "You can't expect miracles, either from them or from me."

"I know." She rubbed a hand across her face, smearing momentary tears. "But I won't be able to rest until I know who he is, and why he chose to murder my baby girl."

Because he's a vampire, and because he got off on it. But I kept the comments to myself. Despite what I might have seen and experienced while caught in Karen's mind, there was no proof as yet that we were dealing with a bloodsucker—nothing other than my instincts and the odd uneasiness in the spirit world, anyway.

I picked my way through the mess and stopped at the bed. The rangers might have taken anything even remotely tied to Karen's murder, but she'd never met her older lover here, only talked to him via her computer. If there *were* something to be found, then it would be something innocuous—something he'd given her that wouldn't raise any sort of alarms. And if he also happened to be a practicing blood witch, then that something would undoubtedly have magic attached to it.

There was no such thing near the bed, however. I

frowned and walked across to the window. There were fingerprints visible on both the glass and the frames, thanks to the dusting of white powder, but I had no doubt they belong to Karen rather than our predator. I'd seen her climbing out, not anyone climbing in, and there'd been no sense of anyone waiting close by.

I crossed my arms and studied the backyard. It was rather small and the grass was heavily overgrown, but there was little else in the way of shrubbery or even trees that would have provided a hiding spot. Behind it, its roof and towers dominating the skyline, was a large, red brick church. Most vamps tended to avoid holy ground, even if they weren't directly affected by it, so he probably would have waited for her out in the street. It was doubtful any of the nearby neighbors would have noticed, especially given the time Karen had climbed out of her window. And a small town like Castle Rock wasn't exactly overrun with security cameras, even in the main shopping strip.

I swung around and studied the room again. Where would a teenager hide something she wanted to keep out of immediate sight but within very easy reach? My gaze went back to the bed—or rather, the pillows, which were lying on the floor near the bed rather than actually on top of it. Given the fact Marjorie had sworn off coming into the room to even change the bedding, it was as good a hiding place as any.

I walked over and picked one of them up. It didn't feel any heavier than a pillow normally would, but I nevertheless opened the pillowcase's flap and rather warily peered inside. There was nothing more than used tissues to be seen. I tossed it to one side, picked up the second pillow, and repeated the process. This time, in amongst all the used tissues was the glitter of gold. I pulled the case free of the pillow and dumped all the rubbish onto the bed.

The chain tumbled out. It was rather fine and obviously expensive, and attached to it was a bloodstone pendant—which was not only a rare and expensive stone these days, but also somewhat appropriate given what we might be dealing with. It was, however, an unusual choice for a dark sorcerer, given bloodstones were traditionally a symbol of justice, and in some cultures believed to ward off those with the evil eye.

I reached for it, but the wash of... not corruption, not exactly, more an utter lack of compassion and humanity... stopped me. Until I was feeling stronger and had more than just the simple ward hanging around my neck to protect me, there was no way I was going to touch the thing.

I looked around on the floor and spotted a pen, which I used to scoop up the necklace. "Do you recognize this?" I asked, holding it up.

Marjorie frowned and walked closer. "No," she said. "But it might have been something her father gave her."

"I was under the impression she didn't see her dad at all." I spotted an envelope near the dressing table and walked over to grab it.

"She didn't, but he did occasionally invite her over to his place when it was her birthday or at Christmas." Marjorie's voice held a bitter note. "She valued his meager offerings far more than she ever did anything I might have done for her."

"Because she blamed you for the breakup." I slid the necklace into the envelope then folded it over to seal it.

"Yes. Her father might have had an affair, but it was all my fault, according to her." That edge of bitterness was joined by a mix of anger and grief. "I know they were close, but her refusal to see—to understand—nevertheless hurt."

"I can imagine." I continued walking around the room, but there was nothing else that spoke to me. Nothing that suggested it might have come from her killer. "Does your ex still live in town?"

"No, he moved back to Melbourne a while ago." She frowned. "Why?"

I shrugged. "If he was still living within the reservation, I'd have liked to talk to him."

"You don't think he had—"

"No," I said quickly. "But if he'd had some contact with her recently, she might have said something to him."

"He won't talk to me at all, but I can give you his phone number and address, if it helps."

I nodded. "I have no doubt the rangers will have already talked to him, but I might try, just in case."

"Thank you." She hesitated. "We've not spoken of a retainer—"

"Because there is no need until we know whether or not I can help you."

She shook her head. "I'm asking you to fully concentrate on finding this man for me, and it's hardly fair that I take you away from your new business for *any* amount of time without offering some form of compensation—especially when it means you'll also have to hire someone to take your place."

All of which was true, but not the main point. Aside from the fact O'Connor had already warned me away, I really didn't want to work on tracking Karen's killer full-time.

"As I said before, I'm not—"

"Five hundred dollars a day," she said. "For however long it takes."

I sucked in a breath. "That's a very generous offer, but—"

"Please," she said, stepping toward me, "you *have* to do this. For me, and for Karen. Neither of us will rest peacefully until this bastard is caught."

A chill ran through me at her words. Though I wasn't entirely sure why, I had a bad, *bad* feeling that even if I *did* walk away from this case, fate was already conspiring to pull me back.

Belle? I said silently. *What do you think?*

I think there's something more happening here than just a teenager's death at the hands of a possible vampire, she replied. *And I don't think we dare ignore it.*

The problem is, I don't know if we're anywhere near capable of dealing with whatever shit is brewing in this place.

Maybe not, but we're all this place has got. And let's face it, five hundred a day is nothing to be sneezed at.

I took a deep breath and then released it slowly. It didn't do a whole lot to ease the trepidation. "Okay, I'll agree. But if the shit hits the fan with the O'Connors—"

"I'll be there to hassle and threaten their asses, never you fear."

I nodded, and then raised the bagged necklace. "Do you mind if I keep this for a few days?"

"No. As I said, I have no idea where it came from."

"Thanks." I tucked the envelope into one of the backpack's pockets, but even so, I could feel the chill radiating from it. It was a sensation that made my skin crawl. "Do you want me to report back daily, or just when I have something?"

She hesitated. "Daily, if you don't mind. Even if

there's nothing to report, it'll ease my mind. It's not as if the rangers are going to tell me anything."

Which shouldn't surprise her, given we were on their land. That lack would probably change once the IIT got here, however, as they tended to be more communicative when it came to the relatives of human victims. "I've got a couple of things to do today, so it'll probably be tonight before I get back to you."

"Good." She reached out and grabbed my hand again. "Thank you. If you send me your bank details, I'll make arrangements to transfer the payments."

Part of me felt guilty over taking her money, even if it was desperately needed. A couple of payments would at least ease some of the immediate stress on our bank account.

I nodded and left, but stopped once I was back in the street, watching a train depart the station as I tried to decide what to do next. While all I really wanted was to go back to the café, I couldn't risk ignoring the warnings of the spirits for too long. If they wanted the wellspring protected ASAP, then that was what I'd better do. I might not be able to put a full spell around it for a couple of days—that sort of magic required time and careful attention to detail—but I could certainly put a warding ring around it. It wouldn't keep out a full-blown blood witch, but it was unclear as yet whether that was what we were dealing with. Certainly the bloodstone, for all that it felt foul, didn't actually reek of powerful magic.

Whether he was more powerful than *me* was something I guessed we'd find out, especially if he *was* here for the wild magic rather than to simply create a little bloody mayhem.

I walked up to Doveton Street then swung right and

headed back to Kalimna Park. Grand old maple trees arched over the road, creating a tunnel of green that was oddly soothing. Most of the houses here looked to be as old as the trees, although there were more modern buildings randomly scattered along the street that stuck out like sore thumbs. As I got closer to the park, the maples gave way to eucalyptus trees, and the roadside vegetation got scrubbier. Eventually the bitumen became dirt and stone, and all too soon I was once again in the park. The road quickly narrowed and the trees crowded closer. Though the morning was definitely warming up, in this place there was a decided chill to the air. But there was no sense of evil, no sense of death. The teenager's soul didn't haunt this place, and of that, I was glad. After the way she'd died, her soul deserved to move on to its next life rather than lingering for all eternity in the clearing in which death had found her.

Of course, if that *had* been the case, Belle could have helped her to move on, although not all ghosts actually wanted to. There were a rare few who'd rather chase revenge than the chance of rebirth.

I continued down the old road. The deeper I got into the forest, the more the noise and bustle of Castle Rock faded. Birdsong filled the air, but there was little else in the way of noise or movement.

As I neared the spot where I'd dived into the forest, the wild magic once again caressed my skin. The fact I was feeling it so strongly when I didn't appear to be anywhere near the source suggested either the wellspring was huge, or that there was more than one of them in this reservation. Which would be unusual but not unheard of.

The road began to climb and I soon came to something of a crossroad. The main road continued on for half a kilometer or so and then gently curved around to the right. The rough, heavily rutted road to my left probably went back to town. The one on my right—which was in even worse repair—disappeared into the scrub. Neither of them looked overly used, although in their current state, anything other than a four-wheel drive probably would have gotten stuck.

The wild magic was pulling me to the right, but there were no signs to clue me in on where it might take me. I grabbed my phone and brought up Google Maps. There was a pine plantation a couple of kilometers up ahead and, behind that, Mount Alexander, but Google was decidedly scant on information about either of them. Changing to street view didn't further my education, as it seemed the camera car hadn't dared risk the track.

I shoved my phone away and studied the road dubiously. I didn't like the idea of going deeper into the scrub without knowing where the hell I was headed, but it wasn't like I really had a choice. Not if I wanted to find the wellspring.

But I'd taken a dozen steps when there was a gentle rustle of leaves behind me, and a familiar voice said, "And just where are you headed, Ms. Grace?"

I briefly closed my eyes and silently swore. Aiden O'Connor was the *last* person I wanted to see right now. But I forced a smile and turned around to face him. "I'm exploring the forest. What are you doing here?"

His deep blue gaze swept me and came up suspicious. "And why would you be out here when you have a newly opened café to operate?"

"Just because it's newly opened doesn't mean I need to be chained to it twenty-four/seven," I replied. "One the advantages of being a boss is that you can ask other people to fill in while you go out for a stroll."

He raised an eyebrow—an action that spoke of disbelief even if little of it otherwise showed in his expression. "So if a stroll is all you intended, why did you visit Marjorie before heading directly up here?"

"That statement suggests my actions are being watched, Ranger, and if that's true, I'd like to know why."

"You can hardly be surprised given you were found with Karen's body last night—"

"*Last* night you said you were aware I didn't kill her—what's changed?"

"Nothing at all."

"Then why the hell am I being followed?"

"Because, as I also said last night, I believe you know a whole lot more than what you're saying. So why are you up here, Ms. Grace? Wouldn't happen to be searching for the elusive stranger, would you?"

His words revived the images—and emotions—I'd been an unwilling partner to, and heat stained my cheeks. "No, I am *not*."

"Then why are you here? Honesty would be advisable, because there are harsh penalties for any human who steps within the boundaries of the O'Connor compound without permission."

I quickly looked around. There was absolutely no indication that I'd entered his pack's home grounds, and surely there should have at least been a warning sign. "Is that where I am?"

"That's where this roads heads, yes."

"So is your compound in the plantation, or up on Mount Alexander?"

"The latter," he said. "And stop avoiding the question."

It took me a moment to even *remember* the question. I hesitated, and then said, "I'm looking for the source of the wild magic."

He raised that eyebrow again. "And why would someone who has claimed to be not much of a witch be looking for that?"

"Because I'm all this place has got, and I need to place some protection around the wellspring in an effort to stop evil from staining it."

"You say that like evil has substance—"

"Because it *has*." I crossed my arms and met his skeptical gaze evenly. "Don't tell me you've never walked into a room and immediately felt either comfortable or ill at ease, because I know that wouldn't be true. Wolves, while generally not psychic, *are* sensitive to currents of stronger emotions."

And not just lust and desire, but also hate and fear.

He studied me, his expression as unreadable as ever. "No witch who has lived within the reservation has *ever* mentioned wild magic."

"Why would they? It's their job to protect and guide it; there would be no need to mention it unless something was going very wrong." I hesitated. "Why did the last witch leave?"

"His residency was revoked." His answer was flat, and filled with both repressed anger and deep hurt.

Which only made me all the more curious as to what had gone on here. But if Marjorie, who was obviously a leading lawyer in this town, had no clue, then there was very little chance that *any* other human living here would. And the wolves certainly *wouldn't* tell me; werewolves were extremely protective—even secretive—of anything related to their pack.

Would the spirits who resided in this place know? It might be worth asking—although surely if they did, they would have already mentioned it.

Not necessarily, Belle said. *They tend to offer information only as required or as asked, remember.*

And yet they have no damn qualms about offering unwanted advice.

Belle laughed. *That's because not only are we seen as a special case, but because my guides do feel rather protective toward us.*

I'm not sure I really want to be regarded as 'special' by the spirit world. Out loud, I added, "And are you my self-appointed follower, Ranger?"

There was little warmth in the smile that touched his lips, which was a shame, because they were rather nice lips.

I frowned and batted the thought away. I didn't need any sort of attraction happening right now, especially to a man who hated what I was with every inch of his being.

"I wasn't following you. I was up here searching for scents and heard your approach." He paused, and just for a moment, something sparked in his eyes—something I would have named amusement if it weren't for his otherwise stony expression. "Silent you are not."

"I wasn't trying to be, either last night or now." I hesitated. "Wouldn't the wind have now erased any scent if it *was* to be found?"

"Yes, but I wasn't only searching for a scent. I was also looking for any indication that a third party had moved through the forest."

"And did you find it?"

He gave me a cool smile and crossed his arms—an action that only emphasized their lean strength, even through the shirt.

"Fine, don't answer." I spun around and started off

down the road again. "If I'm not actually near your compound yet, then I guess I'm safe to continue on my merry way."

I rather suspected I wouldn't be doing so alone, and that suspicion was immediately proven correct.

He caught up with me in three quick strides and then said, "Why did you choose to settle in Castle Rock?"

Because I felt compelled to come here, and because the spirits thought it was a good idea. But I could hardly admit *that* to this man. "The fact that your whole reservation is a tourist destination was part of the reason. It's a lot easier to run a successful business when you have a good stream of people coming through."

"Then why settle here rather than Argyle? That's the main spa town, not Castle Rock."

I shrugged. "We liked the feel of this place better."

He didn't immediately reply, but I could sense his gaze on me. Or rather, on my hair. Again his suspicion rose around me but he didn't give it voice. "Because of the wild magic?"

"Because it seemed like a really friendly town." I glanced at his stony countenance somewhat wryly. "We *did* tell your council we intended doing readings and selling charms at the café."

"And forgot to add the fact you were also witches."

"Damn it, Ranger, if you fall foul of another werewolf, do you blame your whole race for that one wolf's action?"

"No—"

"Then stopping blaming whatever catastrophe happened here on every damn witch you come in contact with." There was an edge of anger in my voice that I couldn't quite control. "I can't change whatever that was. I can't heal it. No one can—not until all those involved are willing to let the wound be healed. And it seems to me neither you nor this reservation is willing to do that just yet."

"You know *nothing* about me or my pack—"

"No, I don't, nor do I fucking want to," I said, in an echo of his own statement. "But you're running a huge risk by not having a powerful, vetted witch here to protect the wild magic, and you'd better pray like hell the darker forces do *not* become aware of it."

"Vetted witch?" he said, voice mild. "Does that mean you haven't gone through accreditation, and therefore are unaligned to any of the major or minor houses?"

I swore internally. Trust me to run off at the mouth and give him a clue like that.

"No, it does *not*," I snapped. "Haven't you got other business to attend to, Ranger? Like discovering the man who murdered the teenager? You're hardly going to find him following me about."

"Maybe," he said. "And maybe not."

If I'd been a wolf, I would have growled in frustration—which probably would have either amused him or made him even more convinced I was hiding something. Which, as far as the case went, wasn't really true. Not when the only thing I was hiding were truths he didn't want to hear.

I bit back my annoyance and continued down the road, the condition of which got worse the deeper we moved into the scrub. And even though I was watching every step carefully, my awareness of the man walking beside me was painfully acute.

"Why is this road so bad if it leads up to your compound?" I asked, more in an effort to break the growing tension—mine, not his.

"Because it's a back entrance rather than the main one." His gaze remained on me. Obviously, he wasn't overly concerned about the possibility of breaking an ankle on this pitiful excuse of a road. "Tell me about the wild magic, and why you feel it's so important."

Surprise had me briefly glancing up at him. "Why? It's not like you actually believe it exists, is it?"

"What I believe isn't relevant right now," he said. "I'm merely trying to understand what wild magic is and why you think it's connected to Karen's murder."

"I didn't *say* it was connected. I just said it being unprotected is a problem."

"Which is what I'm trying to understand." He caught my elbow and guided me around a rather large hole. "Honesty in all matters is advisable. It will help whatever action the council decides to take when the news of your being a witch reaches their ears."

I snorted and pulled my arm away from his touch— and tried to ignore the fact that the heat of it lingered. "I'm surprised they haven't already, given your hatred."

"Despite what you seem to think, emotion neither blinds me nor guides all my actions." He hesitated. "I admit my behavior in that clearing was perhaps a little less than professional, and you are more than welcome to file a complaint—"

I snorted again. "As if filing a complaint against an O'Connor will get me anywhere in a reservation run by O'Connors."

"We only hold three seats on the council, which is no more, and no less, than the Marin and Sinclair packs."

Surprise ran through me. "But this is your traditional land—"

"Which is *why* we hold the area around Mount Alexander in its entirety," he said. "But there was never any question of us ruling this place over the other packs. It would have been unworkable."

As had been proven in some of the older reservations. Obviously by the time *this* reservation had come into being, lessons had been learned.

"And," he continued, "you're once again avoiding the question."

"Wild magic," I said, as the road began to climb and the scrub gave way to the soldier-like lines of pines. "Is not really magic, but rather a force, or an energy, that comes from not only the earth itself, but everything that lives in the soil or flies in the skies. It is the ground we walk on and the air we breathe; it is the rivers and trees and life itself, right down to the micro-organisms that are to be found everywhere."

"All wolves are aware that in life there is power," he said. "But what separates wild magic from the power witches draw on every day? That also comes from the world around us, does it not?"

"Yes, but only a surface level. Wild magic comes from deep within the earth—there are some who suggest its source is the tumultuous outer layers of the earth's core—and that's the reason it so dangerous and unpredictable."

"So these wellsprings are also dangerous?"

"In and of themselves, no. They're simply collection points, and no one really understands why they develop. But, like any source of power, be it magic or man-made, if they are placed under the wrong influence, then they can be deadly."

"How?"

"Have you heard of the High Ridge Massacre?"

He snorted. "It'd be a rare person in Australia who hasn't. It's not often an entire town is all but wiped out in one brutal and bloody night."

"Ah, but that one night was merely the ultimate culmination." My replies were coming out in an increasingly breathless manner, thanks to the steadily rising incline. "What went unsaid in the news reports was the fact that the murder rate kept increasing over a period of months. The final mass slaughter was simply the pinnacle."

I could feel his gaze on me. "And you know this how?"

"Because even a low-class witch like myself hears whispers." I stopped and eyed the road ahead. It showed no sign of flattening out, and my legs were seriously beginning to burn. "How much further until we reach the boundary of your pack's land?"

"Another couple of kilometers." There was a hint of amusement in his voice. "Not far."

"For the fit, maybe." But if I waited for the burn to ease, I'd be here all day. I swung the pack around and opened it up. Thankfully, amongst all the other paraphernalia, Belle had included a bottle of drinking water.

I took a long swig then offered it to the ranger. He shook his head and said, "I'm gathering you believe the wild magic was responsible for both this upswing and the murders?"

"Yes. As I said, the energy that gathers at wellsprings is neither good nor bad, but it can be *stained*—influenced, if you like—by either. The wellspring in High Ridge was newly formed and rather small, but the darker forces

KERI ARTHUR

became aware of its existence before a witch could be assigned to its protection. The wellspring was irrevocably stained, which is why life in that town remains untenable for all who follow the light."

"And this is what you think will happen here?"

"For everyone's sake, I hope not." I stoppered the water bottle and shoved it back in the pack. "But whether you like it or not, Karen's murder might just be the first play in evil's takeover of this place."

"Which is an overly dramatic statement, I'm thinking."

"Perhaps." I shouldered my pack and continued on. "But it might be wise to go read the police reports from that time. As a ranger, you should have access to them."

"I very much doubt those reports will even mention your wild magic."

"No. It'll just show the sudden and dramatic upswing in offenses."

He didn't immediately reply, and for several minutes the only sound to be heard was the rasp of my breathing. His, I noted with annoyance, had barely altered.

I studied the tree-lined road ahead. The caress of wild magic was definitely stronger, but there was nothing yet in that sensation that suggested I was close to the source. Knowing my damn luck, it would be on O'Connor land.

"There hasn't been a witch on this reservation for over a year now," he said. "Surely if our wellspring was going to draw evil, it would have done so."

"It would depend entirely on what protections the last witch placed on it before you ran him out of town."

"We didn't run him out of town," he bit back. "We may have revoked his residency, but he disappeared before we could serve notice. There's still a warrant out for his arrest."

"Have you contacted the Regional Witch Association for assistance? If he's wanted, they would surely—"

Aiden's snort was loud and disdainful. "What? Give away one of their own?"

"If he's suspected of a crime, they would have to."

"And yet they have been spectacularly unhelpful in the past." He shook his head. "We'll take our chances and let the law do its job without the interference of any damn witches."

"We're not all bad, you know."

"I never said you were. I merely said I don't want to associate with any of you."

"And yet, here you are, associating."

Once again his smile held very little in the way of humor. "I'm doing my job. Nothing more, nothing less."

I harrumphed and continued to plod up the final bit of the incline. By the time I reached the top, it felt like I'd run a damn marathon. Any impression that I might have been in okay shape had been well and truly shattered.

The road plunged downward again and was quickly consumed by the regimental lines of green. The mountain that rose on the other side of the valley was rugged and stone-filled, a place of shadows and old, *old* power.

Mount Alexander, I presumed, and home to not only the O'Connor pack but also the wild magic. It could be nowhere else, of that I was certain.

Which meant it was basically impossible for me to access the area without first getting permission from the pack's leaders. As Aiden had already noted, I was a far from silent walker, and while I did know invisibility and scent containment spells, werewolves were capable of picking up the distortion shimmer that was one of the few telltale signs of both.

The flip side, of course, was the fact that it would be just as difficult for anyone *else* to access it. And that at least gave me some time to come up with a way to convince the councilors that the wild magic's source needed some protection—and that it would be better if it came from a more powerful witch than me.

A sharp ring broke the silence and made me jump. Aiden dug his phone out of his pocket and walked down the hill several yards.

I spotted a largish rock on the other side of the road and walked over to sit down and catch my breath. The only sound that broke the silence was the melodious tune of a magpie. Aiden wasn't talking, but it was rather obvious that whatever he was hearing, he didn't like.

After several more minutes, he hung up and met my gaze. His annoyance spun around me, as fierce as it might have been had he been standing right next to me.

"What?" I immediately said.

"It appears you were right."

Amusement stirred through me. "And is that why you're so annoyed, or is it something else?"

The faintest hint of curiosity glimmered through the annoyance as he said, "Do you always try to make light of a situation?"

"When I can, yes." I paused. "What was I right about?"

He thrust his hands on his hips and spun around to study the valley below us. Getting his emotions under control, I suspected, and felt like telling him that it didn't really matter because—for who only knows what reason—I was sensing them anyway.

"That was my sister—"

"Ciara?" I cut in. "The one who's also the coroner?"

He nodded. "She's got the prelim results on cause of death."

Trepidation stepped into my heart. "And?"

The waves of emotion rolling off him got fiercer, making my breath catch in my throat.

"Cause of death was catastrophic blood loss."

"From what?" I knew, God help me, I knew, but something within had to hear it confirmed.

He turned around and his gaze finally met mine again. The blue depths were dark, and spoke of fear and fury combined. "The two wounds on her neck have been identified. We have a vampire on the reservation."

CHAPTER
four

There was little point in wasting air on an I-told-you-so—not when this was one situation where I wished I *hadn't* been correct. "What are you going to tell Marjorie?"

"Nothing," he said, voice sharp. "And neither will you. Is that clear?"

"Crystal." I paused, and then added, "Unfortunately, a vampire may not be *all* you're dealing with."

"Cryptic statements are not something I want or need right now, Ms. Grace," he all but growled, "so whatever it is, just spit it out."

"Ms. Grace was my grandmother's name. I prefer Lizzie." I hesitated. "The reason I couldn't give you much of a description of the vampire is because I think he was using magic to conceal his presence."

He frowned. "I didn't think vampires were capable of magic."

"Most aren't. Those who are were generally capable

of such before they turned, and the magic they use is the blood kind. Which," I added, forestalling his next question, "is magic whose source comes from sacrifices rather than the purer energy of the world. Have there been any recent reports of chickens or other small animals going missing?"

"Not that I'm aware of, but that's the province of the animal management section. I'll check with them." He frowned. "There also haven't been any reports of people being attacked, either."

"He might be moving outside the reservation to feed."

"Yes." He ran a hand through his hair, sending ripples of brighter silver through the dark blond. "The council is not going to be pleased."

No one ever was when it came to discovering there was a vampire in their neck of the woods. "I suggest you contact the IIT and ask them to bring in a vampire specialist."

"Indeed."

He grimaced as he strode toward me. "I need to get back to headquarters, so I'm afraid you're on your own from here on in. The boundary into our compound is the river that lies at the bottom of this valley. Don't cross it unless you wish to land in serious trouble."

"I've gone as far as I intend to today, Ranger."

"Really?" Surprise ran briefly across his expression. "I hadn't pegged you as someone who'd give up so easily."

"It's hardly giving up when there's no point in going on. The wellspring is on your mountain."

"You can tell that from here?"

"Yes. And when you're informing the council about the vampire, then perhaps you can also mention—"

"No. Not without proof."

"So you'd rather risk this place becoming untenable than trust the word of a witch, however tenuous her link to magic?" I shook my head. "I hadn't pegged you as someone who was so closed-minded."

His gaze narrowed dangerously but he didn't say anything. He simply strode past me and headed down the hill. About halfway down, energy stirred and the air shimmered as the internal magic of the wolf—a magic that didn't cause the change, but merely hid the transformation that came from evolutionary DNA adaptions, as well as neatly taking care of everything he was wearing or carrying—swept him effortlessly from one form to another. His wolf was as lean and powerful as his human, and his coat rippled with silver at every movement.

Even in animal form, the damn man was attractive.

He leaped off the road and disappeared into the trees. I pushed upright and began the long journey back to town. It was close to one by the time I arrived back at the café and the sunshine that had been out until that point disappeared behind a gathering bank of dark clouds. I couldn't help hoping it wasn't an omen of some kind.

The bell above the door rang as I entered the café, but the merry sound was almost lost to the babble of conversation. All but three of our tables were full, and the air held a happy resonance that spoke well for our future. I greeted the couple who'd come in for coffee yesterday, and nodded at the rest as I headed toward the back of the room. Belle glanced up and gave me a cheerful grin, even though she'd been aware of my arrival well before I'd even stepped through the door.

"Do you need a hand here?" I asked

"Not immediately." *Go secure things and then have a*

shower first.

I raised my eyebrows. *Are you saying I stink?*

Eau de sweat is strong on you.

I snorted and continued toward the reading room. The air sparked briefly as I entered, a clear indication the spells encircling and protecting the room were active. Incense burned in each corner of the shadowed room, filling the space with the warm scents of cinnamon, clove, lemon, and sandalwood—all of which provided either protection or enhanced focus and concentration. There was a simple wooden table in the center of the room, along with four mismatched but comfortable chairs. A large rug covered the floor and bright lengths of material were draped from the ceiling, not only providing the otherwise drab room with some color, but also hiding the spellwork engraved into the wood. The spell stones we'd placed in each corner backed these up; only an entity of extreme power was going to get into this room.

I walked across to the full-height bookcase that had been built along the right wall. Once I'd moved a decorative candle and a couple of pottery dragons, I placed my hand against the bookcase's wooden back. Energy immediately crawled across my fingers, and after a slight pause, there was a soft click and the wooden panel slipped to one side, revealing an eight-inch-deep empty compartment. The entire bookshelf was actually little more than a cover for thirty-six of these storage compartments, each one matching the size of bookshelf that fronted it. They could only be accessed via Belle's hands or mine. Fingerprint scanners might be the latest evolution in physical locks, but witches had been using a magical version for decades.

I swung the backpack around and placed the foul-feeling necklace into the compartment. Once it was securely locked away, I quickly stored the rest of the pack's items and then headed upstairs to clean up.

The rest of the afternoon passed by relatively quickly. While we weren't inundated with customers, there was a steady enough stream to keep everyone busy. Once the café was closed, I sent Belle upstairs to relax while I finished cleaning up and made us dinner—steak, eggs, and vegetables. While a lot of false witches tended to be vegetarians or even vegans, those of us who dealt with real stuff had to be carnivores. A spell could only be as strong as the practitioner, and *that* meant getting the full range of minerals and vitamins from *all* available sources, be it from fat, dairy, vegetable, or animal.

I carried our meals upstairs. The day had gotten colder as the afternoon had progressed, so instead of eating on the balcony as usual, Belle had dragged the table and chairs inside, squashing them into the small space between the sofa and the TV.

"*I*," she said, as she grabbed her cutlery, "am famished."

"You're in a café surrounded by food. If you don't take the time to eat, you've no one to blame but yourself."

I straddled a chair and then picked up my knife and fork and tucked in. The only sound that broke the silence was the clink of knives against the china.

Belle finally pushed her plate away with a contented sigh and then said, "So, we *are* dealing with a vampire."

"Unfortunately, yes." I gathered the plates and rose. "You want coffee?"

She nodded. "Do you think you could use the necklace you found at Marjorie's to track him?"

Once I'd dumped the plates onto the bench, I

grabbed a couple of mugs and made us both an espresso. "That will depend on what sort of spell he's placed on it."

I had received some training in spell unraveling, but—as usual—I was nowhere near as proficient as either my parents or my brother.

"Juli is a smug wanker," Belle commented. "And you have no idea how often I've thanked the spirits for making me your familiar rather than his."

Juli was the nickname she'd given my brother, Julius, when we were both still kids, and it was one that seriously pissed him off. I grinned. "Oh, I don't know—imagine the fun you could have had making his life utter hell."

"As delicious as that prospect might be, it fails to make me in any way nostalgic for what might have been." She leaned back in the chair and crossed her legs. "I didn't get the impression that what you were feeling from the locket was magic, per se. More a cold inhumanity, which in itself suggests we're dealing with an old vampire rather than one who is freshly turned."

I picked up the two coffees and walked back over. "Just because I couldn't feel a spell doesn't mean it's not there. Especially if he's a strong blood witch."

She accepted her mug with a nod of thanks and took a sip. "And do you think he is?"

"I don't know." I sat down on the sofa and propped my feet on the chair. "Don't suppose the spirits have said anything?"

"About vampires? No. They're just blathering on about darkness headed this way." She paused, her gaze narrowing briefly. "They deny blathering. They merely wish to emphasize the fact we need to be fully prepared for whatever this way comes."

"Which is entirely unhelpful given they aren't inclined

to tell us what comes." I drank some coffee. "I might contact Marjorie's ex tomorrow and see if he's willing to talk about Karen."

"Surely the rangers would have already done that?"

"Yes, but it's not as if they'll tell us what he might have said."

"It's also possible he's as clueless as Marjorie," she said. "Teenagers are notoriously recalcitrant when it comes to telling parents *anything* about their social lives."

"I still think I need to try, if only to cross him off the list."

I studied the darkness beyond the windows, feeling the cold caress of the moon's light even though I couldn't see it. Each moon phase had different benefits when it came to using magic, but when the moon hit its peak, so too did its power. It was *this* power that had werewolves changing—not because they had to, but because they were more in tune to its heat and energy in wolf form. That pulse of life and strength also meant it was the perfect time to perform the more difficult spells.

"The full moon is three nights away," I added, "so I might leave unpicking whatever spell that pendant holds until then."

Belle nodded. "In which case, you'd better grab plenty of sleep. You know the toll that sort of magic takes on you."

"And you," I said. "It's not like I do any of these things alone."

"Ah, but that's what we engine rooms are for."

I smiled, even though it was true enough. The main task of any familiar might be to monitor and protect, but they were also a lifeline of strength—a last resort the witch could draw on. While it was a rare occurrence, there *had* been familiars so completely drained by their witch that death had claimed them. Which, in the case of spirit familiars, meant becoming a shade and never being able to either operate in—or communicate with—anyone in the spirit or the living realms again for all eternity.

"Which is *not* something I'll have to face," Belle commented, as she reached back for the remote and flicked on the TV.

"Unless, of course, you're destined to become a spirit guide or familiar on your death," I mused. "It's not like history has been littered with witch-born familiars, so we could be treading new ground in more ways than one."

"Bite your tongue, woman." Her expression was fierce, but the amusement dancing in her silvery eyes somewhat spoiled the effect. "Don't get me wrong, I wouldn't trade our friendship for *anything*, but how likely is it that I'd be so lucky a second damn time?"

"I don't know," I said. "The next generation of bluebloods could almost be decent by then—"

"I think I'd cut my metaphorical wrists first." She tossed me the remote then pushed upright. "I'm off for a shower."

I nodded and picked up my phone to check in with Marjorie—though I avoided any mention of the vampire. After Aiden's emphatic warning, I really had no other choice. For the next couple of hours, I did nothing more strenuous than watch mindless renovation programs. Once nine o'clock had rolled around, I handed the remote back to Belle and headed for bed.

Sleep found me quickly enough, but so too did the dreams.

At first there was little more than a mire of shadows through which shapes moved. I had no idea whether they were human or animal, and for a while the dream seemed content to let it remain that way. Eventually those insubstantial shapes gave way to a barely lit industrial space—a space that very much echoed the one in which I'd found my sister. A single dark shape moved through it, but even with the shadows all but concealing who or what it was, it seemed broken and ungainly.

As the witching hour was struck, the dream deepened, and the shadows gave way to utter darkness.

In that darkness, I heard a beat.

A *heart*beat, but one that surely couldn't support life, given the long pause between one thump and another. And yet it beat on, gaining strength if not speed.

The darkness shifted and revealed flesh. Flesh that held the blush of blue-white lifelessness. Flesh that was female, and young rather than old.

The image panned out slightly, revealing lips that were as red as blood in a face that was deathly white.

I knew that face. It belonged to Karen.

Behind her, waiting and watching, was the shadow of a man. There was no detail in his form, nothing to give me any clue as to who he might be. Nothing other than the fact he wasn't a werewolf—not with shoulders like that.

The heartbeat became a clock, one that was counting down. Seventeen fifty-nine, seventeen fifty-eight, seventeen fifty-seven....

The darkness moved yet again. This time it showed me an old shack made of stone and roughly split trees. It looked abandoned, but the broken windows had been covered with thick black plastic and there was smoke coming from the chimney. Rather weirdly, under the protective cover of the woodbox next to the front door, sat a dapper pair of black-and-white wingtip shoes. Shoes *that* fancy certainly had no place in the middle of the Australian bush.

The scene faded into darkness so absolute I couldn't see anything else. But I was moving—walking—on ground that was wet, sticky, and warm against my bare feet. The farther I walked, the stronger and deeper that flow of moisture became, until I was battling a gelatinous river that came with a very strong metallic smell.

Fear surged at that, but the dream was relentless, refusing me time to dwell on such emotions. The river continued to climb up my body and I started to lose my footing against the force of it. I was thrashing about, both in the dream and in reality, but the dream's talons were deep within me and would not let go.

The river lifted me up and then swept me over an edge. I plunged down for what seemed like ages before finally hitting something solid. As I sprawled forward face-first, the river became a trickle and shadows began to lift the utter darkness again. I rolled onto my hands and knees and looked around.

All I saw was blood. Blood and bodies. Broken, mutilated bodies, for as far as the eye could see.

Horror filled me and I screamed. The dream shattered and I jerked upright in bed, the scream dying on my lips as I stared, wide-eyed, into the safe darkness of my bedroom.

For several minutes I couldn't move, couldn't even blink. I just sucked in air in an effort to calm my nerves and sweep away the lingering, shadowy wisps of blood and death.

That dream…. I shuddered. Thank God I'd placed spells around both Belle's bedroom and mine—not so much to keep evil out, but to give her some mental space from the constant barrage of my thoughts. She might be my familiar, but she didn't need to be on call twenty-four/seven. *That* would likely drive even the strongest person insane.

I *could* break through the protection spells if it was absolutely necessary, though. I wasn't about to totally alienate myself from her help.

As my heart rate slowed to a more normal rhythm, I thrust the blankets aside and padded over to the wardrobe. I didn't often drink, but there were definitely some times when coffee and chocolate just didn't cut it.

This was one of those times.

I grabbed the bottle of Glenfiddich whiskey I'd tucked away when we'd bought this place months ago, and with shaky hands, poured myself a drink. I gulped it down and closed my eyes as the alcohol burned the few remaining vestiges of the dream away.

Prophetic dreams *weren't* something that generally plagued me. In fact, the last time I'd had one had been when the sorcerer was stalking the blueblood witches of Canberra, and my sister subsequently had ended up as one of the dead. Hers had also been the very last life he'd taken.

That sorcerer hadn't, to my knowledge, ever been caught.

So did the dream mean he was active again? I frowned and poured myself another shot. The initial part of the dream had certainly shown the same sort of warehouse in which he'd sacrificed all his victims, but he'd been neither ill-formed nor ungainly. He'd been a man in his prime, both physically *and* metaphysically.

By the same token, the figure couldn't have been the vampire who'd attacked Karen, either. Even if he *had* been using a glamour to fudge what she was seeing, she would have felt the reality of his flesh if it were malformed in any way.

Did that mean the dream was trying to warn me that the vampire wasn't all we would face in this place? Or was it simply a matter of the spirits' dire warnings to Belle somehow finding form in my dreams?

I slid down the wall until my butt hit the carpet. If that *was* the intent behind the first section of the dream, then the latter was undoubtedly a warning about what would happen if the vampire wasn't caught quickly enough. It was the bit in the middle—the bit about Karen—that I really didn't understand. Karen was dead. I'd felt the life leave her flesh, so I had no idea what the dreams were trying to tell me. Which wasn't really surprising as I hadn't initially understood them the last time it had happened.

And because of that, my sister had died.

I rubbed a hand across my eyes, smearing tears that were a combination of guilt and sorrow. The sane, rational part of me knew that statement for the lie it was—knew that even if I *had* understood the message, Cat would still have died—but the heart and the mind weren't always rational.

For some reason, that thought had my mind slipping to Aiden, and curiosity stirred. I downed the rest of the whiskey then reached for my laptop and booted it up. Marjorie had said that the witch ban had come into effect just over a year ago, so that at least gave me a starting point. But whatever had happened here wasn't likely to be in the national newspapers. It wasn't even likely to have made the regional papers—most reservations had strict guidelines as to what could and couldn't be reported. Only something very serious—something that involved multiple deaths—would have made the newspapers. I hadn't gotten the impression that *that* was what had happened here.

But if the Interspecies Investigations Team had been involved, there might be some information to be found via the freedom of information section on their website. By law, the IIT were required to place a summation of all investigations online. If Mr. Joe Public wanted a full report, then it could be requested. It was meant to reassure everyone that the IIT was above reproach in all its dealings, and while there had been some instances of corruption or favoritism, for the most part, they did a pretty good job under often difficult conditions.

Not that the werewolves of *this* reservation seemed to think that.

Once on the website, I did a search for any mention of the Faelan Reservation within the last year and a half. After a few seconds, three files appeared. I clicked the first one and a PDF sheet opened in a second window. It was a report on one James Barton, a baker at Argyle, whose body had been found three days after he'd been reported missing. His death had been classified as a misadventure—he'd fallen down an old mine shaft, had no phone reception, and had bled out.

I closed that one and opened the second. This one involved a murder in Maldoon, the one of five towns that defined the reservation's borders. The perpetrator—a wolf who'd been on a three-day drinking binge—was currently serving a fifteen-year sentence for murder.

I opened the last one. This summation was brief and to the point but gave very little in the way of information. A witch had been involved in a suspected murder in Castle Rock, but had fled the area before he could be captured.

The timing was right, but the file told me nothing else. It didn't even give me names.

I swore softly and put in a request for the full file. And wondered as I did if the IIT would be obliged to notify the rangers or even the council that it had been requested. Under normal circumstances I wouldn't have thought so, but the lack of names in the summary was troubling.

I checked my e-mails and then caught up on what was happening in the social media arena. When five thirty rolled around, I shut down the computer, grabbed a shower, and headed down to the kitchen to start the day's work.

By the time Belle clattered down the stairs at seven, I not only had most of the prep work done, but also had breakfast ready and waiting.

"Whoa," Belle said as she grabbed some cutlery for us both. "I'm gathering by the amount of food on these plates that you've had a rather nasty night?"

"I dreamed."

She glanced at me quickly. "The everyday 'I've got lots to worry about' kind, or the other damn one?"

"What do you think?"

She swore. "You haven't had a prophetic dream in more than twelve years, so why now?"

"I don't know." I quickly filled her in on what I'd seen and what I'd guessed it might all mean, and then added, "One thing is very clear—we need to track this vamp down, and fast."

"And protect our butts as much as we can in the process," she said, around a mouthful of food. "I think I saw a charm spell in one of Gran's books designed to ward off the undead."

Amusement touched my lips. "Seriously? There's a charm for that?"

"Hey," she said, waving her fork threateningly at me. "Charms have saved our butts more than once, if only because they're such a profitable item."

"Yes, but we've concentrated on the whole 'bring good fortune or find love' end of the spectrum, never anything stronger." Not for the general public, anyway. I picked up some bacon and munched on it contemplatively. "Will such a charm actually work?"

"If it's in Granny's book, it'll work." She paused. "To a degree, anyway. I mean, Gran was killed by a spirit gone rogue after all, and she'd been wearing the appropriate warding charm at the time."

"Awesome. That fills me with so much more confidence."

She grinned. "I might also check if any of our books have anything on vampires and how they turn. The image of those red lips is snagging at my subconscious."

"Mine too," I said, "but I felt the life leave her, so I'm really not sure what the dream is trying to imply."

"Nothing good, I'm sure."

That was a fact that couldn't be disputed, given the river of blood that had almost drowned me. "I'll contact Karen's dad this morning. I might also head over to the tourist bureau and see if they've a map that shows the location of any miners camps in the area."

"It could also be an idea to report in to our ranger—"

I snorted. Loudly. "Even if he didn't loathe the fact I'm a witch, it's highly unlikely he'll take my dream seriously."

Her sudden smile held a seriously wicked edge. "Hey, he told us off for not following procedure, so I think it's only fair we toe the line *completely*, and report every little scrap of information we have to the man."

"Because *that's* not going to piss him off any further." I mopped up the last bits of yolk, then rose and walked into the kitchen to dump the plate. "Have you arranged for Penny to cover my shifts for the rest of the week?"

Belle nodded. "She's quite pleased with the extra work."

"Oh, good." I grabbed my phone from the counter where I'd left it last night and then headed upstairs to make the call to Karen's father.

"Phillip Banks," he said. "How may I help you?"

His voice was cool and polite, but for some odd reason, dislike stirred. "Mr. Banks, my name is Lizzie Grace, and I'm—"

"The witch who found Karen's body," he finished for me. "How can I help you, Ms. Grace?"

His tone remained unperturbed, even when he said his daughter's name. While I was well aware he was on the other end of a phone and that I could be reading him totally wrong, that sense of dislike got stronger. "I was wondering if I might be able to meet with you to discuss your daughter."

"I've already told the rangers all I know. I'm not sure there's anything else I could add."

"I'm not working with the rangers," I said. "Marjorie hired me to try and track down Karen's killer."

He was silent for a moment, and then said, "And do you think you can?"

"I'm willing to try, but there are never any guarantees, whether we're talking about policing, psi work, or witchcraft."

Although, as a rule, bluebloods generally *could*

guarantee an outcome 99.9 percent of the time. It was the reason they held so much wealth and power.

"I've got some business in Bendigo this morning, so I could meet you at say—" He paused. "Nine thirty? Would that suit?"

I glanced at my watch. It was close to eight thirty now, but Bendigo was only a little over thirty minutes away. "That would be great."

"Good. There's a little café called Beans and Greens on View Street. I'll be wearing a blue suit."

"And I'll be the one with the crimson hair. Thanks, Mr. Banks."

After quickly brushing my teeth and changing into a fresh pair of jeans and a dark green sweater, I grabbed my car keys and handbag, and headed back downstairs.

Belle handed me a coffee-filled travel mug and a cookie on the way through. I grinned my thanks and walked around to the car park that was shared by all five businesses along this section of the street. Once I'd safely placed the travel mug into its holder, I started our old wagon and headed for Bendigo. Sadly, the cookie didn't even make it out of Castle Rock.

Beans and Greens was a small but bright café abuzz with people and filled with the gorgeous aroma of roasting coffee beans. I stopped near the entrance and looked around until I spotted a man in a dark blue suit reading a newspaper at a table near the stairs. He would have been in his midforties, with dark blond hair and a suntanned, pleasant face. I ordered a coffee and then walked over. He didn't even glance up. Either the article he was reading was fascinating, or he was one of those people who had no situational awareness. I was voting for the latter.

I cleared my throat. "Mr. Banks? I'm Lizzie Grace."

He finally glanced up. His eyes, like his aura, were mostly brown—a color that spoke of self-absorption. "It's not often we see a blueblood in these parts."

And good morning to you, too, I wanted to say, but bit the comment back. He didn't seem the type to appreciate sarcasm. I pulled out a chair and sat down opposite him. "You're not seeing one now. The hair is a gift from a relation decades back that had a brief but apparently fertile interlude with one while she was in Sydney."

It was a lie I'd told so often it rolled off my tongue as easily as the truth.

"Meaning you're not really a witch?"

I hesitated. I had no idea what links this man might have to either the council or the rangers, so I couldn't risk admitting anything more than I already had. Not that *that* was ever a fault of mine—if I had one thing in common with werewolves, it was a desire to say as little about myself as possible.

"I'm capable of small magic—charms and the like—but not much more, I'm afraid."

"Then how did you find Karen? The rangers were a little light on detail when I talked to them."

As I explained psychometry and its uses to him, I searched his face for any sign of grief. Though both his expression and his eyes gave very little away, there were at least *some* splashes of black in his aura. But there was nothing on the scale of what I'd seen in Aiden's aura.

"And this is how you're hoping to find her killer? Via this skill?"

"Maybe, if I can find something that holds his vibes." I crossed my arms on the table. "When was the last time you talked to Karen?"

He shrugged. "About a month ago."

"Was it usual for you two to speak so infrequently?"

"Yeah. I don't think she's ever really forgiven me for not taking her with me when I left Marjorie."

Which was the opposite of what Marjorie had said. Of course, it was also possible Karen was playing her parents off each other, using the guilt they felt around her to get what she desired. "If you don't mind me asking, why didn't you?"

He grimaced. "Because my work takes me away for days on end, and that's hardly a practical situation in which to raise a kid."

Which was a legitimate enough reason, but I very much suspected the real reason was the fact that having her around might have cramped his lifestyle.

"Can you remember anything about that last conversation? Did she by any chance mention a new boyfriend?"

He was shaking his head before I'd finished. "As I said to the rangers, it was weeks ago. To be honest, even if she *had* mentioned a new beau, it's not likely I'd remember. I tended to let that sort of stuff just roll over me."

It was so casually said, with so little remorse that he'd taken his very last conversation with his daughter so lightly, that I wanted to reach across the table and shake him. Maybe the reason Karen had gotten involved with a much older man was not so much that she was looking to fill a sudden void in her life, but rather, seeking something she'd never really had.

The waitress delivered my coffee. I thanked her and then said, "When was the last time she actually stayed with you?"

He hesitated. "Maybe two months ago?"

"Have the rangers asked if they could search the room?"

"Yes, but I doubt they'll find anything. She really didn't keep anything personal there—just some clothes and books."

Which meant it was probably pointless me going there. It also meant this whole conversation was pointless. Unless....

I leaned forward. "Mr. Banks, would you be willing to try a little experiment?"

His expression became wary. "What sort of experiment?"

"Nothing that's dangerous or invasive, I assure you." I gave him my best it'll-be-all-right smile. It didn't seem to help. "I'll simply grip your hand while you think back to your last conversation with Karen. If luck is with us, I might be able to catch something you've forgotten."

"Mind reading? I'm not sure—"

"No, not mind reading," I cut in, even as I wondered what sort of secrets he was worried about. "It's more... more like a movie that's being shown in a cinema. I'm simply standing back watching events as they happen."

His expression was still dubious. "You can't see what isn't there, though."

"Agreed, but we won't know for sure unless we try."

He took a deep breath and then released it slowly. "If you think it might help catch this bastard, then I guess it's worth a try."

"Take my hand."

I reached out. After a moment's hesitation, he tentatively gripped my fingers.

"It won't hurt," I reassured him.

He smiled. "Is my fear that obvious?"

"I'm afraid so. I'm guessing this is your first experience with a psychic?"

"I've never really believed—" He cut the rest of the sentence and gave me a somewhat rueful look.

"It's okay," I said. "There are more charlatans and tricksters out there than those of us who are the real deal."

He nodded. "What happens next?"

"Just concentrate on what you remember of that night. Think about where you were when she phoned you, and what you were doing while you were talking to her."

His brows furrowed and his fingers tightened against mine. I tried to ignore the distaste that rose and unleashed my second sight. For several seconds nothing happened, but, as I closed my eyes, images began to flit across the back of my eyelids. *There was a room—a living room with leather sofas, an open fireplace, and a vast TV on which football played. Phillip, sitting on one of those sofas, his expression bored as he talked into a phone.*

I couldn't immediately hear what he was saying, but then something shifted and the sound suddenly came on—and so loudly it made me jump.

"I met the most awesome person last night at the club, Dad," Karen was saying.

"I thought you said your mother had grounded you?" There was amusement rather than censure in Phillip's tone.

"Oh, she had, but I snuck out."

"Karen, we spoke about that—"

"It's not like she cares," Karen said. *"She doesn't even bother checking on me."*

"Yes, but still—"

"Anyway," the teenager cut in, *"he was dark and beautiful and totally unlike anyone I've ever met."*

"And has this stunning sample of boyhood got a name?"

"He's a man, Dad, not a boy. And I'm sure he has, but he hasn't shared it yet."

"So you ogled from a distance?"

"Well, yeah, kinda. But he noticed me. He smiled more than once."

"It's obviously true love then."

"Oh, Dad," Karen said, her tone exasperated.

"So if you haven't even talked to him, how do plan to see him again?"

"He'll be at the club again tonight. I'm sure of it."

"You will be careful if he is, won't you?" Phillip said. "Don't be alone with him or anything like that until you know more about him."

"Of course, Dad. I'm not dumb."

Phillip harrumphed, and the conversation moved on to more mundane things like school. I opened my eyes and pulled my hand from Phillip's.

He blinked. "A man. She mentioned a man."

"Yes." I resisted the urge to wipe the lingering sensation of his touch away and picked up my coffee instead. "Do you know what club she was talking about?"

"Not really, but there aren't many choices in Castle Rock. It'll probably be one of the hotels." He paused, frowning. "Although I read somewhere that the old Richards Road Hotel had been recently renovated. That might be worth a shot."

"Karen was underage—and surely well-known in Castle Rock, given Marjorie's prominence as a lawyer. She wouldn't have been allowed entry, would she?"

"Karen was an extremely strong-willed and persuasive young woman," he said. "If she wanted in, she would have gotten in, one way or another."

I had to wonder how, given serving underage persons

not in the company of a responsible adult was illegal in this state and could incur huge fines. But that was something I could follow up with the owners of said nightclub.

"Did you give your daughter a necklace, by chance? One on a gold chain, with a large, bloodred stone set into the pendant?"

He wrinkled his nose. "It sounds rather ghastly, and no, I didn't. I have better taste than that."

No matter how ghastly, Karen would have nevertheless cherished the gift, because it was from him. But his words suggested he'd never really done such things. No wonder Karen had gone searching for something akin to parental love elsewhere.

I quickly finished the rest of my coffee and then pushed to my feet. "Thanks for your help, Mr. Banks."

"You'll let me know if you uncover anything?" His tone was somewhat dismissive. His attention had already returned to the article he'd been reading.

To say it annoyed me would be something of an understatement.

"I sure as hell *won't*," I replied evenly, "but I daresay the rangers will."

"What?" he said, his gaze jumping back to mine.

I gave him a smile every bit as cool as his expression. "Goodbye, Mr. Banks."

Once outside, I took a deep breath that didn't do much to wash the lingering wisps of annoyance from my system, and then headed for my car and home. I parked the wagon in our spot behind the café, and then grabbed the pack and walked over to the Tourist Information Center to see what information they had on abandoned miners cottages. Unfortunately, it seemed that while the

Heritage Park *did* have a number of old buildings on their grounds, there wasn't a list of the many other derelict cottages dotted throughout the region. They *did* give me a list of cottages that had been renovated and were now available for renting, but that wasn't what the dream had shown me. I also discovered—via the woman who was serving me gushing about how wonderful the place now was—that the old Richards Road Hotel had become a themed nightclub called Émigré.

Given I felt no urgency to return to the café—which either meant the place was empty or Belle and Penny were coping just fine without me—I resolutely swung the other way and walked up the hill toward the ranger station. Belle was right—whether he believed me or not, Aiden needed to know what I'd dreamed last night.

A dark-haired woman with a thin face was standing at the reception desk, but the vast room behind her was empty. She glanced up as I entered, but her welcoming smile faded rather quickly. "How may I help you, Ms. Grace?"

I wasn't really surprised she knew me by sight. There weren't any other women with crimson hair in Castle Rock, as far as I was aware. "I need to talk to Ranger O'Connor."

"He's not available at the moment, but if it's important, Ranger Sinclair can see you."

"The definition of importance," I said, with a slight edge, "would depend greatly on whether you believe a psychic whose dreams sometimes foreshadow dire events can hold any truth or not."

"Ah," she said, with a slight blink. "Hold on a moment, and I'll go talk to Tala."

Tala had taken over the investigation into Karen's

death when Aiden had escorted me back to the station, if I remembered correctly. I leaned on the counter and watched the dark-haired wolf disappear into the corridor that led to the cells and the interview room. After a few moments, she returned. Behind her was a dark-skinned woman who was about my height but—if the wisps of silver in her black hair were anything to go by—at least twelve years older.

"Ms. Grace," she said, her voice holding little in the way of inflection. "You have some information regarding Karen's murder?"

"I have. Whether you believe it or not is entirely up to you."

"Any information regarding a murder is treated seriously, no matter what the source." She buzzed open the secure door. "The desk to your far left, please."

I walked over and sat down. She claimed her seat on the other side of the desk and then took out a notebook. "Right," she said, pen hovering above a blank page. "Tell me what you have."

"The vampire is hiding in an old miners cottage." I described everything I'd seen—the wingtip shoes included—and then added, "Karen will not be his only kill if he's not caught quickly."

She paused writing and met my gaze. "Why would you think that? Vampires usually space out their kills by a week, if not more."

"I know, but I think the only rules *this* vampire is living by are his own."

"Again, what makes you think that? The dream?"

"Instinct." I forced a smile. "There's something stranger going on here. It's not just about the kill or a simple need for blood."

"What do you think it *might* be about, then?"

"When I find out, I'll let you know."

She stopped writing again. "If we discover that you are, in any way, interfering with an ongoing investigation—"

"Marjorie Banks has hired me to find the killer." It was pointless hiding the fact, given Marjorie was likely to mention it the next time they saw her. "And you can't actually stop me from doing that—especially if I'm *not* impeding your investigations in any way."

"This is a werewolf reservation," she said curtly. "The rules that apply on the outside do not apply here."

"Then I'll sit back and wait for the IIT to appear," I said. "They're certainly more receptive of help from psychics and witches—"

"The latter of which you claim *not* to be."

"I'm a charm maker. That's not a particularly strong form of magic in anyone's books."

"Mere charm makers can*not* command ghost candles."

If they knew that, it meant they'd been checking up on just what a lowborn witch could and couldn't do. And that, in turn, undoubtedly meant they'd also been checking into my background. While that wasn't unexpected, a *too* thorough search might just throw up more questions than answers. "They can in areas where wild magic exists, and I'm sure you're aware that Castle Rock has an abundance of such magic."

She grunted and made another note. Whether she in any way believed what I was saying, I couldn't tell. I might have gotten a whole lot of unwanted information about Aiden, but instinct was giving me zip when it came to this woman.

"Anything else?" she asked.

I hesitated. It was pointless mentioning the river of blood, but that wasn't the only other thing I'd dreamed about.

"Where is Karen's body currently being held?"

She frowned. "In the morgue, of course. Why?"

"Because I have a strange feeling our vampire hasn't finished with her yet."

Her eyebrows rose, and this time, her skepticism was very evident. "You think he's going to steal her body?"

"Again, I don't really know. I just got the sense that he was waiting for something to happen." I paused, remembering the clock I'd witnessed counting down, and did a quick calculation in my head. "The dream seemed to indicate whatever that is, it would happen tonight at eight thirty."

"I don't suppose it also happened to clarify what that something might be?"

"No."

"Of course not." She paused to write another note, and then met my gaze again. "Anything else?"

I smiled, though it held little in the way of humor. "I think I've stretched the boundaries of your belief enough for one day."

"As I said, all information regarding the case is taken seriously." She rose. "We do appreciate you coming forward, Ms. Grace."

"Say that with a little more sincerity, and I might be tempted to believe you."

"When I have a reason to be sincere, I will be. But you should be aware that I don't believe in psychics."

"I don't expect belief." My voice was as blunt as hers. "I do, however, hope you'll take me somewhat seriously given it was those skills that allowed me to find Karen's body before any of you—despite your noses and natural tracking abilities—could."

She studied me for a moment, and then nodded. Whether it was in acceptance or something else, I wasn't entirely sure.

"Maggie, please buzz Ms. Grace out."

I rose, gave her a nod, and left.

The weather had closed in again in the brief time I'd been in the ranger station, which meant I got absolutely drowned as I dashed back to the café.

"Oh, you poor thing," a woman said, as I all but slid through the door she was holding open. "You're soaked through."

"Yes." I remained where I was, dripping onto the welcome mat, knowing that Belle had already raced upstairs to grab a towel. "I wouldn't recommend leaving just yet, Mrs.—" I paused, trying to remember her name. "—Williams, but if you need to, please grab one of our umbrellas. They're in the pot underneath the coat peg."

"You are a love." She lightly patted my arm. "But my Freddie is coming to pick me— Ah, there he is now. Thank you."

As I stepped to one side, a new BMW stopped in the no-standing zone. The old man sitting inside leaned across and opened the passenger door. She gave me a bright smile and dashed out. I let the café door close, shivering despite the room's cozy warmth.

Our only other customers were a couple sitting in a corner nook, but their attention was on each other rather than anything going on around them. Given the weather's sudden turn, we'd be lucky if anyone else actually ventured in.

Belle reappeared and tossed me the towel.

"Coffee?" she asked.

"I want to grab a shower first, but yes please, and in the largest mug possible."

She nodded and then walked over to the couple to see if they wanted anything else. I wrapped the towel around my hair to stop it dripping everywhere, then slipped off my shoes and socks and padded barefoot through the café and up the stairs. But neither a hot shower nor the bucket of coffee Belle handed me when I went back down eased the chill that seemed to be settling into my bones. I hoped like hell it was merely a cold rather than some sort of portent of evil stepping our way.

I spent the rest of the day helping Mike out in the kitchen, and doing the prep for the following day. When the doors were finally closed and the café once again clean, Belle dropped into one of the chairs and said, "I checked out some of Granny's books after you left this morning. She did have one on vampires—"

"Your gran seems to have had a book on absolutely everything." I walked over to the table and handed Belle a glass of wine. "I would have loved to have met her. Given everything you've said, she surely would have been a force to be reckoned with, Sarr witch or not."

Belle's cheek's dimpled. "Mom once told me there were over a dozen instances where bluebloods actually called on her, for advice or for the use of her library."

"Then I'm surprised they didn't requisition it on her death."

"Oh, I believe they tried, but by that time, all the important books had been squirreled away by my mother. Apparently, she foresaw that her as-yet-unborn daughter would have a greater need of them than the goddamn bluebloods or their library."

I raised my glass and tapped it against hers. "Here's to your clever mother. Long may she continue to blight the aims of the bluebloods."

Belle chuckled. "You seem to forget you're one of said bluebloods."

"Only by birth, and that doesn't count."

Her amusement grew. "*Anyway*, there was a whole chapter on how vampires became vampires."

"In a book about vampires? Color me surprised."

"If I had a peanut, I'd throw it at you right now."

I grinned and motioned her to go on.

"Basically, it comes down to the fact that anyone wanting to become a vampire has to first inject the blood of a vampire into their system once a week over a course of five weeks—"

"Meaning there should have been some evidence of needle marks on Karen's body," I cut in, "and I can't remember seeing any."

"Which is *not* surprising given you weren't looking for something like that at the time, and you can't exactly examine the body now."

"True, but the coroner *should* have picked it up and, given the rangers aren't taking any extra precautions with her body, she apparently didn't."

"Yes, but there's something in the vampire's blood that makes the injection site heal quickly, so there probably wouldn't have been any evidence on Karen's arm by the time she was killed," Belle said. "The fast healing is apparently the reason why the bastards are so hard to kill."

"So did it say what *does* kill them?"

"Yes, in another chapter, but let me finish." She hesitated, but when I didn't say anything, added, "The only telltale sign that someone has shared the blood of a vampire is lips extraordinarily flushed with blood. She called it being blood kissed."

I just about choked on my wine. "That's what I saw in the dream." And what I'd seen in the clearing, when I'd found Karen's body.

Belle nodded. "It would appear that our dear teenager might be well on the path to becoming one of the undead."

"Shit, we have to warn the rangers—"

"I contacted them the minute I read that particular paragraph. They rather politely thanked me and said they would look into it."

"Shit," I repeated. "How long does the transformation take once death has happened?"

"Anywhere between twenty-four and seventy-two hours."

"If the clock I saw is any indication, it'll happen tonight."

"Yes, but we're simply not equipped to handle vampires, Lizzie. The rangers still have your knife, and we can't risk our athames."

"What about wooden stakes? Do they work?"

"Yes," she said again, "but even a newly spawned vampire will be far stronger and far quicker than either of us. It'd be like facing a werewolf with a tiny silver sewing needle."

Which was not something anyone with any sort of sense would ever contemplate. I drank some wine as I considered our options. "What about placing some sort of containment spell around the morgue?"

"It could work, except for one major problem," she said. "We'd have to account for the presence of everyone who works there within the structure of the spell."

"Presuming they're actually working at night. They might not."

"There'd at least be security guards."

"So we give a newly hatched vampire free rein to escape?" Frustration gave my voice an edge.

"No, we hope to hell the rangers take us seriously and place extra guards around the morgue tonight."

"That might not help if the older vamp comes to collect his protégé."

"No, but this *is* a werewolf reservation and our master vamp will know the wolves are more than a match for his speed and strength."

"Which might not help if he's also capable of decent magic."

"We *can't* do anything, Lizzie." Belle's voice was blunt. "Not tonight, and certainly not until we know more about who and what, exactly, we're dealing with."

"I know," I said. "It's just that giving evil free rein has never sat easily with me."

And *that* was what had almost gotten both of us killed twelve years ago. I'd been both ill-equipped and totally underprepared to deal with the monster behind the ritual killings. As a result, I'd not only failed to save my sister, but I'd allowed a killer to get away.

"Maybe," Belle said softly. "That trail of blood they found afterward seemed to suggest he would have bled out before he managed to get to any help."

"And yet they never found a body."

"Which is not surprising when it comes to those dealing with blood magic," she said. "The darker forces they call upon thoroughly enjoy reclaiming their pound of flesh on the sorcerer's death."

"I've spent the last twelve years hoping that's true." Twelve years hoping that by my actions, I hadn't given a killer the time to rest, recover, and plot his revenge.

"Enough remembering a past neither of us are capable of changing," Belle said. "Let's just concentrate on what we *can* do."

I glanced at my watch and then said, "Speaking of changing, why don't we both go upstairs and do just that?"

She blinked, and then smiled. "Are you thinking a little trip to Émigré is in order, by chance?"

"Indeed I am. We can kill two metaphorical birds with one stone by checking out the club and talking to the staff, all while having a nice night out."

"I'm liking the way you think." She drained her glass and then jumped up. "First dibs on the shower."

I laughed as she raced for the stairs, and propped my feet up on her chair, watching the raindrops race each other down the windows as the darkness gathered force outside.

Once I heard the shower shut down, I grabbed her glass and rose, dumping both in the kitchen sink before I went up. It took us close to an hour to get ready, which brought us uncomfortably close to the countdown's end time. And no matter how much I tried not to think about what might be happening in the morgue right now, I couldn't seem to escape it.

The taxi we'd called to take us over to Émigré arrived right on the dot of eight thirty. I hesitated as Belle climbed into the cab's back seat, my senses—both physical and other—attuned for anything untoward. The night was cold and wet, but there was no sense of danger within it, no sense that evil stirred.

Maybe the dream was wrong. Or maybe the

countdown had meant something else.

Maybe.

I tried to ignore the growing sense of trepidation and jumped into the cab. It didn't take long to get over to Richards Road, and once I'd paid the driver, I climbed out and studied the building.

"Whoa," Belle said, as she stopped beside me. "I wasn't expecting something so… bizarre."

Bizarre was certainly a good word. While the main bulk of the building had been painted a flat black, there were weird, almost alien-looking biomechanical forms crawling across the walls and roofline, and they all but covered many of the windows. There also wasn't much in the way of music pulsing out of the building, which suggested either it wasn't very loud or they'd installed the very best in sound deadening. Given this area was a mix of industrial and housing stock, sound management had probably been a permit requirement.

The main entrance rather amusedly looked more like an air lock than a common old doorway. We paid our fee, checked our coats, and then headed into the main room. The music that had been barely audible outside hit full force once we went through a second set of doors, but it was fierce and joyous, and instantly made me want to dance. We paused to get our bearings, and my gaze was drawn to the vaulted ceiling. The huge room had been painted a battleship gray rather than black, and the ceiling again had a series of intricate and intriguing biomechanical and alien forms crawling all over each arch. It looked like something that belonged in a science fiction movie rather than in the middle of a werewolf reservation.

The room itself had been split into two levels. One side of the upper tier held a series of "pods" in which there were seats and small tables, while the other half was dominated by a long bar that was made from twisted metal and glass. The lower tier was devoted to the dance floor, and despite the early hour, it was packed.

"Holy hell," Belle said, awe in her voice. "This place is impressive."

"I wonder why they built it here rather than in a main city center like Melbourne?" I said. "It surely would have been more lucrative."

Belle snorted. "This place is *packed*. I doubt they'd get a better turnout even if it was in Melbourne."

But a city center would have given them a longer period of time before the novelty started wearing off—which I guessed could be true of any business, even one as small as ours. "You want a drink?"

She nodded and led the way across to the bar. I followed in her wake, amused at the way the crowd parted before her. Having Amazonian height and strength did have its advantages.

Of course, it also helped that said Amazon was wearing a barely there red dress that stood out vividly against the more muted tones everyone else was wearing. Even my sapphire blue, formfitting sheath dress seemed dull in comparison.

We managed to claim a couple of barstools—which, following the theme of the place, were shaped like aliens' heads—and then caught the eye of one the bartenders.

"Welcome, ladies," he said, his dark amber eyes glowing with appreciation as his gaze swept from Belle to me and back again. "I'm thinking you're both new around these parts."

He was almost as tall as Belle, and had brown skin and hair that held just the slightest tinge of red. Which, from what I knew of the reservation wolf packs, meant he was one of the Marins.

"We've been in town a couple of months," Belle said, her tone amused. "But this is our first time in the club. What drink do you recommend?"

"Ah, well, that depends on how good a time you want."

"I want a 'hell yeah, dancing on the bar' type good time," Belle said, her smile echoing his.

He laughed. "Then I have just the drink for you— two Death in the Afternoons coming up."

As he walked away, I swung around to study the dance floor. There was an intriguing mix of both young and old in the room, and the atmosphere in the place was warm and friendly, despite the weirdness of the surrounds.

Movement above the dance floor caught my eye. I looked up, and realized a room had been built into the ceiling at the point where all the arches met. It was right above the dance floor and basically built from dark glass and metal, which gave it a full view of the whole room while all but concealing its presence from casual sight.

There was a woman standing at one of the windows. She was little more than a featureless shadow, but there was something about her presence that had unease stirring. Maybe it was the night, maybe it was simply the uncertainty of my dream and what it had meant, but she was almost otherworldly.

I shivered, and, just for a moment, wanted to do nothing more than run. She stepped away from the window and beyond my sight, but that uneasy need to flee didn't similarly fade.

What you need, Belle said, with a glance up at the concealed glass room, *is to stop seeing threats in shadows, and just try to have a good time.*

I'm trying.

Try harder. Especially given this might be our one and only chance before all hell breaks loose.

Thanks for that rather cheery thought.

She laughed. *You're most welcome.*

The bartender returned and handed us each a champagne glass. The alcohol inside had bubbles and a greenish-yellow tinge. Belle took a sip and then grinned. "Oh hell, *yeah.* That's good."

"Absinthe and champagne," he said. "An awesome combination that should be imbibed slowly if you don't wish to be flat out on the floor rather than dancing on the bar."

Belle laughed and held out her hand. "I'm Isabelle—Belle to my friends—and this is Lizzie, my good mate and the co-owner of our café."

"Zak Marin," he said, holding her hand just a little longer than necessary. "Bar person by night, handyman by day."

"A man who is handy never goes astray," Belle all but purred, even as I rolled my eyes. "You'll have to give me your business card."

"Oh, of that you can be sure. Shall I start up a tab for you both?"

"Yes, please," Belle said, and handed him her credit card.

He swiped it through the machine and then handed it back. "I've got to go attend to some other customers, but don't run away on me, ladies. I'll be right back."

"A man who is handy never goes astray?" I repeated, once he was out of earshot. "Seriously?"

"Hey, it worked, did it not? That wolf is all but mine

for the night, Lizzie dearest, so you'd best start looking elsewhere."

"No problem, because I've sworn off men, remember?"

"That doesn't mean you can't flirt and dance a little."

I let my gaze roam across the dance floor. There was no denying that there were some fine-looking men in this room, but that was to be expected in a reservation. You didn't often see overweight or out of shape werewolves— their systems simply ran too hot for that to happen.

Of course, that heat also made them very good lovers—a thought that instantly raised Aiden's image in my mind. I shoved it firmly back into its box and swung back to the bar.

"Maybe." I took a sip of the cocktail and felt the bubbly, licorice-like alcohol burn all the way down to my stomach. "Of course, it's highly likely that after one or two more of these, I'll be dancing on the bar right alongside you."

She laughed. "I'll hold you to that."

I took another sip as our bartender returned. "Got a message from the boss for you, Lizzie. She'd like to see you if you've got a spare moment."

"Does your boss have a name?" I said, even as my heart rate jumped.

"Indeed she does," a voice said from behind me. "And she will introduce herself once you are in her presence."

I jumped slightly and swung around. The man who had spoken was tall and thin, with pale hair and even paler eyes. Not a werewolf, but something else. Something other than human. He gave me a polite smile and added, "If you'll please follow me, Ms. Grace, it would be appreciated."

You want me to come with you? Belle asked, concern in her thoughts.

I hesitated. *No. You weren't invited, and I have a bad feeling it wouldn't be wise to go against her wishes."*

Well, you know I'm only a mental shout away.

I know. I picked up my drink and motioned the pale stranger to lead the way. We made our way along the top tier, past the end of the bar, and toward a pod that was closed off by a wrought iron door that was an intricate mix of vine leaves and skeletal spines. There was an inconspicuous keypad on the right-side wall, and after my escort put in a code, the door slid aside to reveal a set of black glass stairs.

"Please," the thin stranger said, and motioned me on.

I took another drink and then entered the confines of the stairwell. The gate closed behind me and the shadows pressed closer. As I paused, uncertain of my footing, light flared, forming a chain of blue that led the way up the circular stairwell.

At the top there was another metal door, but it opened as I approached. The room beyond was all dark glass and metal, and filled with shadows despite the bright array of lights that constantly swept across the windows. There was a black table sitting in the middle of the room, with a couple of plush-looking chairs at the front of this and a third behind. The room seemed to hold little else in the way of furniture.

"Please, do come in," a soft, slightly accented voice said. "I won't bite, Ms. Grace, I assure you of that."

I hesitated and then moved into the room. "I'm afraid you have the better of me, as you appear to know my name, but I don't know yours."

A figure appeared out of the gloom. Her skin was like porcelain, pale and perfect, with little in the way of lines to suggest her age even though I suspected she was far older than she looked. Her hair was a lush chestnut that had been swept into a loosely bound topknot, and her eyes were a gray so pale there was only the slightest variation between her irises and the whites of her eyes. She was wearing a rich brown dress that looked for all the world like an eighteenth-century riding gown, but her feet were bare.

"My name is Maelle Defour," she said, in the same unthreatening tone. "And I wish to welcome you to my establishment."

I didn't immediately answer. I couldn't, because every instinct I had was again telling me to run, and it was taking every ounce of concentration to stop from doing just that.

Maelle Defour wasn't just a powerful woman of indeterminate age.

She was also a vampire.

CHAPTER
five

Oh, fuck, came Belle's comment. *You want me to magic up a distraction or something?*

No, not yet. Her canines aren't visible, so I don't think she's intending an attack.

If she were, you probably wouldn't know about it.

Thanks for yet another cheery thought. I took a sip of alcohol, trying to act nonchalant when every bit of me was quivering. Which, as a vampire, she'd undoubtedly sense.

"It's a pleasure to meet you, Ms. Defour," I said, glad my voice at least sounded normal. "But I'm afraid I'm at a loss as to why you summoned me."

"Surely not?"

She motioned toward one of the chairs at the front of the desk, and all but glided to the one behind.

I sat down and crossed my legs—an action that revealed a little too much upper leg for my liking. Vampires, I'd been told, considered blood taken from the inner thigh to be far sweeter than that from the neck or the wrist. Which was weird, but I wasn't about to tell a very old vampire that—especially when I was locked in the same room as her.

"I'm afraid you really *do* have me at a loss," I said.

"Ah, well." She interlaced her fingers, her pose somewhat regal. "It is not every day that one gets to meet a blueblood witch."

I didn't make the denial, even though it sprung to my lips. All I said was, "I'm not what you think."

"No one ever is." She cocked her head slightly to one side, her strange gaze narrowing slightly. "You know what I am."

"Yes."

"And you fear it?"

"That would depend on two things."

"Those being?"

"On what outcome you wish of this meeting, and whether you are, in any way, involved with the vampire who has killed a sixteen-year-old girl within this reservation, and may have shared his blood with her."

Even though she didn't move, her pupils contracted and there was a definite sharpening in her attention. "When did this happen? I've heard no whisper of it through my contacts."

"The teenager was found in the forest two nights ago. The rangers had confirmation via an autopsy yesterday that the bite marks on her neck were indeed a vampire's."

"Ah, the Banks girl?"

"Yes. Apparently she'd been meeting with her killer for weeks." I hesitated. "She met him here."

"Impossible. I would have sensed the presence of another on my own soil." Her voice was flat—chilling.

"And I certainly would *not* have allowed it."

"I believe he's capable of the dark arts, and is using it to conceal his presence."

She frowned, momentarily marring the perfection of her face. "This is unpleasant news indeed."

"Then I'm gathering he's not one of yours?"

Cool amusement touched her lips. "My vampires have better sense and—dare I say it—better taste than to share blood with a sixteen-year-old. I can imagine no worse a fate than tying yourself to someone who will not grow beyond the self-important 'the world owes me' attitude of those years."

I couldn't help smiling. "Teenagers *do* eventually grow up and gain some sense—surely that would also apply to those who have imbibed vampire's blood?"

She waved a hand, the motion dismissive. "It still takes far too much time for it to be, in any way, a pleasant experience."

"If he is not one of yours, will you pass on any news you might hear of him?"

"I certainly will pass on anything I might find to you, Ms. Grace, but I have no desire to mix with the werewolves any more than necessary."

"And yet, here you are, running a nightclub that is both staffed by werewolves and enjoyed by them, just as much as the humans."

"This club is a business venture. I meant privately."

There was something in the way she was studying me that had my heart racing. She might mean me no immediate harm, but that look suggested there was something more behind this meeting than just a simple introduction.

I took a drink that failed to ease the stirring unease or

the unwise racing of my pulse. "Are the wolves even aware of your presence here?"

"Indeed they are. I would never step within the boundaries of a reservation without giving the council fair warning of my presence."

So why had Aiden been so adamant that there were no vampires here? "Then the council hasn't passed this information on to their rangers, which I find rather surprising."

"No, because I guaranteed I would shed no blood and feed on only the willing while I am within this reservation. In return, they will not expose my presence to the wider population."

"I hardly think the rangers could be called the wider population."

"Perhaps not, but those were our agreed terms."

I frowned. "You will excuse me if this sounds rude, but how in the hell can they even police such an agreement?"

She smiled. It wasn't an entirely pleasant smile. "You are obviously not up on your vampire history, young lady. I am of the *Defour* line. Our word, once given, is a binding we cannot break. The council is well aware of this fact."

"That almost sounds like the binding is one of magic."

"Indeed. It was—depending on your point of view—either a gift or a curse from a long-ago witch of the Marlowe line."

A statement that made me wonder if she suspected who I was. But how? Hair color alone wouldn't have told her much. The crimson color might be a common trait amongst the three blueblood lines, but it wasn't unusual for it to carry over to the "half-bloods"—those witches born from a union between a blueblood and either a lowborn witch or a common human. And unless they had the ability in life, vampires weren't telepathic. I'd certainly had no indication that she was rifling through my thoughts and memories, and I would have, given I was still wearing a warding charm.

"If you think I am capable of undoing such a spell," I said evenly, "you are sorely mistaken."

"Oh, I am well aware the binding cannot be undone. I have asked greater adepts than yourself many a time over the years."

"Which places us right back to your reason for inviting me up here."

"Is it not always sensible for one such as I to make my presence known to the local witch?" she asked. "It tends to lessen any misunderstandings that might otherwise occur."

"I appreciate that politeness, but it is hardly necessary. Witches have been banned from this place."

"And yet, here you are."

Again my smile held little in the way of humor. "I'm a charm maker with psychic powers. Nothing more, nothing less."

"Oh, I think there's a *whole* lot more to you than you either wish to see or admit," she replied, and rose. "I will inform you if I hear anything about the vampire. But I must also warn you that I am, given the terms of my agreement with the council, unable to do anything about him, as much as I might wish otherwise."

I picked up my drink and stood up. "I'm surprised the council have neither advised you of the vampire's presence nor come to you for advice."

Amusement briefly crinkled the corners of her pale

eyes. "They undoubtedly will if there is a second kill, but most vampires who prefer a full meal rather than a mere sip generally tend to hit and run."

"I don't think this vampire has any intention of running."

"If he has shared blood, I would agree." She made a rather regal motion toward the stairwell. "Thank you for indulging me, Ms. Grace. I look forward to having another chat with you soon."

It was a statement that had trepidation flaring fierce and hard again. But I forced a pleasant smile, said a polite goodbye, and headed out. Her pale assistant opened the door once I reached the bottom of the stairs, and Belle met me near the bar with another cocktail. I downed the remains of my first one and then repeated the process with the second. A warm buzz flooded my body, chasing away the cold threads of dread.

"Want another?" Belle asked, as she plucked the second glass from my grip.

I shook my head. "Not unless you want me dancing naked on the bar."

She grinned. "I might not, but it could be an interesting experience for our ranger."

"What? He's here?" I glanced around but couldn't immediately spot him—not surprising, given the place was packed.

"I saw him talking to the bar staff. It appears he's here for the same reason we are."

"Except he has no idea this place is run by a vampire." I stepped around her and headed for a vacant stool. The alcohol buzz was getting stronger. Perhaps downing both drinks in such quick succession wasn't such a bright idea.

"Are you going to tell him?"

"It's not my place."

"It's not our place to be trying to find this vampire, either, but that hasn't stopped us."

"That's because we have five hundred reasons a day to do so." I frowned at her. "Where's your werewolf friend? I'm in need of some water."

She propped beside me and then waved her hand. Zak appeared a few seconds later. "What can I get for you, lovely ladies?"

"Another cocktail for me, and a sparkling water for my friend here."

"Coming right up."

"Thanks." Belle glanced over my shoulder. "Don't look now, but your hot ranger is walking toward us."

"Probably to interrogate me," I muttered. "Or to bitch yet again about me being in Castle Rock."

"I'm thinking it's something a little more drastic than that," she said. "He does *not* look happy."

"That appears to be a common look for him, especially around me."

"This is more a 'something very bad has happened' expression rather than a mere 'I hate witches' one."

I reluctantly turned and looked. He was walking up the steps from the dance floor, his movements fluid and yet oddly sharp, and his expression as fierce as the flashes of red in his aura.

I held up my hands as he approached. "Whoa, Ranger, I have no idea what you're about to accuse me of, but I promise, I haven't done a goddamn thing."

He stopped several feet away from me and shoved his hands into the pockets of his brown leather jacket. "I'm not here to accuse you of anything. I'm here to ask for your help."

I couldn't help a sharp laugh. "I'm sorry, what? Has hell frozen over or something?"

"Obviously." His gaze flicked past me. "Ms. Kent, I presume?"

"Indeed, but please call me Isabelle." She stuck out a hand. "Pleasure to finally meet you, Ranger...?"

"Aiden O'Connor, as I'm sure you're aware." He briefly shook her hand but his gaze remained on mine. "Well?"

I raised my eyebrows. "You might try saying please. You might also want to explain the sudden urgency for my help when neither you nor your second-in-command have taken my dreams or my psychic skills seriously."

"This is neither the time nor the place for recriminations," he bit back, and then took a deep breath, visibly reaching for calm. "You're right, of course, and I apologize."

Man, that hurt him, Belle said, her mental tone somber. *Hell must have indeed broken loose for him to reach out like this.*

I don't think either of us need to guess what that 'hell' might be. To Aiden, I added, "How did you know I was here?"

"You weren't home, so I checked the hotels and clubs."

And, as Phillip Banks had noted, there weren't that many options in Castlerock. "Did Karen rise, as I predicted?"

"Later than you predicted, but yes." His voice was grim. "And we have five people dead."

"Shit." I rubbed a hand across my eyes. "I'm sorry there's been such a high toll, but I don't really understand why you need me there. The people she killed can't rise as vampires—"

"I'm aware of that," he cut in. "And if that was all we were dealing with, I wouldn't be here."

Ain't that the truth, Belle commented.

"Then why *are* you here? Spit it out, Ranger."

"Karen had help escaping," he said. "We presume it was the vampire who turned her."

"I did say that was a possibility."

"Yes, but there's more. He left a message." He paused and then added softly, "For you."

"No." Fear spiked within me even as the denial passed my lips.

"Yes." He reached out as if to grab my arm, then dropped his hand. "Please, I need you to come and see it."

"Why?" I said, even as I rose.

"Because the only thing we're able to read is your name. Everything else looks like gibberish."

I glanced at Belle. "Some sort of spell, perhaps?"

"It's certainly possible." She smiled at Zak as he returned with our drinks. "But it's unlikely he would have had the time for anything too intricate."

"Meaning your business partner *is* a witch, despite your protestations," Aiden commented. "Doesn't this just get better and better?"

"Look," I said, somewhat testily. "No matter what grief some witch caused you in the past, neither of *us* deserve to be the target of your hatred—especially when you're here to ask for our goddamn help."

"True enough," he said, after a slight pause, "and again, I'm sorry."

I couldn't help suspecting he was sorrier about being forced to ask for our help rather than for his hatred, even if his voice held an edge of sincerity. "Has the message been placed on the inside or the outside of the building?"

"Inside. Why?"

"Was the outside of the building patrolled?" I continued.

"Of course—there were three people, in fact, all specifically hired for that purpose. They were all wolves so should have sensed the vampire well before he had the chance to attack."

"Unless the vampire was using some form of magic to conceal his presence."

He frowned. "I didn't think that was possible."

"If a vampire is capable of magic before he turned, what makes you think he would be incapable after?"

"Nothing more than myths and legend, which—as a werewolf—I should know better than to trust." He shrugged. "But my people are all over the crime scene— nothing untoward has happened so far."

"Which might just mean it *is* a simple message, as you suspect." I glanced at Belle. "But in case it *isn't*, would you mind coming along?"

"It's not the way I'd hoped the evening would end, but I can hardly let you face this alone." *And the fact he's addressed this note or spell to you specifically suggests he might be aware that you were with Karen in her final moments. If he's capable of that, he's probably stronger than we've been presuming.*

That connection was immersive, Belle. All he should have sensed was Karen's thoughts and feelings.

Just because he shouldn't have felt you doesn't mean he didn't.

She motioned for the bill and, once Zak had bought it over, signed it and then leaned forward, whispering something in his ear. He grinned, pulled a business card out of his pocket, and handed it to her.

"If your social life is all sorted, can we go now?" Aiden said, voice holding an edge.

"Totally," Belle said. "After you, handsome."

He raised an eyebrow but did as bid. We collected our coats on the way out and followed Aiden over to his vehicle—an unmarked blue Ford Ranger rather than the green-striped white SUVs that were commonly used within the reservation.

The morgue was situated within the grounds of the region's hospital, and though it was housed in a separate building, it could be accessed from the hospital by a glass-covered walkway between the two and also via the doors set within the walkway. Ranger vehicles and—rather weirdly, given the hospital was little more than a few hundred meters away—ambulances were parked everywhere, and there was a myriad of medical staff and rangers moving around.

I climbed out and took a deep breath. The air was fresh, filled with the fading electricity of the storm that had passed by. There was no immediate sense of magic, dark or otherwise.

There wouldn't be if the spell lies within the building, Belle said.

"This way, ladies." Aiden walked toward the walkway's entry doors.

I shivered, and it wasn't entirely because of the cold. I might not be able to sense any magic, but it was here, somewhere, of that I was sure.

"Where exactly was the note left?" I asked. "Inside the refrigeration room or somewhere else?"

"It's in the small reception area, and it was written before he released Karen."

"Why are you so certain?"

His smile held little in the way of humor. "Because the wolf who'd been guarding the door into the cold chamber managed to set off the alarm before he was killed. The vampire wouldn't have had the time to do anything more than grab Karen and get out of there."

"Ah." I studied the door ahead. Once again I had no sense of anything untoward, and there was no shimmer or spell threads to indicate magic was present. And yet, intuition stirred, suggesting caution.

I glanced at Belle. *Are you sensing anything?*

No, but that's not surprising. You're the stronger witch in this outfit.

Aiden opened the door and ushered us inside. A ranger appeared and handed us blue crime scene booties and gloves; once we'd all pulled both on, we were allowed to continue. I narrowed my gaze as we neared the main door into the morgue; once again, there were no immediate signs of magic. And yet, the gentle pulse of it began to stir, making the small hairs on my arms rise.

I stepped into the room and then stopped. This was obviously a reception area, as there was a desk directly opposite and several chairs along the right wall. There were two doors behind the desk, but no symbols or signs, magical or otherwise.

The message had been painted on the left wall, in what I suspected might be drying blood—a theory supported by the chalked outlines of several body parts lying between the desk and the wall.

There were only two ways our vampire could have wreaked such havoc on a human form—either he'd used some form of spell, or he was extraordinarily strong. And it didn't really matter which of those was the truth—I simply didn't want to confront a man capable of wanton destruction.

I shivered again and forced my gaze back to the wall

and the message. To the untrained eye, it might have looked like gibberish, but it was, in fact, what was commonly known as witch script—an ancient text that only adepts could read, and which had been developed over centuries to prevent the more dangerous spells from falling into the wrong hands.

Which could mean that not only had our vampire been a witch of some power before he turned, but that he'd come from one of the three blueblood houses. And yet *that* was impossible, because it broke the laws of life and death and went against everything witches believed in.

I couldn't read what it said, however. There was some sort of spell interference happening, making it blurry.

It's also blurring for me, Belle said. *Which suggests that whatever the spell is, it's not specifically aimed at you. It might just be a general warning to the reservation's witches.*

Then why would he use my name? And why use witch script if all he wanted to do was warn us away?

I don't know.

Neither did I, and that was what was worrying me.

"Can you read what the message says?" Aiden asked.

"Kind of."

"Meaning what?"

I glanced at him briefly. "It means there's a spell in place stopping me from reading it fully."

"Your charm isn't reacting," Belle said. "That backs up the idea that the spell isn't specifically aimed at you."

"Or it could just mean it's triggered by proximity rather than mere presence." I glanced at Aiden again. "I want your people out of here, just in case my attempt to defuse the spell goes wrong."

He immediately glanced at the brown-haired ranger who'd handed us the booties. "Order an immediate evacuation of the entire facility. I want everyone out to the vehicle area."

She nodded and began talking into a two-way radio. As a stream of people began to leave the area, he added, "I'll get you to head out as well, Jaz."

As she retreated, I said, "I think you and Belle had better do the same."

Aiden frowned. "The IIT would have my badge if I allowed you to remain here alone—"

"If we *are* dealing with a major spell of some kind," I cut in, "then you have little other choice, and they'll know it. I can't be worried about your ass when I'm trying to defuse a spell, Ranger. If you want, Belle can relay everything I'm seeing and doing for your records."

His gaze shot to hers. "You're telepathic?"

She patted his arm comfortingly. "It's okay. I discovered a long time ago that the thoughts of most men aren't worth the effort of skimming."

His expression was anything but comforted as his gaze returned to mine. "Fine. But if you need help—"

"I'll call in Belle. You, Ranger, are to remain outside until I've declared the area safe."

He hesitated, but after a moment, nodded and walked out. I tugged off my heels, handed them to Belle, and then put the blue booties back on.

"Are you sure you don't want me to stay with you?" she asked. "Sometimes two sets of eyes are better than one when it comes to unraveling unknown spells."

"Yes, but if he *has* concocted something nasty, I'd rather have you free to detach me from it." My gaze went to the ranger's departing back. "Thanks to the current clime, we can't exactly call on other witches for help."

"Then please be careful." She touched my arm lightly

and then retreated; a few minutes later, she added, *We're both clear.*

I took a step closer to the wall, and the crawling sensation immediately sharpened. I squatted on my heels and studied the area with narrowed eyes, all senses—both physical and metaphysical—alert. After a moment, I began to see the slight shimmer that indicated the presence of magic. But I wasn't yet close enough to make out the individual threads—or layers—of the spell. Each one was basically a combination of the words and energy used to create the incantation, which were then fused together to make a whole. In some ways, creating a spell held some similarities to the way fleece became yarn—and its success just as often depended on the skill of the weaver.

I shuffled closer. The vampire's magic began to bite more strongly, its unpleasant feel making my skin jump and twitch. But I could at least see the spell now. It had been placed three feet away from the wall in a semicircular shape, and it appeared to be nothing more than a simple concealment spell—a fact that was at odds with the force crawling across my skin. I couldn't see any spell stones being used as anchor points, and that was another indication of the vampire's magical knowledge and strength. Most minor witches tended to use stones, as Belle and I had at the café. There was a lot less effort involved.

I reached out and carefully untwined the first thread from its brethren. As I did, the charm at my neck sprang to life, its warm pulse telling me there was indeed a dark intent behind this spell, even if I couldn't immediately see it. I carefully deactivated the opening line, and then repeated the process with each of the others. As each of the blurring spell's threads came free of the sum, and the words painted onto the wall became clearer, the biting sensation got stronger. It began to feel like I'd stepped into the middle of a swarming bull ants' nest, and *that* was the opposite of what was supposed to be happening.

The final few threads looked unusually dark for this kind of spell, which—when combined with both the stinging and the warning pulse of my charm—suggested something had been attached to one or more of the final lines. And *that* meant the vampire had been here far longer than Aiden had suspected.

I dismantled another thread, leaving two. The bottom one—which was also the final line of the incantation—definitely felt heavier than it should have. Most were nothing more than the spell's list of limitations and closure.

Stop, Belle said, mental tone urgent. *Energy is building under the earth on the outside wall of the reception area.*

I paused, handing hovering over the remaining threads. *Earthquake?*

Not a natural one.

I'm not feeling anything in here. And I should if the spell was strong enough to affect or draw power from the ground outside. *Perhaps you'd better push everyone back farther.*

And maybe you'd better leave those final threads alone, she said. *I'd rather not know what the bastard has said rather than risk your safety.*

You know I can't do that.

A half-dismantled blurring spell isn't dangerous to anyone—

The closure line is too thick, Belle. There's something else here.

Is the message clear enough to read yet? If we could at least get the gist of it, then maybe you don't need to go any further.

My gaze jumped back to the wall. The blurring spell had faded enough to see it was writing, but what it said was still unclear. *He's designed the spell so that it has to be fully dismantled before the message can be read.*

A trap, in other words.

We suspected that going in. I reached out, plucked the penultimate line free, and began to undo it. The final thread hovered in the air, dark, heavy, and extremely unhealthy in its feel. *There's definitely a second spell attached, and it's nasty.*

Nasty as in not witch magic?

I hesitated. *Its construction is witch, but its power comes from blood.*

Then he can't be one of us, she said. *In all the time the six families have been collecting spells and histories, there's never been any mention of a witch becoming a vampire.*

As far as we're aware, I said. *But how else would he know witch script? It's something that's handed down generation to generation rather than taught in schools.*

And because of that, each family had script quirks specific to them, and *that* meant untangling the blurring spell was more important than ever. It could be one way of pinning down who we were dealing with.

I don't think this is a good idea, Lizzie.

Whatever the spell is, I can at least see it. And if I can see it, I can undo it.

A declaration that isn't really comforting me right now.

It wasn't comforting *me*, either, especially given neither of us knew anything about blood magic. That was the sort of information they gave to those who went on to study at the witch university—of which there was only one in Australia—and Belle and I had run *long* before we'd become eligible for that.

And I was never eligible, given I'm a lowly Sarr. She paused. *Everyone is now farther back. I'm not sure whether this is good news or not, but the trembling in the earth hasn't worsened.*

Maybe he just wants to frighten us rather than cause any real damage.

Maybe, she said. *Be careful.*

It's my middle name. I reached out and carefully touched the final thread. It shimmered in response and the stinging peaked briefly then faded, but the unclean feel of the whole thread became stronger. I shivered and forced myself to concentrate, even as sweat trickled down the side of my face. The final thread's fibers slowly became visible—the completion line was indeed intertwined with the threads of a secondary spell. I carefully pulled on the lightest of the three spell lines that made up this final thread, holding it as I murmured a spell to isolate it without breaking the connection to the other two.

The words on the wall shimmered and then became visible. But even as they did, the fiber in my hand began to disintegrate and the other two began to pulse.

The trap had been sprung.

I swore and quickly read the note to Belle. *Vengeance is best given time and served cold. Let them sleep in the knowledge that they are safe, because it will make the moment when my hand rips out their hearts—as they ripped out mine—taste all that much sweeter.*

To that end, I cannot allow any interference. Your death is not personal, Ms. Grace. It is merely a precaution.

Even as my gaze swept across that last word, a wave of power knocked me off my feet, and both the floor and the wall began to shake and buckle.

I scrambled upright, quickly uttering the words of an umbrella spell that would hopefully protect me from the worse of the explosion as I dove for the desk rather than the door and the glass walkway beyond it. I had no idea if

KERI ARTHUR

the former would, in any way, provide additional protection, but the latter surely wouldn't.

Even as I leaped, the wall exploded, filling the air with dust and huge chunks of rocks. The force of it was so damn strong it not only sent me tumbling forward, but down into blackness.

CHAPTER
six

Waking was a somewhat slow and confused process. It came in a series of stops and starts that were filled with voices and dust, the former echoing in my head as sharply as fear, and the latter catching in my throat and making breathing somewhat difficult. There were what felt like boulders pinning me down, but no waves of pain. My body felt bruised rather than broken, and if that *were* the case and not a symptom of shock, then I'd been extraordinarily lucky.

As consciousness sharpened, Belle's voice became clearer. *Don't move,* she said. *The desk and that last-minute spell appear to have protected you from the worst of the explosion, but there are still some bits of wall pinning the lower part of your legs. They're in the process of moving them now.*

They?

Emergency service guys. No one else is allowed inside the building, as the reception area has been declared unstable.

Meaning the force of the explosion had been even worse than it had seemed. I finally opened my eyes, but couldn't see much more than the somewhat battered underside of the desk. And I couldn't turn my head to look at anything else because there was a brace around my neck.

The entire walkway came down in vast sheets, Belle continued, her tone grim. *If you'd been underneath it, it would have sliced you to pieces.*

Which suggests he expected me to run that way rather than toward the desk.

Yes, otherwise the force of the explosion would have also demolished the desk.

He's going to be pissed when he realizes I didn't die in his carefully planned trap. One of the lumps covering my left leg was moved, and pain flared. It still wasn't anywhere near the agony that came with broken bones, but I nevertheless growled at whoever was doing it.

"Sorry," a male voice said. "But the pain relief should kick in any minute now."

"Any minute isn't fast enough." It came out croaky— no surprise given my throat was dry and coated with dust.

We'll need to seriously ramp up both the protection spells around the café, Belle said, *as well as the ones we're wearing.*

Yes. Another piece of rubble was moved, but the drugs were obviously beginning to work because this time I barely felt it.

"Right," the same man said. "We're going to slide you onto a board and get you out of here. Ready?"

"Not really, but I'd rather not stay here."

A man appeared in my limited line of vision. He gave me a comforting smile, but his gaze was on someone else rather than me. "Okay, on three—"

Tension ran through me as he counted down. And despite the drugs, the minute they moved me, a wave of pain hit and consciousness fled once again.

When I next woke, it was to the gentle beeping of a heart monitor and a wall of blue curtains.

"You're in the hospital," Belle said. "There're no broken bones, no spine or neck injury, and no major cuts. You're going to be black and blue, and as stiff as hell for the next few days, but all in all, you're good."

I carefully pushed into a sitting position, wincing as various bits of me protested, then hitched the ill-fitting hospital gown back into place. "Then why am I still here?"

"Because they're hardly able to release an unconscious person." Her voice was dry. "They want you in overnight for observation."

"I can't stay here—"

"You can and you will," Belle said. "You've been unconscious for a couple of hours. They want to be sure nothing has been missed."

"But the vampire—"

"Won't be aware you've survived as yet," she cut in. "Besides, he'll be too occupied with Karen to worry about us for the next couple of days."

I opened my mouth to protest, and then shut it again. She was right. Becoming a vampire was the easy part of the whole process. Learning to cope with all the new sensory input, adapting to the hunger and the need to take human blood without destroying life, as well as understanding the restrictions that came with life as a vampire, would surely take weeks, if not months.

And while I doubted *this* vampire intended to give Karen that long, if he wanted to use her as any sort of weapon, then he'd have to give her a few days, at the very least, to gain some control and sanity.

Unless, of course, it was her *insanity* he wanted.

"That's a definite possibility," Belle said. "He did state he was here for vengeance."

"Did Aiden give any indication he knew what that note meant?"

"No." She grinned. "He's been in to check on you several times, though, which is interesting."

"No, it isn't," I replied. "He's dealing with a magic-capable vampire, and—whether he likes it or not—we're the local authorities on magic."

"All true," she said. "But he could simply have sent one of his subordinates. I'm thinking the man is attracted."

"And I'm thinking you're insane."

Her grin grew. "Possibly. I *have* been hanging around you for a very long time now. That sort of thing can be catchy."

I snorted and whacked her lightly on the arm—an action that probably hurt me more than her.

"The IIT also want to interview you once you're out of the hospital," she continued.

I frowned. "Why don't they just interview me here and now? It'll surely save some time."

"I have a vague feeling Aiden had a word or two in friendly ears," Belle said. "The doctors are refusing to let them in."

"It would seem the rangers aren't the only ones who dislike the IIT," I said.

"It would be fairer to say no wolf likes the IIT," Aiden said, as he came through the curtain. "They do have a tendency to ride roughshod over reservation sensibilities."

"But they also have a job to do," Belle commented.

"And obstructing them is hardly beneficial to either of you."

"Between the explosion site and the coroner's report, they have plenty to keep them occupied for the next couple of hours." His gaze came to mine. "The doctors said you were damn lucky."

"It was certainly lucky I decided to dive for the desk rather than the corridor. Belle said the whole link came down."

"It did indeed." He hesitated briefly. "Are you feeling up to some questions?"

"Sure."

He dragged the other chair up and then sat down. "Ms. Kent said it's sometimes possible to tell which house the script come from—was that the case here?"

"No, and that's weird, because—as far as I'm aware—no one outside the three high houses are taught script."

"A statement that basically confirms the fact you're from one of those families," he commented, with a completely neutral expression.

"It confirms I was taught some script," I replied, keeping my voice even. "But that doesn't mean I'm a full blueblood or that I'm capable of any major magic."

That raised eyebrow once again spoke of disbelief. But all he said was "So does that mean the vampire we're looking for is also a blueblood?"

I hesitated. "I doubt it, if only because the script he used was too pure. It's almost as if he learned it from a textbook."

"And is that usual?"

"No. Basic script *is* taught in witch school alongside regular writing and spelling, but there're no textbooks handed out and every witch house has their own variation. The only existing records of script are kept in the National Library."

He leaned forward and crossed his arms on the bed. His scent played around me, warm and musky, with just the faintest hint of smoky wood. Which was nice—more than nice, actually. It was probably just as well he hated what I was, because I might have been tempted to break my "no more men" rule had he shown even the slightest bit of attraction.

"And has the public got access to those records?" he asked.

"No," Belle said, with an amused glance my way. "It's law that a copy must be kept there, but it's basically locked down. The only people who have access are high-profile bluebloods or government ministers."

"The latter wouldn't be able to read it, though, would they?"

"No," I said. "Not without help. But if someone *did* access it, that would give you a starting point."

"I'll contact the National Library tomorrow morning," he said. "Did the spell itself give you any insight? It was obviously powerful—"

"Yes and no," I cut in. "The initial spell was a basic blurring spell, but the spell that caused all the damage was actually one designed from blood magic."

He frowned again. "Witches don't do blood magic, do they?"

"No," Belle said. "It's considered an unclean magic, and one that stains the soul unto darkness."

"Witch magic," I continued, "comes from both the power of the practitioner and the power that lives all around us."

"So we're looking for a blueblood gone bad?"

"Again, I doubt it. We consider becoming a vampire an abomination of the natural process of life and death."

"Which doesn't mean it can't happen," he said.

"True, but to my knowledge it never has." I hesitated. "If you want to be sure, it might be wise to contact the council and ask them."

"And about more than just our vampire, I think."

"Go for it," I said, even as a sliver of trepidation ran through me. It was highly unlikely an innocent query would raise any alarms when it came to either Belle or me, as our name change wouldn't be listed in the council's records, but I nevertheless preferred to keep *any* sort of contact at a minimum. "But they won't be able to tell you much about either of us—they generally don't keep records of mutts."

"And yet they apparently teach them," he said.

"Only if said mutts come from a highborn family and show an inclination for magic," Belle said. "And even then they're placed into the lowborn schools so that blueblood sensibilities aren't stained by their presence."

"I'm sensing a whole lot of bitterness behind that statement."

"Ranger, you have no idea." She leaned back in her chair and crossed her arms. "The note said he was after vengeance, and that he intended to rip out the hearts of those who'd done him wrong. Are you any closer to uncovering the incident the note referred to?"

"No—"

"And he wouldn't tell us if he did." I glanced at Belle. "That's ranger business, not witch."

"But if he wants our help dealing with this vampire— and he's not dumb enough to think he doesn't—then he had better start sharing *all* information."

"Ladies, I *am* still in the room, remember." Aiden's voice was a mix of annoyance and amusement.

"Totally aware of it," Belle said. "Otherwise we'd be having this conversation telepathically."

His gaze leaped to mine. "Don't tell me you're telepathic as well?"

"You can relax, Ranger," I said. "The only thoughts I can read are Belle's."

"And as I've already said, I have no desire to read yours or anyone else's at this current point." Belle paused, her gaze narrowing a little. "Unless, of course, you give me good reason to do so."

"*That* is hardly a comforting thought." He frowned and leaned back in the chair. "I'll share what I can, and answer what questions I can, in regards to this case. But I expect the same. Clear?"

I nodded. "Then you *do* have an opinion on the note?"

"There's been no murders within the reservation that involve hearts being ripped out of bodies, so it's obviously not meant literally."

"Unless it's an event that happened before you were a ranger," Belle said. "He did say vengeance was best served slow and cold."

"We're checking past files, but it would be hard to stop a murder like that being the subject of gossip," he said. "And it can't have happened too far back, as he's obviously targeted Karen."

"Karen could be an anomaly," I said. "If he intends to be here for some time, then he does need blood."

"You believe that no more than I do," he said. "He made Karen a vampire, and *that* alone suggests intent."

"And it also means Marjorie might be the first piece in his vengeance puzzle."

"Which is why I've placed a watch on her."

I frowned. "But there're only four of you—"

"Six, actually, and Mac's leave has already been canceled," he said. "But that's beside the point. Is there anything else relating to that note or the vampire himself we need to know?"

I hesitated, and glanced at Belle. *Should I mention the pendant?*

I would. He'll shut down if we don't at least appear to be fully open with him, and we need his help if we're all to get out of this mess in one piece.

Another warning from the spirits?

Indeed. They're all gloom and worry at the moment.

Then I'm really *glad I can't hear them.*

"I get the feeling," Aiden said, "there's a whole separate conversation happening that I'm not a party to."

"Yes, but in the spirit of cooperation, I'm now going to tell you what it was about." I flashed a smile that didn't appease the annoyance in his expression. "I searched Karen's room after your people did, and found a necklace that held the stain of dark magic."

"And what did it tell you?"

"Nothing yet, because I haven't actually attempted to examine it." I glanced at Belle. "And given what happened at the morgue, I'm thinking it might be better to do so out in the forest, within a full protection circle."

"Totally agree," she said. "Especially given he's already gone to some lengths to wipe out the local witch."

I frowned. "But the reservation hasn't had an official witch in over a year, so how did he know I was here, let alone what I was? It's not like the charms we sell would have told him that—it's only minor magic."

"Another statement that is somewhat at odds with what you claim you are," Aiden said softly. "So why do you continue this farce?"

"Because it's *not* a farce," I said. "I may be capable of magic, Ranger, but trust me when I say I am not—and never have been—capable of the sort of magic bluebloods can bring into being."

His gaze held mine for several seconds, and then he nodded, just once. Whether that meant he finally believed me or not, I couldn't say. Those insights I'd been getting were decidedly—and rather annoyingly—absent right now.

"Call me Aiden," he said. "The ranger thing is getting annoying."

"And you can call me Belle," Belle said.

The ghost of a smile played about his lips, but didn't quite reach full bloom. Which was a shame, but not unexpected given the grief and distrust he still carried in his aura.

"Did you find anything else in that room?" he asked.

"No." I hesitated. "What are the chances of regaining my knife? I know silver is banned, but it's a great conductor of magic and I might yet need it."

"That's a council decision, not mine," he said.

"So I talk to them?"

"I'll mention it when I make my progress report tomorrow." He pushed to his feet. "I want to be present when you attempt to read that pendant."

"As long as you keep your hatred of magic under control," I said. "Because emotion *that* strong can often have detrimental effects on spells, and that's not really what we need when we're dealing with whatever has been placed on the pendant."

"I don't hate magic—"

"No, just those of us capable of using it," I said. "But that's unfair, Aiden, and you know it."

He didn't say anything. He just turned and walked out.

"That man is going to be a challenge," Belle said.

"Just as well I'm not up for one, then, isn't it?" I touched her hand lightly. "You'd better go home and get some rest."

"Rest? When I have a hot date with an even hotter werewolf planned? Unlikely."

I grinned. "Then have a good time, but not at our place, just in case the vampire does come calling."

"I doubt he'd be capable of that tonight, even if he didn't have his hands full with his vampling. The creation of that spell would have drained him." She rose and dropped a kiss on my cheek. "Try to get some sleep rather than stressing over what's going on."

"Easier said than done."

"I know, but try anyway." She collected her coat from the back of the chair. "I'll bring in a change of clothes for you tomorrow. There's nothing much left of your dress, I'm afraid."

Which wasn't a surprise, given the force of the blast. At least I hadn't lost the shoes as well. "Thanks."

She nodded and left. I reached for the water sitting on the nearby table, then grabbed the remote and turned on the TV. Time, as ever when stuck in a place you didn't want to be, crawled by.

A ward doctor doing his rounds woke me the following morning. He checked the observation chart, gave me a once-over, wrote out a prescription for stronger painkillers if I needed them, and declared me fit enough to leave.

Belle appeared on cue a few minutes later, looking too well rested given her previous hot date declarations.

"Said hot date was a blast, but he had a job booked for seven, so we didn't have a whole lot of time together."

"Sometimes the best times don't take a whole lot of time."

She grinned, handed me a bag, and then pulled the curtains around so that I could change. "Indeed. But all we did this time was talk."

"I don't believe *that* for one minute."

Her grin grew. "Well okay, maybe we did test the waters just a little, but nothing full-on."

"That's very restrained of you." I tossed the sheet off and carefully swung my legs over the edge of the bed. Because of all the painkillers I had on board it didn't actually hurt, but everything felt stiff and the bottom half of my legs had the beginnings of a colorful array of bruises.

"And who knew I was even capable of that, right?" Belle laughed. "We're meeting tonight, barring a sudden disaster or a change of mind on reading that pendant."

"There won't be any change."

"You say that now, but the spirits are suggesting the sooner the better."

"That's because they're not the ones having to expend the energy." I eased off the bed and began to dress. "There is no way on earth I'm going to be ready before the rise of the full moon. In fact, I'm planning to do nothing more than prop myself in a corner of the café, eat cake, and drink tea."

She grabbed my arm to steady me as I shuffled toward the door. "Good plan, but you know how they get—nag, nag, nag."

"I'm so glad you hear them and not me."

"A sentiment they agree with. Your propensity to ignore good advice would drive them insane, apparently."

"I don't really ignore it." I just didn't always do want they wanted with the sort of speed they wanted. Sometimes—as with the wellspring being on O'Connor compound—it just wasn't possible. But spirits didn't exactly get that things in the real world often couldn't happen instantly.

"We'll need to upgrade the spells protecting the ground floor, too," Belle continued. "The current ones protect us more against dark spirits and energy rather than a living force of evil."

Which certainly described our vampire. At least we didn't have to worry about such precautions during the day. For all that Hollywood and novels had screwed with much of the vampire legend, they'd gotten one thing right—vampires couldn't stand the touch of sun. It didn't matter if it was the faintest stray sunbeam, it would turn them to ash quicker than I could say "good riddance."

Of course, that rule didn't stop him hiring someone else to do the deed. But instinct said he wouldn't do that, that he was a man who preferred to make his own kills.

It was a shame instinct couldn't give me a similar insight on where the bastard was hiding.

Once home, Belle headed upstairs, and I made good on my promise to prop myself at a table in an empty corner. The sunshine streaming in through the nearby windows did at least warm some of the trepidation from my soul.

Penny appeared, her expression concerned and, I suspected, all mothering instincts on high. "Are you all right? I heard you were caught in some sort of explosion at the morgue, though why on earth someone would want to bomb a place like that—"

"I'm fine thanks, Penny," I said, before she could go on any further. "But I'd love a cup of chocolate mint tea and a large slab of banana cake."

She wrinkled her nose. "We've sold out of the banana already. I've got chocolate, carrot, red velvet—"

"*That* would be perfect."

Her smile dimpled her features. "Coming right up."

As she walked away, I switched my gaze back to the window. Why would our vampire go to the trouble of turning Karen if his intention was simple vengeance? Why not just kill her? It would have still ripped out Marjorie's heart, but caused *him* a whole lot less trouble.

And what was Marjorie's link to the vampire—was he a past case or was something stranger going on here?

Can't be a past case, Belle said, as she clattered back down the stairs. *He said they, rather than just she.*

Meaning we need to talk to Marjorie about her past.

No time like the present, Belle said.

I smiled at Penny as she approached with my tea and cake. The cup was a cheery Christmas one, which would normally have made me smile. Right now, however, all I could think of was the pall of fear that would quickly dull the brightness of the coming season if we didn't catch this bastard soon.

I scooped up some cake and munched on it as I pulled out my phone and rang Marjorie. While I waited for the phone to be answered, I silently uttered a quick but simple spell that would stop our conversation from carrying beyond the limitation of the small table. There might not be many people currently in the café, but I didn't want them hearing anything untoward. Aiden would *not* be pleased if I started any sort of panic amongst the reservation's population.

"Banks Law Incorporated," a pleasant voice said. "How may I help you?"

"I'd like to talk to Mrs. Banks if she's available, please."

"I'll see if she's free," the receptionist said. "Who may I say is calling?"

"Elizabeth Grace."

"One moment, please."

There was a brief pause in which music played, and then Marjorie's modulated tones said, "Elizabeth? This is a surprise—word on the street was that you were caught in an explosion last night."

The gossipers obviously hadn't wasted any time. "I was, but I was released from the hospital this morning."

"I'm told you were extremely lucky."

Lucky that I'd gone the right way, lucky that I'd had the time to utter a protective spell. "Have the rangers been around to see you yet?"

"Yes. I'm under guard. Some rubbish about me possibly being on a hit list."

Meaning they hadn't told her about Karen? *Shit.* "They didn't say anything else? Ask you anything else?"

"Well, they did ask me if I had any past cases that resulted in clients threatening retribution—"

"And did you?"

"None that I can immediately think of," she replied. "Major crimes aren't prosecuted here, though, but rather in the Melbourne courts."

"And there's no one, either in the reservation or outside of it, that you can think of that might want to harm you or Karen?"

"No, I've got a good reputation and have never received any sort of threat." She hesitated. "Do you think that's why Karen was killed? Because of something I have or haven't done?"

"At this point in time, we're simply exploring all avenues." Which was probably exactly what the ranger had already said, but I couldn't really give her much more right now.

"Do you know why the morgue was hit?" she asked. "The rangers haven't said, but I have a bad feeling it had something to do with Karen."

"Only in a sense." I hesitated, not wanting to be the one to tell her—especially given Aiden's warning. And yet, she deserved to know, if only because Karen's death might be just the first step on the vampire's revenge ladder. "The explosion was the vampire's attempt at erasing any possibility of me interfering with his schemes."

"And Karen? Is her body okay?"

"Yes." I hesitated again, and took a large gulp of tea. It burned all the way down, but it didn't have anywhere near the effect of the Glenfiddich. "Marjorie, if you're not already sitting down, you might want to do so."

"Oh God," she whispered. "What's happened?"

"There's no easy way to tell you this—" I hesitated, and then continued on quickly. "It would appear Karen underwent the ceremony to become a vampire. She rose last night with the help of the vampire who killed her."

For a several minutes there was absolutely no response. I knew she was there, because I could hear her breathing. It was fast, and spoke neither of fear nor grief, but something else entirely.

Something that made my heart and stomach sink.

"Marjorie?" I said, hoping like hell I was wrong, that she *wasn't* seeing Karen's rising as a good thing. "Do you want me hang up? We can talk later, if you'd like—"

"No," she said, and then added more softly, "No."

I picked up the spoon and scooped up more cake. It didn't really ease the vague sense of guilt that I should have—could have—done more to stop Karen from rising.

Short of chopping off her head, that's impossible, Belle said.

Another insight from your gran's books?

Yeah. I was reading it again last night to see if there was an easy way to track her.

And is there?

Normally, you'd have to track her down by finding her maker. You do have another option, though.

If he did sense my presence in Karen's thoughts, he would have taken steps to prevent me tracing her that way again.

It's still worth a try.

It was, but not until I felt stronger. I scrubbed a hand across my eyes, still unable to escape the notion we could have done more to prevent all this.

We did what we could, Belle said, mental tone gentle. *We warned the rangers—we told them about our suspicions. We couldn't have done anything else—not until they were willing to take us seriously.*

And it had taken the death of five good people *and* an explosion for that to happen.

"So does this mean," Marjorie said, voice still soft but vibrating with an odd sort of hope. "That's she's not dead? That she's not gone from my life?"

"Karen's a vampire, Marjorie, and that means she'll have changed in ways I can't even begin to explain—"

"But she's alive?"

I hesitated. "Technically, yes."

Of course, science *was* still debating that one, because many of the processes that were so vital to *all* life—things like sleeping or defecating—were no longer active in vampires. Hell, they really didn't even need to breathe, though most of them did simply to avoid outing themselves when living amongst others.

"Oh dear God," Marjorie repeated, and quietly began to sob.

"Please don't get your hopes up of seeing her anytime soon, Marjorie. You may not see her for months."

If at all. While newly minted vampires needed time to understand and control their sharpened senses, it was their lust for human blood that prevented most from returning home. It was simply easier to cut ties and walk away rather than risk killing those you once cared about.

But a vampire intent on bloody revenge had raised Karen. That she'd actually get the time she needed to regain control was something I seriously doubted—and that placed Marjorie in danger. Karen didn't appear to have a whole lot of respect for her mother, and the man who'd turned her undoubtedly intended to use that lack.

Because what greater revenge was there than to have a desperately ungiving but nevertheless much-loved daughter kill the woman she blamed for all the problems in her life?

The reality was, Marjorie needed to leave town, but I doubted she'd listen to reason. I silently waited a few more minutes and then hung up. She'd undoubtedly ring me back once she'd gotten over the shock.

I dispersed the spell around the table, finished the rest of my tea and cake, then rose and hobbled toward the stairs. Bruises, I discovered, didn't like being moved all that much after a rest period.

Once I'd grabbed my laptop from my bedroom, I continued out to the balcony. The screen was glary thanks to the sun, so I shifted position then opened my e-mails—and immediately saw the response to my request for more information on that third case file from the IIT.

Elation quickly turned to frustration, however. The file had been locked at the request of the Regional Witch Association, and could only be viewed with their permission.

I hit the link they gave me, which took me over to the RWA's website and a permission form. I skimmed through it then backed the hell out of there. The Association wanted far too much information in that form, and while I *did* want to know what had happened here, I wasn't about to risk outing either Belle or myself. It might be true that my family could have found us if they'd tried with any sort of intent, but there was always a risk that a simple query could spark that interest. They'd all but wished me dead in the months after Cat's murder, and that was exactly what I intended to be to them, for as long as I remained alive.

Instead, I searched the IIT's website for any reservation crimes relating to vampires or hearts, but this time found nothing. I tried lengthening the time frame out to twenty years—the longest period the search engine would allow—but the results were the same. The crime the vampire was seeking retribution for really *had* happened a very long time ago, just as his note had implied.

I leaned back against the chair and watched the traffic roll past on the street below. I had no idea where to look or what to do next, and *that* was extremely frustrating when there was only a limited window of time in which this bastard was inactive.

I swore and hobbled back inside, dumping the computer on my bed then grabbing my purse and car keys.

"Lizzie," Belle said, as I reappeared downstairs.

I held up a hand to stop her. "I know, and I tried, but I just can't sit here and do nothing. I'm going to drive around and see if I can spot anything remotely resembling the cabin I saw."

"Wasn't it in the forest?"

"Yes, but there're plenty of dirt roads outside of town, and it could be down any one of them." I shrugged. "I've got to at least try."

"Fine." She reached into the fridge and handed me a bottle of water. "Keep hydrated. The minute you start getting tired, come back."

"Promise."

Her snort was a sharp sound of disbelief. I grinned and left. But three hours later, I was no closer to uncovering where the vamp was hiding.

By the time I got back to the café, it was empty. The bell chimed as I entered, and Penny glanced up from behind the cake fridge.

"Belle's in the reading room, if you're looking for her."

"Client?"

She shook her head. "Not this time, although we did have a good run of people for a while there. Nothing like a newly minted local almost getting killed in a bomb blast to stir up curiosity in the local population."

"As long as they come back, I don't really care."

There was no telltale flash of light above the door to indicate Belle was in the middle of a spell, but I nevertheless knocked.

"Enter," she called. "I'm just finishing up."

"Finishing up what?"

The table had been pushed to one side and the carpet rolled up to reveal the pentagram we'd inked into the floor. White candles burned at each point, their light dancing merrily through the otherwise shadowed room.

"Stronger charms—not only for you and me, but also Penny, Mike, and Frank. I don't want them getting caught up in anything nasty." She held out what looked like a bracelet made with a random selection of colorful strings interspersed with flashes of silver and wood. "One vampire deterrent, at the ready."

Clean, bright energy caressed my fingers as I took it. "How much of a deterrent?"

"It will—if Gran's book is correct—stop them getting close enough to bite you, but it's not going to stop bullets or anything like that." She hesitated. "There's also a warning that the newly turned *could* be immune to them, thanks to the tumultuous state of their mind."

I slipped the bracelet over my left wrist; the pulse of power flared briefly and then died down. "I doubt she'll be sent at us. I think it more likely she'll be aimed at her mother."

"I agree." Belle began snuffing out candles. "It would probably be easier—safer—if the ranger got her off the reservation."

"She won't leave now that she knows Karen has been turned."

"He can force her—"

"And she'll no doubt shove a restraining order right up his ass, and return."

Belle grunted and climbed slowly to her feet. "We can try putting a protection spell around her house—"

"But it won't stop madness getting in—and that's all

Karen will really be right now." Madness and hunger. I hesitated, my gaze sweeping her, seeing the tiredness I could feel through her thoughts. "Go upstairs and rest."

"Yeah." She placed a hand against her back and arched backward. "I'll certainly need the latter if I'm to be in a fit state for tonight's activities."

"Meaning you and the lovely Zak have another date?"

"We do indeed. He's picking me up at seven and taking me to dinner. Dessert is at his place."

Her dimples flashed, leaving me in no doubt as to what she intended dessert to be. "Then I shall prepare a potion to speed up recovery."

"I don't trust the evil gleam in your eyes right now."

"Me?" I said, all innocence. "Do you really think I'd plot revenge for all those shitty-tasting drinks you've forced on me over the last few days?"

"That angelic expression you're going for isn't working." She touched my shoulder lightly. "If you have the strength, it might be wise to ramp up the nighttime perimeter wards down here."

"On it." I stepped to one side to give her room to pass. "I'll be up in ten with that drink."

As she went upstairs, I finished cleaning up and put all the furnishings back in place, then grabbed two of the remaining charms and headed into the kitchen. Mike had already left for the day, but Penny was pulling on her coat in the small alcove that held the lockers, and Frank was sanitizing the benches. He was bald, muscular, and possessed a fine array of tats over both his arms and legs.

"I'll finish off here," I said, and handed Frank a charm. "I need you both to wear these."

Penny accepted hers with a frown. "Why?"

"There's a few bad vibes running about the

reservation at the moment," I said, "These will ward them away."

"Good, because I don't need any more bad luck right now." Despite looking like the last person on earth you'd think would willingly wear a somewhat pretty charm, Frank slipped it on without hesitation. "Will water affect it?"

"No, you can shower in it and all."

"Excellent." He walked over to the lockers and grabbed his stuff. "See you tomorrow then."

"You will."

Once the two of them had left, I finished cleaning up and made Belle's revitalization potion—and stood in front of her to make sure she drank every last drop.

"God, that is *vile.*"

"Welcome to my world," I said, with just a hint of satisfaction. "I want you to block me out tonight. Just relax and enjoy yourself."

She frowned. "You know I don't like doing that—"

"Yes, but we've likely got a day or so before our vampire causes any more problems." I crossed mental fingers I hadn't just tempted fate with that statement. "I *can* break the block if I really need to, so quit worrying and just relax and have fun."

Because at least one of us needed to. I didn't say it, but I didn't have to, either.

She hesitated, and then nodded. "But only if you promise to shout the minute anything untoward happens."

"I will, but it won't." I continued to the living room and the hours slipped by. Zak came calling at precisely seven, and Belle left with a spring in her step, all trace of tiredness gone.

I bolstered the spells protecting the café and was

halfway through eating dinner when my phone rang. I recognized the number and immediately answered it.

"What can I do for you, Marjorie?"

"I'm outside, in the car," she said. "Can I come and talk to you?"

I hesitated. "I know you'd like to know more about Karen becoming a vampire and what it means, but I really don't know enough about the process—"

"I still need to talk to you," she said. "*Please.*"

There was something in her voice, an odd sort of edge that snagged at my instincts. "Okay. I'll be down in a second."

I shoved my meal on the coffee table then brushed off the crumbs as I headed downstairs to open the door. She appeared a few seconds later, her face white and eyes shadowed. I motioned her to the table in the corner and locked the door again.

"Tea?" I asked.

She shook her head and sat without taking off her voluminous red coat. I sat opposite her and crossed my arms, making sure my hands were well and truly out of her reach. Her aura was almost black with grief, despair, and—rather oddly—uncertainty, and it was a combination that had the power to rip past my shields.

"I've been trying to remember," she said, "if there was anything—anyone—whose case might have gone so badly that they'd want revenge."

"And you've thought of one?"

Grief slipped across her aura. Grief and guilt. "It wasn't a case. It's something else."

I waited silently. After a moment, her gaze met mine, haunted and uneasy. "It happened a long time ago. I can't believe it could possibly be the reason behind this madness, but I can't think of anything else."

"Tell me, please." I kept my voice soft. Her mental state was extremely fragile—anything else would have either sent her running or broken her completely.

"I was only a teenager," she said. "The group I ran with were… well, vile, if I'm looking back at it now, but back then, we were the top dogs, the 'in crowd.' We'd even attracted a couple of werewolves."

"So you were born within the reservation?" I asked, surprised.

She nodded. "Mom was already pregnant with me when they moved here. Dad was a cardiologist at the hospital."

"And this event? What happened?"

She lowered her gaze. "A new family came to town. Rumors soon got around that they were into magic and other weird stuff—"

"Meaning they were witches?" I cut in.

She shrugged. "I don't really know. But a few animals had gone missing, and the rumor mill was soon blaming the family."

Missing animals could certainly have pointed to the darker arts being used, but was no real proof. After all, animals *did* wander off sometimes, and either get lost or die. "What happened?"

"Their daughter was enrolled in our school. She wasn't liked." Her gaze rose again; the brown depths were haunted by both shame and regret. "You can imagine what happened."

"Yes."

There was no need to say anything else. Bullying—be it physical, verbal, or even via social media pages—had been an unwanted fact of life back in my day. It was only recently that schools and the government had begun to see and deal with the very real psychological damage it could cause.

But if the girl's parents *had* been capable of magic, then surely they would have done something—cast some sort of spell against the perpetrators. While it went against the witch creed to cause direct harm unto others unless the circumstances were dire or involved the forces of darkness—and no matter how reprehensible the actions of Marjorie's gang were, they would never be classified as either of those—there were certainly spells that could bounce actions and emotions back twofold. That was often enough to stop the hardiest bully in their tracks.

And when it came to dark magic, well, the options were endless.

Of course, either option depended on the child being honest and open to her parents about what was happening, and in a great percentage of bullying cases, they weren't.

"How old were you when all this happened?"

"Sixteen."

A bitch of an age, in more ways than one. "What happened?"

"We were relentless," Marjorie continued. "Day after day, we picked on her. We made her life hell, both in and out of school."

I knew what was coming, but I nevertheless asked the question. "And?"

"She killed herself. Her note said she couldn't take the abuse anymore, and she couldn't see any other way to be free of the pain and humiliation." Marjorie took a deep, somewhat shuddery breath. "I wish I could turn back time and undo what we all did."

It was a wish I could sympathize with, even if for very different reasons. Marjorie's actions, like mine, had caused the death of another, but hers had been done in spite and hate, while mine had been an act of desperation.

But if she was looking for sympathy or even forgiveness, then she was talking to the wrong person. What she needed to be doing was evoking the girl's spirit and asking *her* for forgiveness.

"Can you remember the names of the other people in your group?" I asked.

"Maybe. It was a long time ago." She frowned. "I think there were eight—no, nine—others."

I pulled out my phone and opened the voice recording app. "Tell me the names you remember."

"Morris Redfern still lives here, and Mary Jones died in a car accident when she was twenty-five," she said. "The others moved out of the reservation years ago. I have no idea where they are now."

"Just tell me their names. We can search."

She did so, although for a couple of them, all she could remember was their first names. When she'd finished, she wrapped the ends of her coat more tightly around her body and said, "Do you really think Karen was targeted because of that one event so long ago?"

"It's a possibility we can't ignore." I stopped the recording and tucked my phone back into my pocket. "What can you tell me about the girl? Or her parents?"

"Her name was Frieda." She paused. "Frieda Andersen, I think. We never saw her dad—he apparently had a night shift job somewhere in Bendigo. Her mom didn't work."

"Did Frieda have any brothers? Sisters?"

"No," she said. "But there were a couple of other

women living with them—it was another reason Frieda was mocked. We only ever saw them occasionally, when they came to pick Frieda up from school if her mom couldn't make it."

So the women weren't vampires, although we couldn't yet rule out Frieda's dad as a possibility. While vampires might, as a general rule, be loners, there were always some exceptions. These came in the form of pods—a small group of humans who willingly allowed a vampire to feed on them in exchange for security and an easy life.

If being a vampire's meal ticket could ever be considered easy.

That being the case, however, it meant our vampire couldn't have been Frieda's dad. Vampires were *not* fertile, so the only way he could have had a child was if he'd inseminated one of them before he'd turned—which was certainly possible, I guessed, even if it made the subsequent living arrangements a bit more perilous.

But if he'd had the control to feed from three women without killing them, why take so long for retribution? Why wouldn't he have done it right there and then? It didn't make much sense.

"Where did the family live?" I asked.

Marjorie hesitated, and then shook her head. "It was somewhere on the west side of town."

"But in town, rather than out in the scrub?"

She nodded. So much for the vague hope that Frieda's home might be our vampire's current hideout. "Is there anything else you can tell me about the family?"

"No. As I said, it was a long time ago. That's why I'm struggling to believe it could be related to what has happened to Karen."

"It might not be, but if you can't remember any other event, it has to be considered," I said. "Was Frieda buried here?"

"No. But I can't tell you why."

Maybe they simply hadn't wanted her buried in the town that had all but killed her. Or maybe Frieda shared blood and was about to become a vampire herself, so they dared not risk remaining in the town. "What happened to the family after Frieda's death?"

She shrugged. "They were never seen again, as far as I'm aware."

And I doubted a search would reveal much information on where they'd gone, especially if we *were* dealing with a pod. Not only had it all happened a long time ago, but it was easy enough to get a new identity if you knew the right people or spells—Belle and I were evidence enough of that.

"If you do think of anything else, please call me," I said. "In the meantime, maybe it would be best if you left—"

"No." Her expression switched from guilt to anger in an instant. "Karen is here and I will *not* go anywhere until I see her."

"Marjorie, a newly turned vampire is nothing more than an insane mess. She won't know you. She won't even remember who *she* is. Everything about her has changed, and it'll take time—"

"I'm her *mother*," she said. "I will *not* abandon her."

I hesitated, then pulled the charm from my wrist and held it out. Belle would kill me, but Marjorie needed it more than I did right now. "Then wear this. It will at least offer you some protection from the vampire who raised Karen last night."

Her expression was somewhat dubious as she accepted the charm. "How can something so fragile in any way deter a vampire?"

"Magic can do many things," I said. "Wear it, and it'll hopefully keep you safe."

She slipped the charm over her wrist and then rose. "You'll call me if you hear anything? Either about Karen or the vampire?"

"I will."

"Thank you."

She left. I locked up again and then headed back upstairs. I didn't fancy reheating the crumbed fish in the microwave, so I made myself a cup of tea and grabbed a packet of Tim Tams from the cupboard. It might not be the fuel my body needed, but my soul also had needs, and right now it wanted chocolate biscuits.

I was halfway through the packet when I felt the faint caress of magic. It wasn't witch in origin, but rather dark.

Blood magic.

Our vampire wasn't neatly tucked away somewhere recovering his strength and controlling Karen.

He was out there, in the night, raising hell.

CHAPTER
seven

I grabbed my keys and backpack, then raced downstairs to the reading room. As much as I wanted to stop whatever might be happening out there, I wasn't about to do so totally unprepared. And *that* meant grabbing my athame as well as some of the precious blessed water we had in stock. I had no idea what spell was being cast, but those two items gave me the best chance to combat it. And if I was too late to do that, I could at least cleanse the ritual site.

Once outside the café, I paused, despite the growing urgency. I needed direction. I couldn't afford to run around blindly.

The force of the spell rose again and tugged me left, toward Barker Street. I briefly debated whether to grab the car, then abandoned the idea and simply ran. I couldn't drive and concentrate on tracking the sensations running across my skin. I just had to hope that the location wasn't too far away.

I turned left into Barker Street without really looking, and crashed full force into someone who smelled faintly of warm musk and smoky wood.

Aiden.

His arms went around me as he staggered back several steps, but he somehow managed to keep us both upright. "What's the emergency?" he said, his voice a little hoarse.

Which was no surprise given the force with which I'd hit him. "Someone is casting a spell. I need to stop it."

I thrust away, but he grabbed my arm, stopping me. "Can you track this force in a car?"

"Yes."

"Then I'll drive. This way."

I followed him down the street. Once in his SUV, I wound down the window and closed my eyes. The wisps of energy that was the spell were getting stronger; whatever the vampire was trying to do was reaching a pinnacle. Time was running out.

"Continue straight down Barker," I said. "And floor it."

The truck's big engine roared as we hurtled down the street. "Can you tell what type of spell is being cast?"

"No, but it's blood magic, not witch." I didn't open my eyes, needing to concentrate on the nebulous threads of power rather than the world whizzing past. "Right at the next road."

"Princess Street." The truck tilted alarmingly as he took the corner at speed.

The spell peaked, the power of it so strong—so dark and *wrong*—that my skin twitched and stomach rolled.

"Left," I said, voice tight.

The truck slid sideways for several meters before he got it under control. "Cemetery Road."

Those two words had horror surging. Our vampire wasn't raising hell. He was raising the *dead*.

"He's in the cemetery—"

"What the fuck would he be doing there?"

"Attempting the second part of his vengeance plan, if I'm not mistaken."

"Meaning what?" Aiden's gaze stabbed toward me, something I felt rather than saw. "Trust me, now is not the time for cryptic comments."

I gripped the door, bracing as the vehicle did a sharp right and slipped around on a graveled surface. We'd entered the cemetery.

"Meaning if I'm right, and if we don't stop him, we could be dealing with a zombie."

"Oh *fuck*."

A statement I echoed as the caress of magic died. "Stop."

He slammed on the brakes. As the Ford came to a shuddering, sliding halt, I threw open the door and scrambled out. The energy was fading fast but its remnants led me left, toward the rear of the cemetery.

I raced through the gravestones, every sense on high alert. Just because the main spell had reached completion didn't mean there weren't others here—especially if our caster was aware his plan to wipe me out had failed.

Candlelight flickered through the trees ahead, a faint glow that did little to break the darkness or lift the unease coursing through me. The magic might have faded, but the sense of wrongness was still very much present—one that was now accompanied by a weird sort of anger. It was an emotion that seemed to be coming from the night itself.

I cut through the strand of trees and ran on. Magic stirred anew, but its touch wasn't dark. It was fresh, light, and powerful—wild magic. It was here, in this cemetery, and full of the anger I'd sensed only moments before. It curled around me, urging me on—something I had no idea a non-sentient force could do.

I caught sight of two figures up ahead—one tall and broad of shoulder, the other hunched and cloaked.

Energy surged, and a sphere of what looked like a boiling mass of blood began to form above the two men. The taller of the two made a throwing motion and, as the red mass hurtled toward us, picked up the cloaked figure and ran in the opposite direction. I threw up a hand and started casting a diversion spell. The wild magic gathered around me, weaving itself into the spell and creating a force far greater than I'd intended.

A second sphere formed at the end of my fingertips—it was bright, white, and as deadly looking as its counterpart. It wasn't what I wanted, and I had no idea what it might do, but it was all I had. I flung it at the darker mass flaming toward us, then spun and threw myself at Aiden.

This time, he had no chance to catch his balance, nor did I want him to. He caught me with a grunt and we crashed to the ground as one.

"What the fuck—" he said, the words little more than a wheeze.

"He just threw something at us." I slipped to one side and twisted around. The two spheres continued to arrow towards each other, and the air burned with their joint fury.

"What the hell are *those* things?"

"Ethereal fires," I said. "Dark and light."

The two of them hit and halted, the white merging into the red and disappearing. For a heartbeat, nothing happened. The merged spheres simply hovered above the ground, pulsing and heaving as each spell fought for control over the other, creating a field that rippled out in ever-tightening circles. It was accompanied by a whine that reminded me of an engine being pushed too hard and too fast.

There was only way this could end.

"Cover your eyes," I said, and buried my face into Aiden's side, breathing in his warm, rich scent to counter the bitter fury of the pulsing spheres.

With an almighty roar, the spheres blew apart.

Even though I had my eyes squeezed shut, I was nevertheless aware of the fiery heat that sprayed across the night, and of the wild magic chasing and consuming those droplets. None of them hit us, but the ground sizzled and the stench of burned grass touched the air.

Lizzie? Belle's mental tone was concerned. *Is everything all right? I just felt an almighty rush of power—*

It was a spell, but not one specifically aimed at me. Which technically wasn't a lie because it had also been aimed at Aiden. *I've dealt with it, so there's nothing to worry about. Get back to enjoying your lovely werewolf, and keep those mental shutters down!*

A statement that fills me with suspicion.

I promise, there's nothing to worry about. Not now, anyway. *I'll tell you all about it tomorrow morning.*

If I find out you're holding out, I'll be pissed.

And I'll be pissed if you don't shut the hell up and get back to enjoying yourself.

Her laughter ran down the mental lines. *Fine. I'm gone.*

The slight buzz that was the connection between us

shut down again. Around me, silence had again fallen and the sense of danger slipped away. I carefully lifted my head. The night was empty of any sort of magic, wild or dark, but we were completely surrounded by thick patches of burned grass. The wild magic had saved us, by both enhancing my spell and then protecting us from the fallout.

That scared me, almost as much as the power the vampire could so readily call into being.

I wasn't the local witch. I wasn't even a *vetted* witch. The wild magic shouldn't have even recognized my presence, especially when I had yet to enter the wellspring to commune with it.

But it wasn't just *that*—it was also the anger I'd sensed within it. I'd always believed wild magic wasn't sentient, but if that were true, how in the hell could it have been angry?

Was Belle right? Did the wild magic not only hold some form of awareness, but was it also the reason I'd felt compelled to come here?

But that raised yet another question—why me? If the magic within this reservation were capable of calling a witch to it, why wouldn't it have called to someone far more capable?

Aiden pushed to his feet. "What the hell sort of spell was that red sphere?"

"A nasty one."

"Which you destroyed with one of equal power," he said. "And that is yet another indicator you're not what you claim."

"Except it wasn't all me. The wild magic subverted my spell and created something I had not intended." I paused as instinct suggested that whatever had happened here tonight was just the start of things—but the start of what, it wouldn't say. I rubbed my arms, though it did little against the gathering chill. "I did warn you it was dangerous."

He briefly scanned the graveyard. I had the suspicion he was searching for the magic he didn't have the capacity to see or feel. "I thought you said the wellspring was in the O'Connor compound?"

"The wellspring is, but the wild magic itself isn't restricted to that area. As I said, it's everywhere on this reservation."

"Ah." He offered me his hand. "I have to tell you, I'm struggling to believe any of this."

"Which is hardly surprising given your less than stellar opinion of both magic and witches." I placed my hand in his and let him pull me up. "We'd better go see what he was doing."

He didn't immediately release me. "You look rather pale—are you all right?"

I nodded. He hesitated, and then stepped to one side to allow me to pass. But his grip moved from my hand to my elbow, as if in readiness to catch me should I stumble or fall. I didn't object—my legs were more than a little wobbly. It had been a long time since anyone of power had tried to kill me—over twelve years in fact—and this bastard had now tried twice.

"Is it really possible to raise the dead?" Aiden asked.

"If you know the right spells, yes." I glanced at him. "I don't know those spells, in case you're wondering."

A slight smile touched his lips. "Are you sure you're not telepathic like your friend?"

"Trust me, your thoughts are totally safe from me, Ranger."

"Aiden, please, especially given I'm going to need your help to catch this bastard."

That raised my eyebrows. "So hell really has frozen over?"

"Possibly." His voice held just a touch of self-deprecation. "Certainly it's something I would have thought impossible a year ago."

The candles were still burning up ahead, which meant our vampire either hadn't closed off his pentagram or he hadn't used one. Even for those of us who followed the path of light, their usage often depended on what sort of spell was being created or on what sort of magic or spirits were being called forth.

"I can smell blood," Aiden said. "It's fresh."

"He would have had to make a sacrifice if he was raising the dead." I paused. "How strong a scent are we talking about?"

He glanced at me, his expression one of curiosity rather than anything else. "Why?"

"The longer a body is in the ground, the bigger the sacrifice has to be. Reconstituting flesh isn't easy."

"I'm not sure whether to be relieved or not by that statement."

"Opt for the former," I replied. "It means he should be out of action for the next day or so."

"Should is also not a word I find comforting in this sort of situation."

A smile tugged at my lips. "This bastard does keep doing things he shouldn't be able to."

As we drew closer to the grave, it became evident that the two candles I could see were it—and that, in turn, meant there was no pentagram.

My gaze slipped from the candles to the grave itself.

It was open, and the earth had been flung in all directions, suggesting the vampire's magic had simply punched through it to get to the body. With more than a little trepidation, I looked at the gravestone.

Mason Redfern, son of Emma and Morris Redfern. He'd been buried thirteen days ago, and had only been sixteen years old.

The same age Frieda Andersen had been when she'd committed suicide, the same age Karen was when she'd been killed.

I doubted any of it was a coincidence.

"Do you know how Mason died?"

"Car accident," Aiden said. "His car ran off the road and hit a tree. No one is sure why."

"Why was he driving when he was only sixteen?"

"Teenagers are allowed to drive solo at that age within the reservation as long as they obey a rather strict set of criteria." He shrugged. "Up until Mason, we'd had no major accidents."

"Was he drunk?"

"There was no alcohol or drugs in his system. We initially suspected he either fell asleep at the wheel or was trying to avoid something and lost control, but that was before we discovered bullet holes in his rear tires." His gaze settled on mine. "Why?"

I hesitated. "I was talking to Marjorie early this evening. I think I know what all this is about."

"And you're intending to enlighten me, I hope."

"Yes, but not here."

He grunted and stepped past me. I grabbed his arm to stop him from getting any closer. "Wait."

"Why?"

"Because the earth at the far end of the grave is

stained with blood and who knows what else." Just because I couldn't feel any magic right now didn't mean it wasn't here. "At the very least, I need to cleanse the area before we go near that grave."

His skepticism was on full display, but all he did was motion me to proceed. I swung the backpack around and unzipped it. The precious bottles of holy water were still intact, despite the roughhousing they must have gotten. I pulled two free then handed the pack to Aiden and walked to the end of the grave. There was no sign of active magic, but the memory of it stained the earth as strongly as the blood. I uncorked one of the bottles and began the purification spell. As I spoke, I poured the water over the bloody soil, until it was completely covered. Then I uncorked the second and continued around the grave, just to ensure no taint remained. Mason would be laid to rest here again once we caught him, and the combination of holy water and the spell should ensure that he could at least rest in peace. Without these precautions, any spell remnants left in the soil might have kept at least some parts of his body awake, if not aware.

I closed off the spell then glanced at Aiden. "It's safe to approach now."

Aiden stepped up to the grave and studied it silently. "The casket looks as if it was smashed open from the inside."

I nodded. "Reanimated flesh is surprisingly strong."

He raised an eyebrow. "You've had experience with them before?"

"No. It's simply one of the things they teach us at school."

"Not at my school, they didn't." A smile flirted with his lips, but faded all too quickly. "How dangerous will

Mason be? How long will the magic keep him alive?"

"I can't honestly answer the latter, because it usually depends on both the spell and the practitioner." I hesitated. "But in this case, I can't imagine he'd be active for more than a few days."

"Why's that?"

"Because he was raised for one simple purpose—to kill his father."

"*Morris*? Why?"

"Let's go back to the café and I'll tell you."

"Okay." He hesitated. "I know the Redferns quite well. Mason was their only child, and his death hit them hard. This is going to shatter them."

I walked around the grave and headed back to his truck. "Not as much as their decaying son smashing his way into their home and trying to kill them will."

He fell in step beside me. "Is there any danger of that happening tonight?"

"As I said before, this spell *should* wipe our sorcerer out, but he's also a vampire and I've never come across that combination before, not even in any of the reference books I've read." I rubbed my arms against the chill continuing to steal across my body. "It may be that he'll send Mason after his father as soon as possible, because while the blood magic raised him, it's the strength and will of the practitioner that feeds him."

Aiden shrugged out of his jacket and offered it to me. "Here, put this on."

"I'm fine," I said, unable to keep the surprise from my voice.

"No, you're damn well not," he all but growled. "So take the damn jacket and stop being silly."

I did. And immediately felt better for it. "Thanks."

"I'm not always a bastard," he said. "Despite appearances to date."

"So I'm learning." And maybe, just maybe, he was beginning to look beyond his instinctive hatred of witches, and see the person rather than the power.

He opened the truck's door, ushered me in, then ran around to the driver side and started the engine. "What's the best way to stop a zombie?"

"Shoot the fuck out of them," I said. "Head shots work best. Decapitation is another option, but that means getting a little too close to them."

"Not the answer I was expecting." He smiled again. "Can we stop him from getting into the Redferns' house? Morris doesn't own a gun, but I doubt he'd be able to shoot his own son even if he did."

I hesitated. "Placing salt across all entrances is one of the few myths that holds true, but it won't stop our vamp if he's with Mason."

He turned left onto Cemetery Road then glanced at me. "So it's not true that vampires can't cross a threshold uninvited?"

"It is, but he's also a witch. He can simply raise a force to blast the salt away."

"Meaning I'd better go talk to Morris and Em tonight."

"And tell them what? Their son's a zombie?" I studied him. "Why on earth would they even believe something like that?"

"They won't," he said. "Hell, I'm not entirely sure I believe it yet, and I've seen the grave. But I can't *not* tell them, either."

I guess he couldn't, if only because the opened grave would be discovered in the morning by the cemetery staff.

Silence fell as the streets sped past. He eventually pulled into the driveway of a small weatherboard house and then stopped. "You'd best stay here. I'll go talk to them."

I nodded. He climbed out and walked up to the small porch. The light came on as he neared the front door, and a woman with brown hair and a bright smile ushered him inside.

I locked the doors, then crossed my arms and hunkered down in the seat. In a matter of minutes, I was asleep.

It was the sound of the truck's engine that jerked me awake. I blinked rapidly and shoved upright, looking around for a moment before I realized we'd already left the Redferns' house. I rubbed tired eyes and then glanced at Aiden.

"Everything okay?"

"Sort of." His expression was grim. "I told them Mason's grave had been desecrated, but not that he'd found new life as a zombie."

"Which leaves them unprepared if he turns up."

"They weren't likely to believe that even if I had told them." He shot me a grim glance. "Few rational people would. Zombies belong in books and movies, not real life."

"Yes, but that doesn't negate—"

"What I *did* say," he continued, cutting me off, "was that there'd been a number of robberies in the area, and the perpetrator's description matched Mason's. I asked them to call me if they saw someone who looked like him."

Which wouldn't really help them, because by the time anyone got there, the damage would already be done.

Aiden must have guessed what I was thinking, because he added, "I've also ordered Byron onto watch duty."

"He's another ranger, I take it?"

"Yes, and just in case our vamp does make an appearance, I've told him to grab a cross and sharpen some stakes." He glanced at me again. "They do work, don't they?"

I smiled again. "The stakes do." And at least a werewolf had the speed to make them a practical weapon. "The cross would need to be blessed before it is in any way effective."

"And another myth hits the skids." He pulled into a parking spot outside the café. "Do you want me to come back tomorrow? You were pretty solidly asleep for a while there."

I hesitated, then shook my head. "You need to know what Marjorie told me so you can warn all those involved."

"All?"

I climbed out of the truck and walked across to the front door. "Does the name Frieda Andersen mean anything to you?"

He shook his head. "What has she got to do with it?"

"Everything." I ushered him inside then walked across to the coffee machine. "Drink?"

"Strong black would be good."

"Instant okay? Or do you want the real stuff?"

He smiled, and this time it reached his eyes. He really did have nice eyes when they weren't cold and filled with hatred. "Instant *is* real as far as I'm concerned."

As I put the kettle on, he leaned on the counter, watching me for several seconds before adding, "Tell me about Frieda."

I did so as I made our drinks. He accepted his mug—a basic, no-nonsense white one—with a nod of thanks and then said, "Isn't thirty years a long time to wait for revenge?"

"For the average person, yes. But we're not dealing with that."

"No, I guess not." He drank some coffee and surprise briefly touched his expression. "Your instant is a *whole* lot classier than ours."

"That's because we don't buy supermarket shit. Would you like some cake?"

He glanced at the cake fridge and said, "Are those brownies as good as they look?"

"Better." I grabbed a pair of tongs and got a couple out. "So you were never told about the Andersens?"

He shook his head. "I would have been only one when it all went down, and my parents have never mentioned it."

Meaning he was only a year older than me. Nice. "Marjorie gave me a list of names, but she only knew the whereabouts of a couple."

"I gather you took notes?"

I nodded and got my phone out. "I'll send you the recorded file if you'll give me your number."

He did so. His phone beeped as it received the file. "Thanks," he said, after glancing at it briefly. "Did Marjorie tell you much about the Andersens?"

"Not a whole lot, but from what she did say, I suspect they might have been a pod." He raised an eyebrow, so I quickly explained what that was and then added, "It might be worth chasing down Frieda's birth certificate. If our vampire is her father, that should give us his name."

He nodded. "There's one thing that puzzles me in all this—if our vamp was a witch in life, why would he have even bothered to turn?"

"Many believe that the process of turning cures the flesh of all its previous ills. Whether that's true or not, I couldn't say." I shrugged. "Would there be some kind of record of the Andersens in the reservation's archives?"

The Faelan Reservation had, like most of them, diluted the restrictions and requirements for non-werewolves to settle within the reservation just over fifteen years ago—something Belle and I had discovered when we'd been researching the area before we'd decided to come here. But the stricter rules had certainly been in place at the time the Andersens had been here, and that meant they would have been fully vetted by the council beforehand.

"I'm not sure how long the records are kept, but I'll get someone to check." He raised the half-eaten brownie. "This is extraordinary, by the way."

"All thanks to kitchen magic," I said. "Which is not, in any way, connected to real magic—just in case you're thinking I'm trying to spell you or something."

"I wasn't. I'm too busy simply enjoying."

So was I. For the first time since I'd met him, he actually appeared relaxed in my presence. His aura still ran with grief, but the flashes of distrust and hatred had muted. They certainly weren't gone, and would no doubt flare back to life with one wrong statement or move, but it was at least a step in the right direction.

What that direction might be—and whether I actually wanted it—I couldn't say. Not only was there my vow of no more entanglements to consider, there was also the fact he was still very much a stranger. He could be married with a dozen kids for all I knew.

I finished my brownie and licked the chocolate from my fingers, well aware that he was watching me even though I wasn't looking at him.

"When I was talking to the Redferns," he said, his tone slightly deeper and edged with a tension that had my pulse rate rising. "I asked if I could borrow something of his."

He reached into his pocket and then placed a watch on the counter between us. The face was shattered and part of the band was missing. "Would it be possible to track Mason's current location through it?"

"Possibly." I reached out, but didn't touch the watch. I didn't need to. The waves of wrongness rolling off it were evident enough from a couple of inches away, and it made me want to knock it far away. "What reason did you give his parents for needing it?"

"Mason's death is still an open case because of the shot-out tires, so I simply told them we were following a new lead and that we needed the watch he'd been wearing at the time of the accident. They gave it to me without question."

"Do you think it's possible our vampire killed Mason?"

"Don't you? Both our vampire's note *and* his actions make it clear he's intent on making his victims suffer before he kills them. It's not much of a leap to presume he was behind Mason's so-called accident. Especially given tonight's events."

"True."

I studied the watch for a moment, my arms crossed on the bench and fingers clenched. I really didn't want to touch the thing. Fear and desperation might have filled Karen's last remaining moments on this earth, but her passing hadn't stained the locket with evil or wrongness. The vibes coming off the watch felt like what I imagined hell would feel like, only without the heat.

Presuming the myths of hell being hot were, in fact, true, that is. The darker spirits could probably have told us, but no witch I knew would ever risk summoning or conversing with them—especially for a question as inane as that.

"Can you use the watch?" Aiden asked.

My gaze rose to his. "Yes, but it won't be pleasant. The desecration we witnessed at the gravesite vibrates through his remains and, subsequently, this watch."

"If you'd prefer not to touch it, then don't. We'll find him the old-fashioned way."

"The old-fashioned way might just take too much time. I'll try tomorrow." I stopped and then swore. "I'm such an idiot."

Amusement touched his lips again. "You're many things, but I wouldn't have said an idiot is one of them."

"Thanks. I think."

His smile grew. Brownie goodness really was the way to this man's heart—or, at least, into his good books.

How long it would last was another matter entirely.

"What did you remember to cause that outburst?"

"That I can track vampire Karen the same way I tracked human Karen—via her necklace."

He frowned. "Didn't you say you were going to do that tomorrow night, when the moon was full?"

"Different necklace. That one has our vampire's stain on it. I can't risk using it without being in a full protection circle."

"Ah." His expression suggested he really didn't understand why, but was going along with it anyway.

"That stain could be a spell of some kind," I said. "Given he's a blood witch, and much more powerful than me, I can't risk an attempt to explore it without being fully protected."

"Or you might end up in another situation like last night?"

"Exactly."

"Not something we need."

"Agreed." I glanced at the clock on the wall and saw it was nearly ten. "Do you think it's too late to give Marjorie a call?"

"That depends on whether or not she knows Karen has become a vampire. We've not mentioned it."

"I told her when I was talking to her earlier." I hesitated. "She deserved to know."

"I agree, but the council overrode me. They didn't want to risk untoward rumors."

I raised my eyebrows. "You've got two vampires and now a zombie running around Castle Rock. That's fact rather than a rumor."

"Yes, but the last thing we need is a population in panic. We've enforced a news lockdown—nothing will be reported in either the papers or on television—"

"It doesn't need to be. The gossip vine in this place knew all about that explosion and the fact I was caught in it within minutes."

"Yes, but they don't know *why* it happened." He grimaced. "We're keeping an eye on the vine's main players, and hosing down spot fires before they become anything stronger. As I said, we don't need people panicking. It'll just make the task of finding this bastard that much harder."

And we certainly didn't need that. I pulled my phone out of my pocket and called Marjorie.

"Banks residence," she said. "How may I help you?"

"Marjorie?" I held the phone away from my ear so Aiden could hear the conversation. "It's Lizzie—"

"Have you found Karen?" she cut in. "Is that why you're ringing?"

"No," I said. "But if I can borrow that necklace again—the one you gave me when I first tracked her down—I might be able to do so."

"Oh." She sounded deflated—depressed. Still hoping for a miracle despite everything I'd said to her. "But yes, of course you can borrow it, if it'll help bring her back to me any quicker."

"Bring her back?" Aiden murmured. "Did you not tell her what a newly turned vampire is like?"

I placed a hand over the phone and said, "I tried. She couldn't see past the fact Karen was alive."

"Christ, what a mess."

"Tell me about it."

I lifted my hand as Marjorie added, "Are you coming over tonight to get it?"

I glanced at Aiden. "Up to you," he murmured. "You're the witch, not me."

There was no rancor in that statement for a change. "I'll drop by in the morning to grab it, if that's okay with you. It's been a long day and I'm not sure—"

"Someone's at the door," she cut in. "Hang on a sec."

There was a clunk as she put the phone down, then footsteps as she walked to the front door. A chain rattled as Marjorie said, "Who's there?"

If there was a reply, it was too soft to hear. But my

heart was beginning to beat a whole lot faster, and trepidation crawled across my skin.

"Hello?" Marjorie said again. "If that's you out there, James Maldoon, I'm going grab you by the ear and drag you back to your mother. Don't think that I won't."

Still no reply. Marjorie muttered something I couldn't quite catch but didn't open the door. Instead, she walked away.

Don't walk, run, I wanted to scream at her. *Run and hide, and don't come out until we get there.*

But even as I thrust upright, there was a heavy thump followed by the sound of wood splintering. Aiden was already on the move, barking orders into his phone as he stalked toward the café's door.

It wouldn't save Marjorie. Nothing would. Not now.

But we had to try.

I grabbed my coat and ran after Aiden, my phone held to my ear so I could hear what was going on.

"James," Marjorie warned, voice annoyed. "Enough, or I'll call the police."

Another crash at the door. This time, glass shattered. Marjorie's footsteps stopped, and then she was running. "Elizabeth?" Her voice was high and filled with fear. "Are you still there? Someone's trying to break into my house—"

"I know." I slammed the café door shut and quickly locked it. Aiden was already in his truck and motioning me to hurry up. "I'm with Ranger O'Connor now. We're coming, Marjorie. Is there a room you can lock yourself in?"

"The bathroom, but—"

"Go there now." I jumped into the truck and held the phone to my ear with my shoulder, grabbing the seat belt as Aiden reversed out of the parking spot at speed. "Lock yourself in, and don't come out until you hear my voice."

"But surely—"

"Marjorie, get into the bathroom—*now!*"

Her footsteps told me she was finally obeying. Then a soft, almost tremulous voice said, "Mom?"

My heart skipped several beats. That voice belonged to Karen, and I very much doubted she was alone. While vampires did gain strength and speed on turning, Karen was still a newborn in vampire terms. She wouldn't have had to time to understand the power that was hers, let alone the strength to partially shatter a wooden door.

For that same reason, she should also have been nothing short of mad right now, her mind torn apart by sensations and need.

And yet that soft, uncertain question had her sounding anything but.

"Don't stop," I urged Marjorie. "Just get into the bathroom and lock the door. We're only minutes away, Marjorie."

"But that was Karen, I'm sure of it."

The certainty of approaching doom pounded through my veins. If she didn't obey, if she didn't get into the bathroom, she'd die.

And her death would be far from pleasant.

"It wasn't Karen, Marjorie." My voice was flat and calm, free of the fear and the tension that was pulsing through me. "You have to trust me. I don't care what you think you heard, it was an illusion. A trick. Get into the bathroom."

"But what if it—" She broke off, and then added, her voice broken and hushed, "It *is* her. I can see her."

"It's not Karen. It's someone who looks like her."

Someone who was wearing her skin but whose mind was in the control of a man who wanted revenge. "Get into the bathroom, Marjorie. Don't open the goddamn door."

"She's crying, Elizabeth. My baby is crying. I can't—" The rest of her sentence ended in a sob.

I glanced at Aiden.

"We're a minute away." His voice was harsh. Tense.

"Go faster," I said, even though I knew he was already redlining the engine.

On the other end of the phone, Marjorie added, "Karen? Is that really you?"

"Yes," came the soft reply. "Please Mom, you have to open the door and let me in."

"Marjorie, no!" I shouted. "Ignore her and just get into the fucking bathroom!"

I doubted she even heard me. Against all the odds, the daughter she'd thought she'd lost was standing outside her door, sounding sane and very lost—a little girl who just needed her mother. It was the very opposite of what I'd told her Karen was likely to be, and Marjorie had no defense against it.

But it was a lie. I knew it in my heart, felt it in every inch of my soul.

It was a lie, and that lie was about to kill.

"Marjorie," I screamed. "Don't!"

There was no response. Footsteps echoed as she returned to the door.

"Karen," she breathed, her voice filled with wonder. "It *is* you. You've come back to me."

"Yes, Mom." Karen's tone was still soft. "I have come back—for you."

For a moment, there was nothing but utter silence.

Then the screaming began.

CHAPTER
eight

The screaming rose to a pitch and then abruptly cut off. But that didn't mean there was silence—far from it.

And those sounds.... It sounded like a wild animal tearing at its prey. I closed my eyes and tried not to imagine what was happening, with little success. All I could see was Karen's bloody face as she ripped and tore into her mother's throat.

Aiden swore, threw the truck around a corner, and came to a sliding stop outside Marjorie's place. I scrambled out the door and raced through her gate, an immobilization spell springing to my lips. They were designed for the living rather than the dead, but vampires were still flesh beings so technically, it should work. Besides, it was the best I could come up with on the fly.

Aiden overtook me and raced up the steps two at a time. I finished the spell and cast it into the house. A heartbeat later, someone screamed, the sound high-pitched and feminine. Karen. Her master had probably bolted the minute Marjorie had died. Raising Mason, and then controlling Karen so strongly that she sounded her normal self, would surely have left him running on a thin edge of strength. He wouldn't want any sort of confrontation with me, let alone a werewolf.

Aiden slowed as he approached the front door, his gun drawn and held at the ready. He motioned me to stop, then, with a deep breath, carefully edged around the splintered doorframe and disappeared inside. There was no immediate response from Karen and tension wound through me.

Then she screamed, a sound followed by three quick gunshots.

Silence fell again. I clenched my fists and, after a moment's hesitation, crept toward the door.

What I saw was not Karen or Aiden, but rather Marjorie. She was lying on the floor, on her back, her head surrounded by a halo of dark blood and bits of flesh, a look of horror frozen onto her face.

And her throat... dear God, her throat.

My stomach rolled. I spun around and bolted for the stairs. I'd barely reached the garden when everything I'd eaten that day came surging up my throat and I was seriously, violently ill.

"Sorry," Aiden said softly, a few minutes later. "I should have warned you."

I hadn't even heard him approach. But I guess vomiting so hard it felt like your innards were trying to jump past your lips did tend to mute all other senses.

"Hardly," I somehow managed to say. "You were too busy trying to stop Karen... did you?"

"You stopped her. I just killed her." His voice was

clipped. "Here, wash your mouth out with this."

A glass of water appeared near my face. "Thanks."

I rinsed my mouth out a couple of times, then drank the remainder. My stomach didn't feel any easier, but at least my throat wasn't as raw.

I straightened and turned around. His gaze swept me briefly, his expression hinting at concern. "Do you want me to drive you back to the café?"

I hesitated, then shook my head. "You've work to do here. I'll walk back—it's not that far."

"Are you sure? That might not be a wise decision, given our vampire is still out there somewhere."

"He'll be on the run." There was far more certainty in my voice than I actually felt. "Even the most powerful of dark witches have their limits. I think ours might have reached his tonight."

"Which only means we should be out there trying to find him."

"Unless you know where that cabin I saw in my dreams is, you probably won't," I said. "Even then, he'll have all sorts of concealment spells around it."

He glanced past me as lights swept around the corner and a green-striped SUV pulled to a halt beside his. Tala, his second-in-command, climbed out and came striding towards us. She gave me a brief nod and then said, "What's happened?"

"Karen murdered her mother. Is Ciara on her way?"

"Yes. What happened to Karen?"

"I shot her." He glanced at me. "I figured what worked for a zombie might work for a vampire."

Meaning the shots I'd heard had been at her head, not her heart.

"Zombie?" Tala's gaze shot from Aiden to me and

then back again. "Did I miss something?"

"Plenty." His voice held a note of weariness, but I guessed it had been a long day for him, too. And it hadn't ended yet. "I'll tell you later. Right now, we have a crime scene and two bodies to deal with."

"I'll get the kit."

As she returned to her car, I said, "I'll leave you to it."

He nodded. "Don't forget I want to be present when you try to find either Mason or our vampire."

"Sure." I reached out then froze, not exactly sure what I'd intended. I made it a wave instead then spun around and walked away.

Another car pulled up as I walked out the gate, and Ciara climbed out. She grabbed her kit from the rear seat of her car then nodded my way as she headed for the house.

I shoved my hands into my pockets and kept on walking. The night was hushed and there was no trace of energy in the air. The wild magic, like the vampire, had disappeared.

I walked back to the café without incident. I hung my coat on the hooks near the door then headed for the stairs, but a whisper of wrongness pulled my gaze to the counter and made me pause. The broken watch sat on the bench, glinting softly in the café's low lighting. I couldn't leave it there, out in the open, emitting that sort of energy. We'd worked hard to create a happy vibe in this area, and I wasn't about let this thing corrupt that. I walked into the kitchen to grab a pair of tongs, then picked the watch up and carried it into the reading room. Even though I held it at arm's length, the sensations that continued to roll from it had my skin crawling.

And, rather oddly, they were getting stronger—something that shouldn't be happening, given Mason's strength came from our vampire, and our vampire should be well and truly hitting the wall after everything that had happened tonight.

Unless, of course, he was feeding.

Vampires might not generally seek nourishment in their own backyards, but our vampire wasn't intending to stay here. If we didn't find him before his revenge plans had reached full fruition, I had no doubt he'd simply slip into the night, never to be heard from again.

I thought about ringing Aiden to warn him, but in reality, there was little point. It wasn't as if I was even sure there *had* been an attack—it was just a vague suspicion thanks to the emanations from the watch.

Once it was securely stored, I headed upstairs to wash the sweat and the foul feel of magic from my skin, and then wearily climbed into bed. I was asleep almost as soon as my head hit the pillow.

It was the awareness of being watched that woke me. But there was no rancor in that gaze, no heat or harm, and the brief flash of tension that had risen with wakefulness quickly evaporated.

I stretched the kinks out of body then opened my eyes. Belle leaned a shoulder against the doorframe, her shoes swinging lightly in one hand and her expression one of concern.

"Your thoughts are all kind of ugly," she said. "What the hell happened last night?"

The spells I'd placed around our bedrooms were preventing her from reading those thoughts, which was why she wasn't seeing the details. And for that, I thought grimly, she should certainly thank me.

"Plenty happened." I threw the blankets off and climbed out of bed. "How was your date?"

"Awesome, but don't change the subject."

"I'm not, but you need to shower and grab some sleep, and I need to get downstairs and get the day's prep done."

"I'm not going anywhere until you tell me—"

"No," I said firmly. "It'll take too long and your eyes are practically hanging out of their sockets. Not a great look if lover boy drops by today."

"I can assure you with more than a little smugness that Zak will be incapable of doing very much at all today." Amusement touched her lips and crinkled the corners of her eyes. "A werewolf's stamina has nothing against that of a woman who hasn't had decent sex in weeks."

I snorted. "That doesn't alter the fact that you need to rest—for my sake if not yours."

"Well doesn't *that* statement ease all my worries," she said. "Just give me the bare bones."

I hesitated then grabbed my clothes and began to dress. "Only if you promise to then drop it and get some rest."

"Done. Give."

Memories stirred, as did fear, but I somehow managed to shove both back into their boxes. I wasn't ready to deal with either right now.

"Bare bones," I said, voice tight. "Last night our vampire raised the dead, and then he sent Karen after her mother. Aiden and I didn't get there in time and both are now dead."

Belle's gaze widened. "Holy fuck—"

"And," I continued grimly, "Aiden wants me to make

an attempt to find the zombie using the kid's watch, and I'll need you to be at full strength in case something goes wrong."

She blinked, visibly shaken. "And to think we'd imagined Castle Rock was going to be a nice, sleepy little town in which to settle down."

"It probably was until they ran the local witch out of town and left the wild magic to its own devices."

Her gaze narrowed. "Meaning what?"

"Bare bones, remember?" I waved a hand toward her bedroom. "Go rest."

"As if I can after that sort of news," she muttered, but nevertheless pushed away from the doorframe and walked into her room.

I headed down to the kitchen and, for the next six hours, lost myself in the daily routine of running the café and looking after the customers. Belle came down just as the lunch rush hit, meaning we had little time to think, let alone talk. From my perspective, that was a very good thing.

Aiden arrived just as demand was beginning to taper off, and claimed the table in the corner of the room—the one I usually sat at. I finished serving a young couple, aware all the while that he was watching me, and then walked over.

His usually bright eyes were bloodshot and there were dark circles underneath them. "You look as if you need a nuclear-strength coffee."

"I'm not sure even *that* would be strong enough." He scrubbed a hand across his unshaven jaw then leaned back in the chair. Weariness seemed to ride every inch of his body; even his usually vibrant, if dark, aura was muted. It was almost as if he simply didn't even have the strength to maintain his rage and grief. "It's been a rather long night."

"Something of an understatement, considering it's almost two in the afternoon. Have you eaten?"

"I haven't had the time."

And didn't really have it now, if his expression was anything to go by.

"Can we talk?" he added.

I nodded. "Just let me grab your drink—"

"I'd rather not talk here," he cut in. "I don't want to start untoward rumors."

I couldn't help smiling. "Which is exactly what you'll get if you and I disappear upstairs for a private chat."

A somewhat reluctant-looking smile tugged at his lips. "Probably, but better that than the truth."

"At least you prefer me over a zombie," I said. "But don't worry, no one will overhear us here—I'll make sure of it."

He raised his eyebrows but didn't say anything as I walked back to the kitchen. I ordered him a deluxe burger with the lot then went behind the counter to make his coffee and my tea.

"Your ranger is looking a little worse for wear," Belle murmured, as she plated up a couple of cakes. "But it rather annoyingly makes him look even more attractive."

That it did. "Can you join us once you finish doing that? Penny should be able to cope with the remaining customers."

"Will do."

I picked up Aiden's coffee and my tea, and headed over. He accepted his mug with a nod of thanks and regarded its cartoony Christmas decorations with some amusement. "I get the feeling you're one of those people who is heavily into Christmas."

"I am, but you also looked as if you needed some cheering up." I pulled out the chair next to him and sat down. The table was small enough that our knees brushed, but he didn't pull away and neither did I. And there was something very comforting about that. "I asked Belle to join us. She needs to know what is going on."

"Why?" His tone was rather blunt. "What is the relationship between you two? Because there are all sorts of rumors circulating—"

"We're not lovers, if that's what they're saying," I cut in with a smile. "Never have been, never will be."

"And yet there's definitely a relationship between you that goes beyond mere friendship," he said. "Even blind Freddy can see that."

I took a sip of tea and silently cast a spell to ensure the couple sitting at the nearby table would hear nothing more than incomprehensible murmurs.

"Belle's my familiar," I said softly. "That's why we can share thoughts, and why we're so close. She's my conscience and my strength, and I wouldn't be alive today if it wasn't for her."

Surprise ran across his expression before he got it under control. "I thought familiars were generally either cats or spirits?"

"They are. As far as anyone is aware, this is the first time one witch has become the familiar of another."

"You said she's your strength—do you mean literally, mentally, or magically?"

"All three. Familiars are guides and advisors, but also provide an additional source of physical strength should a spell require it. But because Belle is also a witch, I can also draw on her magical skills, combining them with mine if necessary."

"So she also has a familiar?"

"No."

"Then what the hell does she get out of the whole deal? Not a lot, from the sound of it."

"That's unfortunately very true." Although at least becoming my familiar *had* bolstered her spell-casting strength and abilities. In fact, even though she hadn't been tested since puberty, I'd hazard a guess that they were now very close, if not equal, to my own. We still had our own separate skill sets, but when it came to general magic, we were equals.

"I'm surprised she's not at least a little bit bitter about—" He paused, his eyes widening a little as Penny came over with the food I'd ordered for him. "That's an impressive-looking burger."

"You looked as if you needed a good feed," I said, with a smile of thanks to Penny. "And it's hard to be bitter about something the spirits keep telling you will be the best thing to ever happen to you. Or so she said at the time."

"I don't think I want to know what you mean by spirits—not until I've digested all the current information, anyway." He took a bite of the burger and something close to bliss touched his expression. "Man, this is *good*. Are you sure don't add a little touch of magic to your food?"

"If ensuring our food is nothing short of mouthwatering can be considered magic, then we certainly do," Belle said, as she sat down opposite him. "But over the years we've discovered quality generally works better than any minor spell we could actually incorporate into our food production."

"If that's the case, what happened in Peak's Point?"

"You've been checking up on us," Belle said,

amusement clear in her tone.

"Of course. Nor have I finished." He took another bite then added, "Peak's Point—explain."

"We were outsiders who came in and showed up the entrenched businesses," I said. "Let's just say they didn't appreciate it."

"The local cop I spoke to said that you were behind a sudden rise in the rat population."

"That cop," Belle said, "sat on his fucking hands and mouthed platitudes while his bastard mates harassed our customers and suppliers, and generally made our life hell."

"And," I added, "magic can't make rats breed like rabbits, but it certainly *can* call to the unseen population of them that is in every town, and invite them to infest a certain premise or two."

Amusement twitched Aiden's lips. "So if there's a sudden rat infestation at the ranger station, I'll know I've seriously pissed you two off?"

"If you seriously piss us off," Belle said, voice mild, "you'll be dealing with far more than a rat infestation."

He studied her for a moment, obviously uncertain whether she was joking or not. She was, but I wasn't about to tell him that. It might do nothing to gain this man's trust, but if the events over the last few days hadn't already done that, nothing would.

"What happened after I left Marjorie's last night?" I asked.

"The usual. We might be dealing with a vampire and her victim, but that doesn't actually change procedure." He glanced at me. "Although Ciara wants to know if there's anything specific she needs to do with Karen's body."

I glanced at Belle. Given she'd read her gran's book

on vampires, she was the expert, not me.

"The old legends apparently have it right," she said. "Decapitation, stake them through the heart, then burying them under soil blessed with holy water."

"Can a priest do the latter, or does it have to be incorporated within a spell?"

"No. And holy water originates from priests, not us," I said. "Have you talked to Karen's dad about her funeral?"

He nodded. "I told him the explosion at the morgue had taken out a good portion of the refrigeration room and that he wouldn't be able to have an open casket at his daughter's funeral. He accepted it without fuss."

Of course he did. It meant he wouldn't have to pretend any real emotional connection as he looked upon his daughter for the last time.

That's a bit harsh, Belle said. *It's not like he totally abandoned the kid. He did at least see her.*

An uncaring dad is often worse than an absent one. And I knew *that* from experience.

I got the impression Phillip Banks wasn't really uncaring—I think he simply put his own comforts and desires ahead of everyone else's.

"I'm once again getting the impression there's a whole separate conversation happening that I'm not a part of," Aiden said.

Belle reached out and patted his hand. "Don't worry. You'll get used to it after a while."

"I'd rather you just talk to each other like normal people," he said. "Especially when you're in my presence."

"But we're not normal people," Belle said sweetly. "And you seriously do *not* want to hear every little thing we're telepathically discussing. It might just make you a little uncomfortable."

Amusement crinkled the corners of his blue eyes and made my pulse skip a beat or two. Disheveled or not, this man was seriously attractive when he smiled.

"I'm a werewolf. There's not much that will make me blush."

"Even when it involves two witches?"

"Depends what those two witches are doing," he replied evenly. "And to whom."

I just about choked on my tea, and Belle laughed, a contagious sound that broke the boundaries of my spell and had people looking around with a smile.

"I think there's actually a half-decent person underneath that cool and unemotional exterior of yours, Ranger," she said. "It's a shame you don't unleash it more often."

"How do you know I don't?" he asked. "As I've said before, neither of you know much about me or my pack."

"Nor did you wish us to," I reminded him. "Or has that now changed?"

He met my gaze, and I watched the amusement die. It wasn't replaced by the all-too-familiar wariness or distrust, but it wasn't exactly offering any hope of friendship, either. "I honestly can't answer that question."

I nodded, even as I hoped my unruly hormones took note and didn't step any further along the attraction line.

"Then I'm gathering you're here now not so much to talk, but because you want me to try finding Mason via the watch?"

"Yes. But also to tell you there was an attack last night—our vampire fed on an old couple not too far from Marjorie's." He paused, gaze narrowing as it swept my face. "You don't look at all surprised."

"No, because when I returned home last night, the vibes coming off the watch were strengthening, not diminishing. Given Mason's life comes from our vampire, it had to mean he'd fed."

"You should have contacted me—"

"And told you what? It's not like I could tell you who he'd attacked or where." Wasn't as if he'd actually had the people free to go looking.

"You'll have to release some kind of statement soon," Belle commented. "Not even a full press blackout will stop the rumors now that there's a desecrated grave *and* four people dead."

"That is the province of the council, not us." He pushed his empty plate away. "I relocated the Redferns this morning, and have them under twenty-four-hour guard. Will that be enough, or will Mason still be able to find them?"

"Mason's a zombie," Belle said. "He has no memories and no ability to think for himself. He is simply a creature at the whim of his master's needs and desires."

"Then what is the likelihood of our sorcerer being able to locate them?"

"Highly probable," I said. "Finding spells aren't all that difficult. All he needs is something of theirs."

"I haven't the manpower to place a watch on the Redferns' place." His tone was grim. Frustrated.

"I doubt you'd need to," Belle said. "As that note said, he's been plotting this revenge for a long time. He's undoubtedly already taken what he needs."

"Which might just explain the car break-in they reported a month ago," Aiden said. "It happened at night, but all that was taken were the spare house keys they keep in the center console. They changed the locks the next day."

"By which time, our vamp had already sent someone in to take what he needed," I said.

"Probably." He picked up his coffee and finished it. "Are you up to making an attempt—"

He stopped, his gaze moving past Belle as a mix of annoyance and hostility touched his expression. "Damn."

I leaned back and saw two men enter the café. Both were tall and dark-haired, wearing gray suits, dark sunglasses, and an official air.

"The IIT?" I asked, my gaze returning to Aiden.

"Yeah." He pushed to his feet. "Call me when they finish."

"You aren't sticking around?" I said, surprised.

"They won't allow it." His lips twisted. "Especially given I punched the shorter of the two in the face the last time they were here. It put something of a dampener on our relationship."

"*That* is one story I'd really like to hear," Belle said.

"And one you're unlikely to." He touched my shoulder lightly as he moved past. "Be wary of these two. I suspect they'll treat witches with almost as much respect as werewolves."

A statement that makes me even more curious as to what went down, Belle said. *I wouldn't have said our chief ranger was the type to lash out without reason.*

From what I can gather, the last time they were here involved a witch who was never found, and the death of someone who was close to him. Aiden walked past the two men, offering them a polite nod they did not return. Obviously, the bad feeling was mutual. *Wolves are notoriously protective of those within their packs, so it might not have taken much.*

Given how controlled that man is, I'm disagreeing. Belle

pushed to her feet. *Aiden's not the type to let emotion overrule common sense.*

Except when it comes to witches.

Despite his obvious distrust of our kind, he's treated us far better than many in the past. A smile touched her lips. *And now, I shall flee and leave you to the mercy of the IIT.*

Coward.

Totally. She gathered Aiden's plate and cup, and then left, her laughter ringing lightly through my mind.

I looked up as the two men stopped in front of the table. "This is looking rather official—are you gentlemen here to arrest me or something?"

"John Hart, Interspecies Investigations Team." The taller of the two flashed his badge. "This is my partner, Terry Blume. May we sit?"

They were claiming chairs before I could answer, so I didn't bother.

"We need to talk to you about recent events," he continued. "Is there somewhere more secure we could go?"

I gave him my politest smile—a sure sign of hackles being raised. And it wasn't so much what he said, but rather the way he said it—in that bored, you-are-not-worthy tone I'd heard far too often in my youth. It was an interesting attitude to take given these two had to be dealing with witches on a regular basis. While the majority of bluebloods *did* restrict themselves to Canberra in order to be close to the Federal Government, there were advisory high witches connected to all State Parliaments, and the lowborn houses were scattered far and wide.

"Yes," I said. "But there's no need to go anywhere else. We're quite safe to talk here."

"Meaning you've spelled the area?" Blume said.

"I have indeed. What can I do for you gentlemen?"

"You can start off by telling us about yourself," Hart said. "Because we've checked regional records, and the Association has no listing for either you or your partner."

"No, they don't."

"Care to explain why?"

"If you'd care to explain this line of questioning."

He raised his eyebrows—an action that was barely visible over the top of his dark sunglasses. "I simply find it interesting that these events have occurred not long after two unregistered witches arrived in town."

"We arrived three months ago, Mr. Hart. Given the first incident occurred two months later, I wouldn't exactly call *that* close."

The two glanced at each other. "What happened a month ago?"

"Car break-in." I smiled sweetly. "It's only a theory that the thief who took the house keys from the Redferns' car was indeed our vampire, but it's one that becomes more likely given recent events."

"Meaning the refleshing event that occurred last night?"

"It can hardly be called a refleshing, as even dark magic can't replace what putrefaction has already taken." I paused as the charm around my neck began to pulse in warning. "And whichever one of you gentleman is trying to invade my thoughts, give it up. I'm well protected, both mentally and magically."

They shared another look, which made me suspect they were both telepathic.

And they're also well protected from mental invasion, Belle said. *It appears to be some sort of electronic shield rather than a magical one. I'm not able to get past it.*

I wasn't feeling any sort of energy output, but if science had developed enough in recent years to create a wearable shield against telepathy, then they'd probably gone that extra step to ensure it wasn't detectable.

"Why would there be no Association record of either you or Ms. Kent?"

"Because it's not a requirement for half-breed witches to register their presence when entering a new state," I said. "You won't find our names mentioned in the high council's records of vetted witches, either. Neither of us bothered undertaking that particular process."

"I thought it was a requirement of the high council that all half-breeds be vetted?"

"It is. Doesn't mean it always happens."

The two men contemplated me for a moment. I found myself wishing they'd take off their damn glasses— it was hard to get an indication of what they might be thinking when I couldn't see their eyes.

A little breeze incantation can fix that problem, Belle said. *More than happy to do the honors.*

Tempting, but don't think it's a good idea to get them offside right now.

I'm thinking I don't care.

And I'm thinking that's *a bad attitude. We don't need them setting the Association on us.*

The Association doesn't scare me.

In and of itself, no. But it would only take one photo up to the high council to reveal our true identities. And while my parents might not care about either of us, I still had no desire to risk any possible contact or interference from them.

"To the suspicious," Blume said, "your determination to avoid interaction with both the regional and high councils suggests you have something to hide."

"Or that we simply have no desire to get involved with officialdom." I picked up my cup and rose. "If you're not here to discuss the recent murders, gentlemen, then I have nothing more to say to you."

"Please, sit," Hart said. "We are merely trying to establish your credentials as a witness."

I snorted, but sat back down. "Do you make a habit of interrogating witnesses like they were criminals, then?"

"No." Hart plucked a piece of fluff from his suit sleeve. "What can you tell us about the magic-wielding vampire?"

"He's using blood not regular magic," I said, and gave him a full rundown on everything I knew or suspected. I might not like either of them, but as I'd said to Aiden, they were here to do a job. "I take it you've contacted the Association for help?"

"Indeed." Blume glanced at his watch. "They should have a representative here within the hour. He or she will probably wish to speak to you."

Undoubtedly. Whether I wanted to speak to him or her was another matter entirely.

"Are you able to tell us anything about the reanimated corpse?" Hart said.

"I'm thinking you two probably know a whole lot more about zombies than I do."

"Well no, because it's not something we've actually come across before." There was a note in Blume's voice that suggested amusement, even if his face remained deadpan. "Central Victoria isn't exactly a hotbed for the undead."

"Which doesn't mean there aren't any vampires in the region."

"Of course not," Hart agreed. "But most have the

sense to stay under the radar and out of trouble."

"If most of them did that, you two would be out of a job."

"Not as long as there's magic, or humans living within werewolf reservations," Blume said. "How long does reanimated flesh last?"

"As far as I know, for as long as the sorcerer's strength holds out. Given he fed last night, that could mean another week, at least."

The two shared another glance. "He fed?" Hart asked.

"So I heard from the grapevine," I replied, hoping I hadn't just landed Aiden in trouble. "An old couple was apparently found dead this morning. It's not much of a leap to connect it to our vamp, given he would have been in desperate need of sustenance after his efforts last night."

"Speaking of which," Blume said. "I believe one of your skills is psychometry?"

I gave him a bland sort of smile. "That's what the advertising on the café windows says."

"Meaning if we found something belonging to either the Redfern kid or our vampire, you'd be able to find them?"

Obviously, Aiden hadn't mentioned either the watch or the pendant. I opened my mouth to tell them, then closed it again. As much I really didn't want to attempt locating our vamp or zombie through either item, I also had no desire to get Aiden offside. We had to live on this reservation once this mess had been sorted out—slipping back into the O'Connor pack's bad books wouldn't help achieve that aim.

Besides, the vibes I was getting from these two had

old prejudices resurfacing, and that only inflamed the desire *not* to help them.

"Perhaps," I eventually said. "But psychometry isn't as reliable as location spells. It might be easier—and quicker—to wait until the Association witch gets here."

"I personally agree," Hart said. "But given the violence appears to be escalating, we need to cover all bases."

"Fine." I crossed my arms. "But whatever you bring me needs to have been in close contact with skin. And in the case of our vampire, I suspect that's going to be difficult."

"Indeed, but if what you're saying is true, then if we find our zombie, we'll find our vampire."

"In theory, yes, but we are dealing with someone who is a very strong blood witch. It's more than possible he'll counter any such attempt with a diversion spell."

Blume frowned—something that was evident only by the creasing in his forehead. "I know it's possible to spell against magical intrusion, but I didn't think it was possible to do so against psychic powers."

"You can spell against anything. All it takes is the knowledge and the power." I rose again. "If that's all, gentlemen, I need to get back to work."

They stood as one. "Please remain contactable. As we've said, the regional witch will want to speak to you."

"Undoubtedly."

This time, Hart seemed to catch my unspoken reluctance. "It *is* in your best interests to assist our investigation, Ms. Grace. Failure to do so will have unfortunate consequences."

"I've answered all your questions," I said, unable to keep the slight tartness out of my voice, "and agreed to do a psychometry reading. How, exactly, am I failing to help your investigation?"

"Anything you tell the rangers must also be passed on to us," Blume said, as if I hadn't spoken. "Failure to do so will be seen as noncompliance."

"Anything I tell the rangers will surely be passed on as a matter of fact, wouldn't it?" I asked, feigning innocence.

"In theory, yes. But just in case—" Hart paused and retrieved a business card from his pocket. "Please call us direct, day or night."

I accepted the card without comment and watched them walk out the door.

"If you do call them," Belle said, as she stopped beside me, "I suggest you do so at night—the later the better."

"A most excellent plan, my friend."

As much as I wanted nothing more than to go upstairs with a bottle of alcohol and forget everything, I very much suspected we didn't have that sort of time to waste. Our vampire would be active again tonight, which meant we only had five more hours of daylight left to try and find our zombie. I also had to unpick whatever spell had been placed on the bloodstone—although it was totally possible that it wouldn't even be active now that Karen was dead.

But that was something I could attempt tonight, when I had the strength of the full moon and the protection of a pentagram behind me. I wasn't even going to go near the thing until then.

"It might also be wise to use silk gloves with that watch," Belle said. "It'll mute some of the foul sensations rolling off the thing."

"Good idea." I got my phone out and sent Aiden a text. I wanted him by my side when I attempted to find Mason, and not just because he'd demanded it. I simply didn't want the responsibility of having to take the kid down when—*if*—we found him. His soul might be long gone and his body no longer capable of independent thought, feeling, or memory, but I was witch enough to want to avoid killing if it was at all possible.

Aiden's response was almost immediate, and stated he'd be here in ten minutes. I shoved the phone back into my pocket. "How much holy water have we got left?"

Belle wrinkled her nose. "Only a couple of bottles. I've sent out some feelers to see if there're any priests in the area willing to supply some more."

"The association's representative might be able to point us in the right direction."

"If," Belle said, "said representative hasn't got his nose stuck as far up his butt as those IIT chaps."

I grinned. "It could be just us. We do have a tendency to almost immediately get on people's wrong sides."

"Not everyone," she said. "Zak was absolutely delighted to see me last night."

"That's because Zak is a sensible werewolf anticipating hot sex."

She grinned. "And he's already rung me a couple of times today—one night was not enough, apparently."

I glanced at her as I stepped to one side to allow Penny past. "Meaning it was enough for you?"

"Hell no, but there's a whole lot of truth in the old 'play it lean, keep them keen' saying."

I raised my eyebrows. "Since when is *that* an old saying?"

She waved a hand airily. "I don't do mean, so it

makes a whole lot more sense my way."

I snorted softly. "As if you're going to resist that man for too long."

"Oh, I don't intend to." Her smile faded as seriousness touched her expression. "But after last night's events, I have every intention of being with you when you attempt to unravel the spell on that bloodstone."

I nodded. As determined as I might be that Belle have a life outside the confines of being my familiar, I did in truth need her there, just in case the magic on the bloodstone was either far darker than it felt, or triggered an evil beyond the protection of the pentagram.

"I won't be doing anything before midnight," I said. "That does give you a little time with him, if you wanted."

"As tempting as that is, I need to rest. One of us needs to be at full strength."

Which *I* certainly wasn't. I might be ignoring it, but tiredness still rode me and there were niggling aches all over my body. What I needed was twenty-four hours of decent sleep and several large meals of steak and veg, and right now I couldn't see either in my immediate future.

"Meaning you're in need of another potion boost." Belle paused, and a somewhat devilish smile touched her lips. "I think I'll make one for our ranger, too. He was looking a little ragged around the edges."

"Don't make it too foul-tasting," I warned. "He'll probably think you're trying to poison him."

"He'll think that anyway. He's not the most trusting werewolf on the reservation right now, but we can work on that."

"No, we can't. Leave the man alone."

She raised her eyebrows at me, the amusement on her lips growing. "Maybe I will, and maybe I won't."

"Belle," I warned.

She laughed and slapped me lightly on the shoulder. "I'm just joking. I mean, when have I ever interfered with your social life?"

"There was that time in Nerang—"

"You would have been old and gray before that man got up the nerve to ask you out."

"And then there was Jake, in Coolangatta—"

"The surfer." She sighed. "He was absolutely delicious, I agree, but he unfortunately had a stable of at least six others, and he never had any intention of getting serious."

"Too bad if unserious was all I actually wanted."

"The day you do casual is the day your father comes groveling on his hands and knees to beg forgiveness for his treatment of you." She moved past me. "In many respects, you and Karen have similar issues."

I hadn't really thought about that, but it was—rather sadly—true. Like her, I was ultimately seeking the love I'd never really had as a child. But for me, it didn't come in the form of a father figure, but rather someone who would accept me as I was, with all my faults, and love me regardless.

It was, apparently, a very large ask.

I walked into the reading room, collected the backpack, and began gathering a selection of potions and salt mixtures, one of the remaining bottles of holy water, and Belle's silver knife. While I risked Aiden confiscating it as he had mine, it was better that than being without some form of physical weapon. Sometimes, evil simply didn't give you the time to develop a spell or use a potion.

With everything gathered, I grabbed a pair of silk gloves from of one of the drawers and pulled them on.

While the foul vibes of wrongness rolling off the watch still made my skin crawl, the sensation was muted enough that I could hold it without my stomach rolling too alarmingly.

By the time I returned to the café, Aiden was waiting for me—and he had one of Belle's potions in hand.

"She wants me to drink this." He was studying the concoction with a whole lot of trepidation. "And she won't say what's in it."

"Sometimes it's best not to ask." I accepted mine with a nod of thanks and tried to ignore the awful smell coming from it. "It's also best to drink it quickly, without drawing in the scent."

Which was what I did. He watched me with narrowed eyes, as if waiting for me to keel over. I smiled. "If Belle's intention was to either poison or spell you, Aiden, she wouldn't need a noxious-smelling drink to do so. It really is just a potion to boost your strength, as she said."

He hesitated a moment longer, then downed it in several quick gulps. A shudder ran through him. "God, that stuff is as foul as it smells."

"She does it deliberately, I'm sure." I glanced at her. "I'll be back by sunset."

She nodded. "Be careful. Both of you."

We left the café. Once on the pavement, I paused and cracked open my psi senses just enough to get some hint of location. It tugged me left again.

"Are we walking or driving?" Aiden fell in step beside me. "Because my truck is nearby."

I hesitated. "Walking, I think. I am getting a signal from the watch, but I risk overwhelming my senses if I open the gate too much."

"So the hellish feel of the thing remains very much

present?"

"Yes."

"Which means I should be able to scent him as we get closer."

"Possibly. It would depend on where he's being kept and what sort of spells surround the area."

"Ah."

The watch tugged me left again, this time down Hargraves Street rather than Barker. Aiden silently followed, his hands in his pockets and his stride matching mine. He was close enough that his scent teased my nostrils but not so close that our shoulders brushed. I wasn't entirely sure whether to be glad about that or not.

We moved out of Castle Rock's retail area and into residential. The watch continued to lead us farther away, until we reached an area where there were no sidewalks and housing blocks gave way to acreage.

"If we continue down this road," Aiden said. "We'll end up on Stephenson's Track."

I glanced at him. "Is that a good thing or bad?"

"Neither, really. It simply skirts a large area of bush."

"Are there roads through the area?"

"Calling them roads would be rather generous." His gaze met mine, amusement creasing the corners of his eyes. "In fact, the back track to the O'Connor compound you were on would be a major highway by comparison."

"I'm glad I have decent walking shoes on, then."

The watch continued to pull me on, but the sensations rolling off it were stronger, suggesting we were getting closer to our target. We eventually reached a three-track intersection, and I paused. The pulse of foulness was now so strong my stomach was twisting, but I couldn't see a building of any sort. Surely our vampire wouldn't risk keeping his creature out in the open? This area might be wild, but the tracks weren't overgrown, and that meant people still used them.

"Have you lost the signal?" Aiden asked.

"No. Quite the opposite." I swept my gaze across the scrub again. "Are there any buildings near here?"

"Not really. Not in this area. But there are quite a number of old mine workings scattered about."

"Ones that run horizontally into the mountain or down?"

"Both."

"We might be looking at the former, then." I took the left fork and the ground began to rise. My still-bruised legs didn't appreciate this development and began to ache in protest.

I really, *really* wanted to stop. But that annoying inner voice—the one that had dreamed of bloody rivers and bodies ripped apart—suggested *that* would be a bad idea.

My skin began to twitch and shudder under the sheer force of wrongness coming from the broken watch. I tugged the right glove over my hand, folded the watch inside of it, and then held it out to Aiden. "You take this. Otherwise, I'm going to vomit."

He took it without comment and tucked it into his pocket. The sense of wrongness immediately eased, but didn't entirely go away.

"Can you smell anything?"

Aiden's nostrils flared as he took a deeper breath, and then he shook his head. "Nothing that shouldn't be here, at least."

"The strength of the vibes coming from the watch suggests we're close, so you should be able to smell him if he's near." I paused, gaze sweeping the area and my other senses on high alert. "I'm not seeing or sensing any sort of magic that would explain the lack of scent, though."

"There's an old mine not too far away. Maybe he's so deeply underground it's simply impossible to smell him."

"Possibly," I said. "But if he's not there, I'll try with the watch again."

He didn't say anything, just stepped past me and led the way up the steepening slope. I followed, suddenly aware of the rustle of eucalyptus leaves, the crunch of twigs under my feet, and the melodious chatter of the various birds. They were normal, everyday sounds for an area like this, and should have set my mind at ease.

But they didn't.

I might not be touching the watch, but I didn't need to. The sensation of wrongness—of death—was so strong it felt as if every breath was filled with its foulness.

After another ten minutes of walking through spindly trees and mounds of mine waste, Aiden stopped on the edge of a small clearing. Ahead, cut horizontally into the steep hillside, was an old shaft. The entrance was little more than five feet wide, and what looked to be old sleepers shored up the roof and the sides. There was no immediate indication that anything or anyone had been near this place for some time, although the rough, stony ground wouldn't have held footprints even if someone had been. If it weren't for the foul waves that continued to batter my senses, it would be easy to presume no one had entered this clearing for a very long time.

"Anything?" Aiden asked.

"He's here."

"I'm sensing an unspoken *but* in that statement," Aiden said.

"That's because I don't trust the fact that there

doesn't appear to be anything *else*."

His gaze scanned the area then came back to mine. "Surely a vampire capable of magic could very easily erase any indication of movement to or from that shaft?"

"Yes, but there should still be some indication of magic having been used, even if it is little more than an echo."

I squatted and studied the ground between the mine and us. There was absolutely nothing to indicate magic had ever been used here, and unease crawled through me. Our vampire had meticulously planned every step so far, so it was very unlikely he'd leave his zombie unprotected.

Unless, of course, he was also here—but I very much doubted the man who owned the dapper shoes I'd seen in the dream would willingly rough it at a place like this.

"What do you want to do?" Aiden asked. "It'll be dark in a couple more hours."

And our vampire would be active. He didn't actually add that, but that was nevertheless what he meant.

"Follow me," I said. "If I say stop or run, do so."

He nodded. I stepped into the clearing, every sense alert for the tiniest hint of trouble. My skin twitched and burned as we drew closer to the mine's entrance, but if there was any sort of spell here, it was very well concealed.

"Stop," Aiden said, even as he grabbed my arm in warning.

I did so, my heart seeming to lodge somewhere in my throat. "What?"

"Trip wire."

He pointed to the ground several feet in front of us; after a moment, I spotted what looked to be fishing line strung across the width of the clearing.

"A trip wire would explain the lack of magical

protection."

"Maybe he simply ran out of magical strength after everything that had happened last night," Aiden said.

"That would depend on whether he fed on that old couple before or after he came here."

"I guess it would." He touched my back lightly, as if in reassurance. "Wait here while I go investigate."

He followed the line to the right and disappeared into the trees and scrub. I shifted from one foot to the other, suddenly uneasy about being left alone in this place.

"It's connected to a goddamn shotgun," he said. "And it's primed to fire."

It was a trap that sounded almost *too* mundane for our vampire. I rubbed my arms against the rising chill in my body. The tripwire went limp and, a moment later, Aiden reappeared, the shotgun held in one hand.

"It's loaded with cheap shot," he added. "Which means more deformation and a wider spread pattern."

"I'm guessing that's a bad thing?"

"It ensures coverage over the widest possible area to cause as much damage as possible," he said. "It might not be the only trap, either, especially if you're not sensing any magic."

He made the gun safe then leaned it against an old log.

"You're not bringing it with us?" I asked, surprised.

"We dare not use it in that mine—not when we have no idea how sturdy it is. A shotgun blast might not be powerful enough to bring anything down, but I certainly don't want to take the risk."

"What about your gun? Won't that present the same problem?"

"Maybe, but I'm not about to leave it behind."

"Not even when you're going running, apparently."

Amusement briefly touched his lips. "It's a ranger's motto to always be prepared."

"I thought that was the Boy Scouts?"

"Same, same." His smile faded. "I'll lead from here on in."

I wasn't about to object when his physical senses were far stronger than mine. He stepped forward carefully, testing each bit of ground before putting his full weight on it. It made for slow progress, but that was infinitely better than getting caught in whatever other macabre trap our vampire might have set.

We were maybe a dozen steps away from the mine's entrance when a slight tremor ran through the ground. Aiden immediately stopped, his body tense and head cocked slightly to one side. There was no further movement, so he took one more cautious step.

It was one too many.

Without warning, the earth gave way, and we were falling into darkness.

CHAPTER
nine

Even as we plunged down, Aiden somehow twisted in midair and grabbed at the pit wall. His fingers found purchase and he instantly reached for me. His hand locked around my arm and a grunt of effort escaped his lips—a sound I echoed as I came to an abrupt stop. For several heartbeats, we gently swung back and forth. I didn't dare breathe, and my heart hammered like crazy. I stared at the crumbling edge of shoring he was holding on to, waiting for that moment when it gave way and plunged us both into darkness.

A darkness that was very, *very* deep, given the stone and dirt that had fallen with us had yet to hit the bottom.

Lizzie, what in hell—

Not the time, Belle. Chat later.

"I need you to grab the plank closest to you and swing your weight onto it." Aiden's words were little more than a hiss of air, and beads of sweat had broken out across his forehead.

"Will it hold my weight?" I said, even as I reached for it.

"It's got more hope of holding your weight right now than I have."

As if to emphasize this, his grip slipped and I dropped an inch or two before he caught me again, this time at the wrist. His "Hurry, Liz," was little more than a pant of air.

I quickly dug my fingers into the soft soil behind the plank in an effort to get a better grip. The entire length of it shuddered and bits flaked off. But for the moment, at least, it held. I pulled myself closer, and managed to wedge one shoe into the small space between two horizontal boards. It didn't make me feel any safer. Didn't make me feel any further away from death.

I repeated the process with my other foot, but the wood crumbled as my weight went onto it and my shoe slipped. The abrupt shift in position and weight sent me twisting around, wrenching my shoulder *and* undoubtedly Aiden's. He hissed but didn't say anything.

He didn't need to.

Ignoring the panic pulsing through me, I tried again, this time reaching a little further along the plank. It held.

"Ready for release?" Aiden asked.

Hell, no. My knuckles went white as I instinctively tightened my grip over the old bit of wood.

Then I nodded.

Aiden immediately released me and lunged for his section of shoring with his now free hand. I did the same, grabbing the brace so fiercely that splinters dug into my skin and fingernails. Pain flared, but it was totally drowned in fear.

227

I closed my eyes, my body shaking with the effort of holding on. Dirt, stones, and small bits of wood rained around me as Aiden began to climb. I wanted to follow, but fear held me locked in place.

After a few minutes, there was a grunt of effort and the shower of debris briefly increased before lessening again.

"Hang on, Liz. I won't be long."

"I'm not going anywhere." It came out little more than a hoarse whisper, but it was a sound that echoed ominously.

His footsteps ran away from the shaft. After several overly fast heartbeats, a long, loud howl cut across the silence, the sound of desperation and urgency. Aiden might be calling for help, but would it come fast enough to be of any use?

More soil came down. I forced my eyes open and looked up. Half of Aiden's body now hung over the shaft's edge, but he wasn't anywhere near close enough to grab me. He threw his belt—which was wrapped around one wrist—down, but it, too, fell short.

"You're going to have to climb."

"I'm not sure—"

"You're strong enough to do it," he cut in. "Believe it, and do it."

Believing wouldn't help one little bit if the damn bracing gave way, and that was a serious possibility given the heavy smell of rot in the air.

But what other choice did I have? Remaining locked in position until my arms gave out wasn't any more appealing. I swore under my breath and studied the next board. It was wet and fragile-looking, but the board above it was just beyond my reach. I tightened my grip on the current slab of wood then carefully stretched up and pulled on the next one to see if it crumbled. It didn't, so I gripped it tight then shifted one foot. Once it was securely in place, I stepped my other hand and leg up. One plank down. Plenty more to go.

It was a nerve-rackingly slow process, and one that quickly took a toll. Neither my strength nor my legs had fully recovered from the blast, and even Belle's potion wasn't stopping the latter from expressing their displeasure rather strongly. And my arms were beginning to join in on that particular chorus.

But even worse was the fact that the shaft's edge was beginning to crumble under Aiden's weight. He hadn't yet pushed back to avoid being dropped into the shaft again, but he would soon have to.

Desperation surged and I lunged for the next beam. It fell apart as soon as I touched it, and for one terrifying instant, momentum threw me backward. My grip on the lower board held, and I quickly pulled myself back to the wall, sucking in great gulps of air and trying not to think about what might have happened.

"Aiden? What the fuck is happening? Are you okay?" The voice was male, but not one I recognized.

"If you've got the climbing gear in your truck, René, go get it," Aiden said. "And hurry."

I didn't hear the other wolf leave—my heart was still pounding far too loudly.

"How secure is the shoring you're hanging on to?" Aiden asked.

I glanced up and was immediately greeted by another shower of dirt. "Secure enough, I think—why?"

"Then stay where you are," he said, and pulled back.

I closed my eyes and prayed to whatever gods or

spirits might be listening to give him help. I didn't want to die. Not now, not in this place.

Die? Belle mentally screamed. *What the hell—*

Still not a good time. I need all my concentration and strength right now—

So why haven't you tapped my strength?

Because that's not that sort of strength I need. It's okay, Aiden's working on the problem.

Then tell him to get his rear into gear!

Trust me, he is.

Even as I said that, dirt showered down again. I looked up through narrowed eyes to see Aiden slip over the edge and rappel toward me, one hand controlling his rope while he held a second in the other.

"I have never been so glad to see anyone in my entire life," I muttered.

He stopped beside me, but his smile was quick and tense. "Let's get this around you."

He wrapped the other rope around my waist and tied it securely. "Okay, slow and steady, René."

The slack was taken up and the rope around my waist tightened. "Grab the rope, brace your feet against the wall, and climb. René will keep a steady tension and he won't let you fall, no matter what."

I nodded, released one hand to grab the rope, and then repeated the process with the other. Step by slow step, I climbed. Aiden paced me, keeping close and offering encouragement. When we reached the shaft's rim, I threw one leg over, hauled myself up in a somewhat ungainly fashion, then scrambled to my feet and ran for the trees, where I collapsed onto my knees and let reaction set in.

Another howl bit across the silence—this one shorter

and holding no urgency. Then Aiden was beside me, gathering me in his arms and holding me close.

"It's okay," he said softly, his breath warm as it brushed past my ear. "We're okay."

"I know," I said through the tears and hiccups. "It's just the relief."

"If this is relief, I'd hate to see happiness." I could hear his amusement even if I couldn't see it. "And I think my shirt is going to need a serious wringing out."

I laughed, as he'd no doubt intended, and pulled back a little. As I did, he shifted one hand from my back to my waist and brushed the moisture away from my cheeks with the other. His fingers were warm against my skin, his touch gentle. I licked my lips and tried to ignore the flick of desire, only to have any hope of control shattered as his gaze followed the movement and became heated. Between one heartbeat and another, the desire to resist—to *not* get involved with anyone else again—fled. All I could think of—all I wanted—was to kiss this man. I leaned forward imperceptibly and, in a moment of perfect synchronicity, our lips met, the kiss a teasing promise of heat and possibilities.

And that's *all* it was.

He pulled away so abruptly that the cold afternoon air hit my face as sharply as a slap. I blinked as his eyes lost their heat and his expression settled into one of careful neutrality. Annoyance surged, but at my own moment of weakness rather than *his* sharp retreat.

What the hell was I thinking? It wasn't as if he hadn't made his opinion of me clear. I might have seen desire—might have even felt it—but it was surely nothing more than relief. Nothing more than a brief need to affirm life after such a close brush with death.

Footsteps approached and it was only then I remembered we weren't alone. I glanced around. The man approaching was shorter and broader of shoulder than most wolves, with dark reddish hair and brown skin.

I smiled up at him as he stopped beside us. "Thank you so much for helping rescue—"

"There's no need for that," he cut in. "You're just lucky I happened to be in the area." He held out his hand. "I'm René Marin."

I smiled and shook his hand. "Lizzie Grace."

"The witch who owns the new café with the amazing cakes?"

Interestingly, there was no rancor in his question, and definitely no underlying distaste. The O'Connors might hold witches in very low regard, but it appeared the other packs didn't.

My smile grew. "The very one. Next time you're near, drop in. Cake and coffee will be on the house."

"That's an offer no sensible man could resist." His gaze shifted to Aiden. "You need anything else?"

"Just the flashlight, if you don't mind."

René nodded. "I'll be back in five."

Aiden nodded, then rose. He undid the climbing gear then offered me his hand, his grip decidedly impersonal. Obviously, that very brief slip toward attraction was not going to happen again.

It should have made me happy, and yet, it didn't.

Nor should it, given you're both fighting what is ultimately unavoidable—

Says who? I cut in.

Says me after seeing the unspoken—and certainly up until this point, unacknowledged—desire surging between the pair of you, Belle said. *Oh, and color me ecstatic that you're safe. But if you can*

232

avoid such calamities in the future, I'd appreciate it. I'm far too young for gray hairs.

Idiot. To Aiden, I said, "Did you have any idea René was in the area, or was that call simply a wide cry for help?"

"The latter, but I was hoping he was close." He untied the rope from my waist and began to roll it up. "He's been reworking one of the old mines a couple of miles further down for some weeks now."

"Why would a werewolf work an old mine?"

"There's still plenty of gold in these hills, and these days we have better methods of finding it than they did back in the gold rush heyday." He shrugged. "A lot of folks also use metal detectors around the tailings, with various degrees of success."

"And here I was thinking this reservation was one of the richer ones."

"It is, thanks to all the tourists coming to the mineral springs," he said. "But no matter what you or others might think, the three packs here aren't lolling around getting fat on the profits. Nearly all of it is plowed back into the reservation, and most of us work."

I raised my eyebrows at the bite in his tone, and said mildly, "Generalizations suck, don't they?"

He stared at me for a beat then a somewhat rueful smile touched his lips. "I guess they do."

It wasn't an apology, but it was probably as close as I was likely to get. I crossed my arms and turned to study the mine. "Is it normal for a vertical shaft to be so close to the entrance of a horizontal one?"

"This entire area is littered with both, and yes, some of them are dangerously close." He shrugged. "Safety wasn't much cared about in the heady days of the gold rush."

"Meaning there might be another shaft between the one we fell into and the entrance of the horizontal one?"

"No, not in this case," René said, as he came back into the clearing. "But you were both damn lucky not to be killed. Flooding was the reason both shafts were eventually abandoned, and old Cutter's has a hundred-foot drop into water."

Which meant that while the fall itself might not have killed us, getting out might have been next to impossible, given the timbers closer to the water would surely be rotten by now. And a shaft *that* deep might mute any cry for help made.

Aiden handed René all the climbing gear then took the flashlight with a nod of thanks. "How far into the mountain does the horizontal shaft go?"

"A couple of hundred feet, at least." René wrinkled his nose. "It isn't pleasant in there, though."

"We're not going in there for the scenery."

René's grin flashed. "I guess not, given neither of you have anything near the proper equipment. You want me to stick around, just in case something else goes awry?"

Aiden hesitated. "Yes, if you can. I'd hate to risk being trapped again."

"That shouldn't be a problem. The place is wet but pretty solid."

"So a gunshot isn't likely to cause any problem?"

Speculation rose in René's eyes, but all he said was, "No."

"Good." Aiden glanced at me. "Ready?"

"No, but that's irrelevant."

"You don't have to go in—"

"Just because I haven't felt anything untoward

doesn't mean it isn't here, Aiden. Whether I like it or not, I have to go on."

Unsurprisingly, he didn't argue. I followed him across the clearing, watching every step as we skirted around the still-disintegrating edges of the vertical shaft. Aiden flicked on the flashlight as we stopped at the entrance of the horizontal shaft, and swept the beam across the darkness. There was nothing to see other than old wooden beams and rough-cut stone walls that glistened with moisture.

"I can't smell anything other than wood rot and mold," he said. "There's nothing to indicate our Mason is close."

"He probably wouldn't be stored this near to the entrance." It might have made things easier for both our vampire and us, but the risk of discovery would also have been greater, especially if magic wasn't being used to distort the stench of Mason's rotting flesh.

Aiden stepped carefully into the mine. In the distance, water dripped, a melodious sound that oddly matched the soft echo of our footsteps. I rubbed my arms against the chill of the place and did my best to ignore the damp smell of rot that pervaded the air.

As we moved deeper into the mountain, the tunnel began to slope downward and the ground became slippery. I brushed my fingers against the rough wall to help keep balance, and tried to ignore the trailing touch of moss and who knows what else.

After several more minutes, we came to a T-intersection. Aiden stopped and swung the flashlight's beam in both directions. The tunnel to our right dropped sharply and disappeared into dark, still water. The one on the left came to an end about twenty feet in.

Leaning against that rear wall, his flesh putrid and

crawling with bugs and larvae, was the thing that had once been Mason Redfern.

I might have thought I was prepared for the reality of a zombie, but I'd been very, *very* wrong.

"Fuck," Aiden whispered. "I knew it would be bad, but this—"

"Is unforgivable," I finished for him.

What had been done to Karen was bad enough, but she'd at least willingly injected vampire blood, even if she'd had no idea that the man who was guiding her through the process—a man she thought cared for her—was only using her to destroy her mother.

But this... this was flesh without life, without heart or soul. It was a crime against nature itself, and one for which there could be no forgiveness.

I could understand the vampire's desire to lash out at those who had hurt him, but no child should have to pay for the sins of their parents.

And the fact that Mason *was* made me so damn angry it was all I could do to resist the urge to race out of here— to somehow find the monster responsible for this and end it. End him.

Aiden swept the light slowly around the small chamber. "Are you seeing any signs of magic?"

"No, but there has to be something here, as we should be smelling Mason's rot given how close we are."

"I think it's something of an understatement to say I'm glad we're not." The flashlight's beam centered on Mason again. "So, a head shot?"

His voice was matter-of-fact, but there was something underneath it, a timbre that spoke of abhorrence—both at what had been done, and what he now had to do.

I nodded, my mouth suddenly dry. Mason's head *did* have to be removed, and not just to stop the vampire from using him again, but also for the safety and sanity of his parents. They'd already gone through enough heartache—they didn't need to know their child's remains had been given life via magic so he could be used as a weapon against them.

But knowing what had to be done was a totally different matter to actually doing it.

Aiden handed me the flashlight, his expression giving nothing away. Nor did he say anything. He simply raised his gun and took aim.

I wanted to look away, but resisted the desire. Not because of some macabre need to watch the shattering of bone and decaying flesh, but because it somehow felt disrespectful to do anything else.

While this rotting vessel might no longer hold life, it was always possible Mason's soul had not moved on. Some didn't, especially if they were killed before their time. And while I wasn't Belle, and had no way to see or contact him even if he *were* here, I could at least offer him a prayer of peace.

Which was what I did as Aiden fired.

Six shots. That was all it took. Six quick shots to finish what time and decay had already started. With no head and shattered legs, he was now beyond the reach of magic, no matter powerful.

"I'm going to enjoy killing this vampire," Aiden said softly. "And nothing, not the IIT or anyone else, is going to stop me. Not after this."

I touched his arm lightly; I might have well been touching steel. "I think you'll find the IIT won't argue with that sentiment. They want this ended every bit as badly as you do."

"Perhaps."

His gaze met mine, his expression cold—angry. Not at me, not even at the IIT, but rather the situation. At the deaths and destruction that had shattered this otherwise peaceful reservation.

The insights, it seemed, were back—although it didn't really take psychic powers to guess at his emotions and thoughts right now.

"Do we need to do anything about the rest of Mason's body?" he added.

I shook my head. "He needs to be reburied, of course, but we're running out of daylight and it probably wouldn't be wise to retrieve him until tomorrow morning."

"Agreed." He plucked the flashlight from my grip and stepped around me. "Let's get the hell out of here."

By the time we'd exited, the shadows were beginning to close in. René was squatting against a tree on the far side of the clearing, but rose as we approached.

"Everything okay?"

"Yes." Aiden handed him the flashlight. "But the mine is now a crime scene, so don't go in there."

"So it *was* gunshots I heard?"

"Yes."

Aiden's tone remained as neutral as his expression, but the anger and frustration continued to vibrate through him. It might be under the surface and very well controlled, but I suspected it wouldn't take much for it to be unleashed.

"I'm going to place a clearance order on the entire area for a day or so," he continued. "So if you've got anything expensive at the mine you're working, I'd grab it.

But be out of the area before sunset."

René nodded and left.

"What are the chances of the vampire returning here tonight?" Aiden pressed his fingers against my spine and guided me toward the somewhat vague path that had brought us up here.

"He has no need to come back." His touch left me as soon as I stepped onto the path, but the heat of it lingered, a mocking reminder of our altogether too brief kiss. "He'll know Mason is now beyond his reach the moment he wakes."

"I suspect he's not going to be pleased."

"I suspect you're right."

In the fading light, his hair glinted with silver, but the stubble lining his chin was dark enough to look black. It was an odd but rather nice combination.

You need to give up denying you're attracted to the man, Belle commented. *Because you're certainly not fooling anyone. Not even your own hormones.*

Okay, so I'm attracted. Admitting it doesn't change the situation, Belle.

Give him time and space, and you just never know.

Except that I do know.

I could almost see her frown. *You didn't mention another dream.*

Because I didn't have another one. It's just intuition.

Your intuition has been wrong on occasion.

But not often.

No. She paused. *Still, I live in hope that in this case, it is.*

The foolish part of me that never seemed to tire of having my heart broken secretly hoped the same thing. But there was no point in voicing a desire the universe and the man seemed determined to ignore.

We reached the rough road and made our way back to the district's heart. By the time we reached the café, darkness had fallen and weariness had settled into my bones, making every step an effort.

"Would you like to come in for something to eat?" I dug the keys out of the backpack and opened the door.

He shook his head. "Thanks for the offer, but I'm dead on my feet." He hesitated, and grimaced. "And *that* is a saying that will never again seem so harmless."

"No." I touched his arm lightly. Anger and horror still vibrated through him, even if its force was more muted. Whether that was due to control or sheer tiredness, I couldn't say. "Thanks for saving my butt today. If you hadn't caught me—"

"I did, so don't even think about what-ifs." He raised a hand and lightly brushed something from my cheek. Whether it was debris or merely an excuse to touch me, however briefly, I didn't know and didn't care. "Get some rest, because it's totally possible we might have to call on your services again tonight."

"For both our sakes, I hope not." I hesitated. "Night, Aiden."

"Night." He dropped his hand, but his fingers, I noted, were clenched.

I went inside. By the time I'd turned to lock the door, he was gone. I placed the watch and Belle's knife back into their compartments, but left the rest of the items in the pack. I could deal with them tomorrow, when I had more energy.

"Grab a shower," Belle said, as I wearily climbed the stairs. "I'll heat some lasagna for you when you're done."

The hot water washed the grime and the smell of death from my skin, and went some way to easing the ache in my muscles. But no matter how long I stood under the stream of water, my face raised and my eyes closed, it didn't wash away the memory of Mason's empty, broken face, or the stump that had remained once Aiden had finished firing. I eventually gave up and got out.

"Dinner is ready," Belle said, retrieving the plate from the microwave as I walked out wrapped in towels. "I've also made a pot of ginseng tea."

"Thanks." I grabbed a tea towel before accepting the hot plate, then moved across to the couch. "Are you going out tonight?"

"No, I told you that this afternoon." She raised an eyebrow and sat next to me. "Have you forgotten the full moon and the bloodstone?"

I swore and scrubbed a hand across my eyes. "Aiden obviously did, too."

"I'm not entirely surprised, given this afternoon's events." She began pouring the tea. The sweet scent of licorice root drifted through the earthy, woody aroma of the ginseng—a combination designed to boost strength and help relieve pain and stress. "I feel sorry for Mason's parents. This travesty will hit them hard."

"They may never know." I scooped up a mouthful of lasagna. "Aiden has them holed up at a safe house somewhere under full watch. He could very easily arrange for Mason to be reburied before he releases them."

"I hope he does, for their sake." She took a sip of tea. "It might be better if we skip investigating the bloodstone tonight. You look wiped—"

"Yes, but the waning moon hasn't the power of the full. I really think we'll need it—"

"What you need," she said, in a tone that would brook no argument. "Is rest—something the doctors were quite adamant about, and something you're yet to properly do. Besides, a waning moon still holds plenty of power, and between it and us, there shouldn't be a problem."

She was probably right, of course, but the need to unravel the mystery of the bloodstone and the man who had spelled it nevertheless pulsed through me.

Time was running out; he might still have people to wreak havoc on in this reservation, but if we didn't catch him soon, we wouldn't.

"Now *that's* a cheery thought," Belle muttered.

Wasn't it just? "Are you going to call Zak now that I'm not having a go at the pendant?"

She hesitated, and then shook her head. "There's plenty of time ahead to further explore the delights of that man. It'll probably do us both good to have an early night."

I nodded and finished both my meal and the tea, by which time, my eyes were becoming so heavy it was hard to keep them open. I eventually gave up and just went to bed. Sleep hit almost as soon as my head hit the pillow.

I woke with a start some hours later. My heart raced and the bitter taste of fear filled my mouth. For several seconds I did nothing more than lie there, the blankets pulled up close to my nose and my eyes wide as I stared into the darkness. There was no sound other than the slight ticking of the old clock downstairs, and I had no idea why I'd woken in such a state.

And then I felt it.

A tremor. Not in earth, but rather across my metaphysical senses.

Someone was attacking the wards and spells that protected this place—and it didn't take a genius to figure out who. I all but fell out of bed then scooped up a T-shirt from the floor and my phone from the bedside table before bolting for the door—and had to do a quick two-step to avoid crashing into Belle.

"What the fuck is going on?" She thrust a hand through her wildly matted hair. "There's been no alarm, but it feels like—"

"The bastard is attacking our spells and wards." I gave her my phone. "Ring Aiden. I'll go downstairs and bolster the spells."

"Be careful," she said, even as she unlocked my phone. "He's not alone."

"How many can you sense?"

"One other." She wrinkled her nose. "A hired thug."

"Can you incapacitate him?" I pulled on my T-shirt as I headed for the stairs.

"Yes, but not until I ring Aiden. Go."

My footsteps echoed as I clattered down the stairs—something the men outside would undoubtedly hear. It didn't really matter—the vampire would have felt it the minute I became aware of his attack.

I ran through the dark room and placed my hand on the old front door, my fingers spread wide. The energy that pulsed across my fingertips was heated and angry. He was close, so damn close, to fully unraveling the threads that protected us—and it was doubtful the wards alone would stand up to him once he did. They just weren't powerful enough on their own.

Fear surged, but I ruthlessly thrust it aside. I had no time for it—I needed every ounce of control and concentration I could muster.

Through narrowed eyes, I saw both the failing threads of our magic, and the blot of his pressing down on them, undoing them, destroying them.

"You're not getting in that easy," I muttered, and began pushing back. The remaining threads flared as I carefully picked them up and wove a strengthening spell into them. It would drain me faster than adding additional layers to the protecting spell, but the latter would take time, and that was the one thing we didn't really have right now.

The blot of darkness grew heavier, the weight of it threatening to buckle my knees. I forced them to lock and kept going, but even as the remaining threads thickened and grew stronger, he pushed back with a force so great my knees *did* buckle, hitting the floor so hard a grunt of pain escaped.

That collapse saved my life.

The inside of the door where my face had been exploded inward, filling the air with a deadly shower of splinters. A heartbeat later, something hit the rear of the café and what sounded like an entire mountain of plates and cups crashed to the floor.

I didn't look around. I didn't even twitch. I simply kept my hands pressed to the door, my fingers enmeshed in the remaining threads, uttering every spell of strength and resistance I knew.

It wasn't going to be enough. He was simply far too strong for me.

One of the three remaining threads grew taut and then snapped. The force of it rebounded through me, making my body shake and my head pound. Instinct and desperation had me reaching for Belle, and a heartbeat later, she was with me, as one with me, her power and her knowledge mine to use. I threw everything we had at the final two spell lines, quickly bolstering their ability to resist. Then I pulled one hand away and uttered a simple spell, one designed to do nothing more than knock the vampire off his feet. Hopefully, it would be enough to shatter his concentration and stop—however briefly—his unrelenting attack.

I said the final line of the incantation and then cast it forward, physically and mentally. A heartbeat later there was a loud grunt, and the black force shredding our magic dissipated. I took a deep, shuddering breath, and felt Belle do the same. I quickly released her and instantly felt the weakness run like water through my limbs. I closed my eyes and leaned my forehead on the door. But I couldn't stop feeding the thread lines yet—the vampire was still out there. I could feel him. Feel his evil and determination. Any minute now, he would pick himself up and resume his attack….

The sharp sound of sirens cut through the air, and relief surged. Aiden and his rangers were coming; if our vampire had any sense, he would not hang around.

"You win a second round, witch." The voice was deep, well-modulated, and so damn close he had to be standing on the other side of the door. "But the next round will be mine."

I didn't reply. I couldn't. The waves of hatred and corruption seeping through the door that separated us were all but suffocating me.

He left—something I knew only by the sudden ability to breathe clean air. A sob escaped, and tears of relief and exhaustion started coursing down my cheeks.

Outside, tires squealed as several trucks skidded to stop. Doors opened and footsteps echoed.

"Lizzie?" Aiden said. "Are you there? Are you okay?"

"Yes. Go after him. I'm fine."

"Duke, take care of this scum. Mac, you're with me."

Footsteps departed. I took a deep breath and—using the door as a brace—pushed to my feet.

Belle? You okay?

Yeah. Her response was immediate, if weak. *I've been keeping the thug immobile.*

Fuck, you should have released your hold on him the minute I—

And let him run? she bit back. *No fucking way. He was paid a measly grand to shoot the two of us—the bastard's obviously too stupid to be allowed to roam the streets alone. He's lucky I only froze his movements rather than erase what little intelligence he actually has.*

It was a threat that spoke volumes about the level of her anger. Making someone little more than a vegetable theoretically could be done by strong enough telepath—and she was certainly that—but it would be a very dangerous action for her to take. While I had no idea if the witch creed of harming no others would bleed over to her psychic abilities, it was certainly a possibility. And a risk I'd rather she *not* take.

A sharp knock on the door made me jump. I sucked in air in an effort to calm my shattered nerves and then said, "Yes?"

"It's Ranger Tala Sinclair. Open up."

I tied up the ends of the strengthening spell to stop it leeching any more energy from me, and then looked through the newly created peephole in the door. Tala wasn't alone—the shorter of the two IIT men accompanied her, as did a woman I didn't recognize.

I wasn't going to greet any of them wearing a T-shirt that barely covered my butt.

"Hang on while I go grab some clothes."

I bolted upstairs, pulled on an old pair of track pants,

and then returned to open the door.

"I believe you've already met Officer Blume." Tala's voice and expression were carefully neutral. "But let me introduce you to Anna Kang, a representative from the Regional Witch Association."

Anna was a middle-aged woman possessing what could be described as the typical features of the Kang line of royal witches—an oval face, high cheekbones and a prominent nose, and mono-lidded eyes. Her hair was as vivid as mine, but cut extremely short.

Given her heritage, it was rather interesting that she was working for the RWA, as it was a position that normally wouldn't be considered suitable for someone of the Kang line. They tended to be mystics more than spell casters, believing that everything in this world—be it flesh, earth, or plant—had a spirit associated with it, and that interaction and understanding with that spirit was necessary if witches wished something done.

But there were always outliers, witches born to royal lines who didn't live up to family expectations. Perhaps she was another of them.

She held out her hand, and after a moment, I clasped it. Energy stirred, brief but probing—hers stronger than mine. No surprise there. Even if I had been at full strength rather than shaking with fatigue, the result probably wouldn't have altered.

I broke contact and moved aside. "Please, come in out of the cold."

You want me down there? Belle asked.

No. The rangers might be aware you're a witch, but it appears no one else is. Let's keep it that way.

Blume and his cohort must know—surely the rangers would have mentioned it.

I'm not worried about the IIT. I'm worried about our regional witch investigating the backgrounds of two witches of Marlowe and Sarr heritage, and stirring curiosity in the wrong places.

You have something of a fixation with your parents finding you of late, Belle noted. *Is there something you're not telling me?*

It's just a niggle in the back of my mind. It's probably nothing, but still… let's not tempt fate.

Blume led the way to the biggest of our tables. "Why was the vampire attacking you? I would have thought it'd be in his best interests to avoid a direct confrontation."

"He's well aware that I'm no match for him magically." I all but collapsed onto a chair opposite him. "Besides, it's not the first time he's attacked me."

"No, but it makes little sense to do so as openly as he did just now, and with a hired gun at his side." Blume's brown eyes narrowed as he studied me. "That speaks of haste and anger, which is odd behavior for a man who has so meticulously enacted his plans up to this point."

"Such a person is also likely to react violently when anyone interferes or otherwise upsets those plans."

"Which leads me to ask again, why now? Why tonight?"

"It's probably got something to do with the fact we tracked down and killed his zombie this afternoon."

Blume's gaze shot to Tala's. "You lot are supposed to inform us before taking any such action against our target."

"The vampire wasn't the target, but rather his creature." Tala's voice was mild, but annoyance lurked in her expression. "And Ms. Grace was uncertain as to whether it was even possible to trace someone who'd been dead for weeks."

"That is *not* the point," Blume snapped, then made a

visible attempt to regain control of his annoyance. "We've been down this track before, Ranger. If you and your boss continue to flout the rules, we *will* issue a formal complaint to authorities."

Tala raised an eyebrow, obviously unperturbed by the threat. "If you cared to check your partner's voicemail, I think you'll find we did, in fact, leave a message stating our intentions. It's hardly our fault if he didn't bother listening to it."

"I *will* check the authenticity of that statement," he said. "And hadn't you better start securing the crime scene and collecting evidence?"

Annoyance flicked across Tala's features, but all she did was smile and move toward the rear of the café and the shattered teacups.

"Just how *did* you track Mason?" Anna asked. "Via a finding spell?"

Her eyes were several shades darker than Belle's— more a slate gray than silver—which suggested her heritage might be mixed despite the classic nature of her features. It could also explain why she was here.

"No, because I'm a far stronger psychic than a witch." I leaned my arms on the table. Weariness was a drum beating fiercely through my system now, and it was all I could do to keep upright.

"So you used your psychometric skills and a personal item of his to track him?" When I nodded, she frowned and added, "I would have thought both the desecration involved in raising the dead and the malevolence of the man behind it would have made any personal item all but untouchable."

"I used a silk glove to separate it from my skin."

"Ah. Good thinking."

"Where is the body now?" Blume said. "It will need to be appropriately dealt with—"

"Which has been done." My voice was tight as I fought the images that instantly rose. "He just needs to be reburied and blessed."

"And have you a similar means of finding the vampire?" Blume asked.

"If you can find me a personal item of his, then yes, I'll have the means. Until then, I'm as clueless as the rest of you."

"Somehow," Anna murmured, "I'm doubting that."

I didn't glance at her. I didn't dare.

Blume got his phone out and placed it on the table between us. "Right," he said, as he pressed the record button. "A full report on both this afternoon's and this evening's events."

"What, now? You have to be fucking kidding—"

"The sooner you comply, the sooner I can be out of your hair."

You want me to do a little mind tinkering? Belle asked, sounding a little too eager. *I'm sure I can find a way through his shields if I try hard enough.*

As much as I'd love to say yes, it's probably not the best idea with everyone else in the room.

I resolutely made the required report. It was quick and to the point, but it nevertheless took more minutes than I really wanted to waste.

"Anything else to add?" Blume said when I finished.

Nothing that I want to tell you. I shook my head.

He stopped recording then glanced at his phone as it beeped. "They've lost the vampire's trail again."

"No surprise, given what we're dealing with," Anna stated.

"I take it there's no point in trying a location spell this evening?" Blume asked.

"We could try, but he'll probably counter any such effort. It's better to try tomorrow when the sun has forced him to sleep."

Blume grunted and rose. "Then I will see you tomorrow."

He was barely out of the door when Anna switched to attack mode. Her expression sharpened and her demeanor became more intense. My guard instantly went up, though against what I wasn't entirely sure. It wasn't as if she could read me. The spells in this place might be battered, but they weren't defeated. I'd feel any attempt she made to short-circuit or slip past them.

"Who produced the spells that protect this place?"

It was a question I certainly *hadn't* been expecting. "I did—why?"

"Because their construction is unusual."

I forced a smile. "Because—as I'm sure you're well aware—I'm not a vetted witch."

"Accreditation has nothing to do with it, as *that* is little more than an allegiance ceremony." She paused, her gaze narrowing. Her magic played across mine, but it wasn't an attack. It was, instead, the sort of examination an entomologist might give a newly discovered bug. "All incantations have strict lines of structure—it is a formality that is deliberate, and one intended to protect both the witch and the world from which we draw power."

"Are you saying my magic is dangerous?"

"Possibly, given it not only possesses little in the way of recognizable structure, but also an unrestrained wildness. I've never come across anything like it."

"The wildness is easily explained—I cast a spell in the

cemetery last night, but the wild magic caught and altered it."

"That is not unheard of, and generally why it is recommended not to cast when near a wellspring," she said. "But it doesn't explain the wildness in your magic."

"It does if remnants of the wild magic were still clinging to me when I boosted the layering protecting us." I shrugged. "As to the unstructured nature of my spells, well, it isn't altogether surprising given my lack of official training."

Which was only a half lie—I certainly hadn't received any training after I'd run from my family and Canberra. But witches from the royal line started learning spells and control almost as soon as they could walk. By the time I'd left home, I'd had more than sixteen years of study behind me. I might not have honed my skills by moving on into university, but my knowledge was nevertheless fairly extensive.

It just wasn't as extensive—just as I wasn't as powerful—as any of my siblings'.

Her expression remained unconvinced. "Even if you didn't receive formal training—and I find that highly unlikely—why is there no record of you in the archives?"

My heart began to race. This was *not* a line of questioning I really wanted to get into. "Because I'm not from Victoria."

"Perhaps, but there's also no record of you in the South Australian archives, and that is where you told Hart you were from."

"No, I said Belle and I had come here from South Australia. I didn't say I was born there." I shrugged, feigning nonchalance. "If you're looking for my birth certificate, try Darwin. But it's not going to tell you much other than the name of my parents—who are Kate and Lance Grace, if you must know."

"What year were they assigned to Darwin?"

"My parents weren't witches, but rather psychics. The hair and the little magic I possess come from my grandmother, who was the result of a brief dalliance with a blueblood. She was both unregistered and unvetted."

"Which rather conveniently means there's no way of checking your story other than checking your birth records and tracking down your family."

"Good luck with the latter," I said, with a very real edge of bitterness in my voice. "Because they want as little to do with me as I do with them."

"Because of your magic?"

"Yes." I didn't bother hiding either my anger or the lingering hurt. It was real, even if the rest of the story wasn't. "Neither of them shared my grandmother's attraction to witches or magic. They spent my growth years trying to smother the skill."

"Which is a perfectly believable explanation for the free-spirited nature of your magic."

And not one she actually *did* believe, if her expression was anything to go by.

"Why the third degree?" I asked bluntly. "In case it's escaped your notice, that bastard has tried to kill me twice now. How about using your considerable power to track him down rather than trying to unravel my unremarkable past?"

"Fine," she said, her expression hardening. "Why did you lie when Blume asked if you had any means of tracking the vampire?"

"It wasn't a lie, because I'm not sure I *can* track him. All I have is a piece of jewelry he might have given

Karen." I shrugged again. "Whether he's held it long enough to enable me to find him is debatable."

"So why haven't you made an attempt?"

"I was intending to tonight, but sadly the zombie quest and another attempt on my life sidetracked me."

If she heard the sarcasm, she ignored it. "I wouldn't have thought you'd need the power of the moon to bolster your resources."

"Then you thought wrong."

Her smile was polite but her eyes gave the game away. They glittered with annoyance. She waited until Tala had walked past, and then said, "May I see this pendant?"

Though it was posed as a question, it really wasn't. I rose and walked down to the reading room to collect it.

Anna held out her hand when I returned and I dropped the bloodstone into it. She frowned, and once again a strand of her power reached out, this time examining the pendant as she rolled it over in her hand.

"There is definitely some sort of spell attached to this stone, but it's been very cleverly disguised."

"Hence the reason I wanted the moon's help."

She nodded. "Now that I've seen this, I can understand your caution. The spell threads alter composition and appearance from different angles."

"It also feels foul."

"That is natural, given blood has been used in whatever incantation has been placed on this."

"Do you think you'll be able to unpick the spell, or even trace him through it?"

"Possibly." She closed the fingers around the pendant. "I'll try tonight. It would be a shame to waste the power of the moon."

I hesitated. "Do you want some help?"

"You've barely enough strength to stay on that chair." She patted my arm—a comforting gesture that nevertheless felt patronizing. "I'll cast a full circle—between that and the moon, it should be more than enough to cope with the likes of our vampire."

"Except our vampire has studied the dark arts and appears to have at least *some* working knowledge of common witch spells," I said. "And given what happened to me, I'd also be very wary of the wild magic if you're heading into the woods. It's unguarded, so—"

"No," she cut in. "It's not."

I frowned. "But the rangers told me the assigned witch had been evicted over a year ago—"

"Be that as it may, his presence remains." She rose. "Gabe is a friend. I'd know his touch anywhere. Good night."

I stared after her, confusion swirling. Surely even the most powerful witch around could not hide from three wolf packs for over a year. Someone, somewhere, would have seen or scented him.

Aiden appeared, giving Anna a brief nod before striding toward me. "Are you okay?"

I nodded. "There's nothing wrong with me that a good fifty hours of sleep and several slabs of steak wouldn't fix."

A smile tugged at his lips. "I take it, then, that Blume wasn't too rough?"

"No—although he did threaten to report the lot of you if you didn't start passing on information."

"It's not the first time they've threatened that, and it probably won't be the last." He stopped opposite me and shoved his hands deep into his coat pockets. The energy that radiated off him was fierce and filled with the heat of the night. While the full moon didn't actually force werewolves to change, it took a lot of willpower to ignore its call to run wild and free. "We didn't catch the bastard."

"So Blume said. Do you think magic was involved?"

"Possibly, given the trail went cold between Creswyn and Friar's Point for no damn reason." He rubbed his jaw. "I've asked the Sinclairs to keep an eye out, as the Point is part of their range."

"If he *is* there, wouldn't they have sensed him by now? I thought you said packs don't allow uninvited strangers on their lands."

"The Sinclairs have a somewhat more relaxed attitude to it than either the Marin or O'Connor packs." He glanced around as Tala approached. "All done?"

"For now." She looked at me. "I'll need to get a formal statement for our records tomorrow, though, if you're up to it."

"As long as it's in the afternoon rather than some ungodly hour before noon, it should be okay."

"Done," Aiden said. "We'd better let you get some rest."

"Thanks."

It was only after they'd left that Belle came down, looking every bit as tired as I felt. Her gaze hit the mess of broken cups and plates, and her expression dissolved into dismay. "The bastard has taken out some of my favorite pieces."

"Better them than my head."

"I guess." She laughed and ducked away from my halfhearted attempt to whack her. "Let's clean up this mess in the morning. I seriously can't face it right now."

"Agreed."

She turned around and headed back upstairs. I trailed

after her and, for the second time that night, was asleep before my head hit the pillow.

Warmth touched my skin who knows how many hours later. It was so light it was barely even a caress, but it was one that was both familiar and yet oddly alien. For several seconds I wasn't even sure if it was real, or merely the last hurrah of a dream I couldn't remember.

Then it ran across my skin again, its touch flame-like and oddly filled with a sense of urgency.

I opened my eyes to discover a wisp hovering in front of my face. The same wisp, I thought, that had answered my request for help in the forest.

The minute it noticed I was awake, it darted to the door then spun around and returned. It was pretty obvious it wanted me to follow.

I climbed out of bed and pulled on jeans and a sweater while the wisp hovered next to my shoulder, its light pulsing at an ever-increasing rate, seeming to suggest impatience.

"Okay, okay, I'm coming." I grabbed my coat and headed for the door. "Belle? You awake?"

"I am now," she mumbled. "What's up?"

"There's a wisp in our hallway and it wants me to follow him."

"The lunar effect is certainly in full force tonight." She appeared in the doorway. "You want company?"

"No. I just want you to lock the door and get some damn sleep. I'll give a mental yell if I need any help."

"Yell loud, otherwise I won't hear you over the protection spells around the bedrooms."

The wisp darted between us then spun away.

"I think it's urging you to get a move on," she added.

"I think you're right." I clattered down the stairs after

it but detoured into the reading room to grab Belle's knife and the backpack. After tonight's events, I wasn't about to head anywhere without more immediate means of protection. Incantations were all well and good, but they weren't of much help in situations that gave you no time for spelling.

Once outside, the wisp darted forward, forcing me to run or risk losing it. I wasn't entirely surprised to discover it was leading me back to Kalimna Park. Once again the trees grew close, their branches looming overhead and blotting out the moon's light. It didn't matter, because I could feel her power pulsing through my blood.

The wisp finally dived off the road and into the trees. I slowed and followed. I'd already crashed through this place once—I had no desire to repeat the process, especially when I had no idea what lay at the end of this journey.

The wisp darted back and forth, seemingly determined to make me hurry. I tripped over a couple of times but did at least avoid getting my clothes snagged or my face cut this time.

Once again the land began to rise, and a sense of déjà vu hit. We were approaching the clearing in which I'd found Karen.

Trepidation stirred. I caught the flyaway ends of my coat and hugged them closer, but it didn't make me feel any warmer. Didn't do anything to ease the growing conviction that death once again would be found in that place.

We reached the top of the hill and the trees once again thinned out. The wisp shot forward, just as it had the first time, its bright light flooding the clearing.

Lying in the middle of it was Anna's broken and bloody body.

CHAPTER
ten

I fought the instinct to run over to her. The specter of death wasn't hovering nearby, which meant she was hurt and unconscious rather than in any immediate danger of dying, and it was more than possible that this was yet another trap.

I studied the clearing through narrowed eyes but couldn't see any indication of evil. Nor was there any sort of shimmer to indicate magic was present, although remnants of it floated in the air, the broken threads glinting softly whenever the wisp's cool light caressed them.

I carefully moved forward. The wisp spun in a quick circle, once again urging me to hurry. I didn't. I had no idea what had happened here, and no desire to run into any more trouble. I might not be able to see any active spells, but those floating thread remnants indicated magic *had* been in use. And while I'd undergone full witch training—up until I'd fled Canberra and my family, anyway—I had no doubt there were avenues of magic, and mountains of spells, that I had absolutely no awareness of. It was more than possible that these threads were not actually broken, but part of one such spell.

The closer I drew to Anna, the more apparent it became that she'd been caught in some sort of explosion. Much of her upper chest had been burned—and, in some places, quite badly. I grabbed my phone and called in the medics, then stepped warily into what remained of the protection circle. While most of its energy had seeped out through the break, the remaining remnants spoke of its power. It was far stronger than anything I could have formed, and yet it hadn't been able to withstand the force brought against it.

If I *had* attempted to unravel the spell around the bloodstone, I probably would have ended up dead rather than merely burned and broken.

The wisp's light began to pulse, its rhythm matching Anna's increasingly erratic breathing. I scanned the inner sanctum of the pentagram yet again, and then took that final step, my heart pounding so fiercely I swear it was trying to tear out of my chest. Nothing untoward happened, but I didn't dare relax. This attack, like almost every other one the vampire had been involved in, spoke of planning. I wouldn't put it past him to have placed a final "gotcha" to ensure his scheme did not go awry a third time.

Close up, Anna's condition looked even more critical—there were some areas of skin so severely burned it looked charred. Had the pendant exploded? It would certainly account for her injuries, though surely any such spell would have been so intense—so metaphysically heavy—that someone with Anna's knowledge should have at least seen the trigger before she tripped it.

I dug out the two bottles of water I had in the backpack, pulled the stopper off the holy water, and carefully poured it over the worst of her burns. I had no idea if it had any advantage over regular water, but if it *did*, then those areas certainly needed it. When it was gone, I continued the process with the drinking water, until the remnants of her shirt was soaked and the tremors assailing her eased just a little.

Until the medics got here, there was nothing else I could do for her other than keep an eye on her breathing and hope she didn't go into full shock.

I got out my phone again, and called Aiden.

"Liz?" His voice was husky and tired. "Is there another problem?"

"Yes—I just found Anna. She's badly hurt but alive."

"Fuck," he all but groaned. "What's happened?"

"She tried unpicking the magic on that bloodstone pendant I found."

Sheets rustled as he climbed out of bed—which surprised me, given the full moon. Tired or not, I would have thought he'd be out running under the moonlight with the rest of his pack.

That other, more foolish part of me also noted there was no background murmur of protest, or indeed any other sound to indicate that he was sharing the room with another. It certainly didn't mean there *wasn't* someone in either his life or his bed, but the ridiculously attracted part of me couldn't help hoping that was exactly what it meant.

"Where are you?"

"In the same clearing I found Karen in."

"I'll be there in ten."

I battered away the mental images of him getting dressed. However pleasant those images might be, it was hardly appropriate for my hormones to be getting giddy when there was someone lying unconscious and in trouble at my feet. "I've called the medics."

"Good. Don't move—but don't take any risks, either."

"I won't." I hung up, put the phone away, and waited.

Precisely nine minutes and three seconds later, the wisp's light went out and Aiden appeared. He was once again wearing loose-fitting sweats, but this time his feet were bare and his hair was as scruffy as the whiskers lining his chin. A small pack was slung over one shoulder.

He paused when he saw me, his gaze quickly sweeping the clearing before returning. Though his expression gave little away, I nevertheless felt both his frustration and relief. The latter had my pulse skipping a beat or two.

"The medics are a minute behind me." He strode forward. "Is she still alive?"

"Yes, but severely burned."

He knelt beside me, his knee brushing mine. "It looks like she was caught in an explosion."

"There must have been some sort of spell attached to the pendant, as the closed circle would have stopped an outside force from getting in or attacking her."

He glanced around as two men entered the clearing and motioned them over. "So the force of the explosion also erased her pentagram?"

"I think so." I rose and stepped away to give the medics room. "I can't see how else this could have happened."

"Have you done a search of the area yet?"

"No, but we need to. There's no sign of her athame, and she would have used it to cast the circle."

"I take it an athame is made of silver?"

"Yes, although the handle will be wood and the blade single-edged rather than double."

"Single-edged or not, I wouldn't want anyone accidentally stumbling onto it. Not with the damage that stuff can do to us." He handed me a flashlight and then motioned toward the area on the left. "You check that side, I'll check this."

I nodded. Using the top point of the pentagram—the one traditionally representing spirit—as my starting point, I started walking up and down, carefully examining every inch of the clearing. I couldn't find anything, though the lack of bloodstone shards was hardly surprising. The small stone would have disintegrated under the force being channeled through it.

I was walking back to my starting point when a bright flicker in the trees to the right caught my attention. I paused, and the light pulsed again. The wisp might have fled when Aiden had walked into the clearing, but it hadn't gone too far.

I switched direction and hurried into the trees.

"Liz?" Aiden said.

"Hang on," I replied. "I just have to check something."

Again the wisp's light pulsed. I climbed over a felled tree trunk and saw what it had wanted me to find—Anna's athame. I took out my phone, took a couple of photos to record its position for Aiden, then tugged my sleeve over my hand and carefully picked it up. While silver couldn't cause me any harm, most witches from royal lines tended to be rather fussy about who handled their ceremonial items. I had no idea if Anna was one of those, but it was better to be safe than sorry.

There was no physical evidence of damage to either the blade or the hilt, but even through the protective layer of my sleeve, I could feel the uneasy energy clinging to the knife. It was the same sort of energy that had been used against the café's defenses this evening, and it was all the confirmation I needed that the vampire had also been behind this attack.

Not that I ever had much doubt about that.

I glanced up at the wisp. "Thank you so much for all your help tonight, my friend."

The wisp spun in a circle and emitted a ridiculously high-pitched noise. I had no idea what it meant, but it seemed rather pleased with itself.

I climbed over the tree, then returned to the clearing

"Is that her athame?" Aiden said.

I nodded. "The symbols on the hilt—which represent peace and harmony—are the ones traditionally used by the Kang line of witches."

"Is there anything else on it? A spell remnant or something?"

"It's been stained by whatever spell was behind the blast, but that's it, I think. I'd still advise against anyone touching it with bare hands, just in case."

"Given it's silver, you can be sure none of us will." He studied the knife for a second, his expression wary. "What are the chances of tracing the vampire through the staining?"

"None at all."

I glanced around as a twig cracked and saw Hart step into the clearing. He looked as ragged and tired as I felt, and that inordinately cheered me up.

His gaze swept the scene then hit mine almost accusingly. "What the fuck was Anna doing up here?"

"Trying to trace the vampire."

"She sent me a text stating she intended to, but I wasn't expecting it to happen tonight or in the middle of goddamn nowhere." He thrust a hand through his hair. "Is she going to live?"

One of the medics glanced up. "Yes, but you may not be able to talk to her for a couple of days."

Hart nodded, his expression gloomy. "This bastard certainly seems to have luck on his side."

"Indeed," Aiden agreed. "Did you uncover any information about Frieda Andersen or her family?"

"We tracked down her birth certificate. Her mother's name was Jenny Andersen and her dad John." He grimaced. "The former has apparently disappeared off the face of the earth, and the latter has retired and is living in the Adelaide hills."

"Have you talked to him?" I asked. "Did you ask why he and his wife split?"

Hart's gaze flicked to me in a somewhat dismissive manner. "There is no need to, given we've confirmation he was still there as of yesterday, and so cannot be our vampire."

"Yes, but from what Marjorie told me, the man Jenny and Frieda were living with had a small stable of women. That suggests a pod, and John might at least be able to confirm that if indeed she left him for a vampire."

His eyebrows rose. "No one else I've talked to made any mention of a pod existing within the reservation."

"Did you actually ask anyone else about Frieda's family?" Aiden asked.

"Of course I did. Everyone mentioned they were strange, but no one mentioned anything about a pod."

"Well no, but it's an easy enough conclusion to draw after the fact." And it wasn't like vamps went about advertising their presence—that was the surest way of getting booted out of a town.

Hart grunted, his expression even less pleased than usual. "I'll request someone talk to him."

I watched as the medics carefully slid Anna onto the stretcher, then said, "You'd also better contact Anna's family. They'll need to know about this."

"I do know how to do my job," Hart snapped, and followed the two medics from the clearing.

"If you're not careful," Aiden murmured, "you'll join Tala and me on IIT's most-hated list."

"That warning comes about a day too late, I think." I glanced up at him. "Can I ask you again about the previous witch?"

The amusement that had been teasing his expression quickly fled. "Why?"

"Because Anna said something really interesting when I was talking to her, and I'm just wondering if it was possible."

"Can you seriously not talk in riddles right now? My brain isn't up to handling it."

I smiled. "She said Gabe was still here—that she could feel his presence and his magic here."

"Impossible," he said. "Even with magic, there is no way he could avoid being scented or seen by someone in the reservation."

"That's what I said, but if the impossible *is* true, then I need to find him. He might be able to help counter the strength of our blood witch." I hesitated. "At least tell me the circumstances under which he left, even if you don't want to give me full names."

He studied me for a moment, his expression closed and giving very little away. "Fine, but not here and not now. I've got to record the crime scene, and we both need some sleep. I'll drop by later today."

I hesitated and then nodded. Despite the growing sense of time running out, it wasn't as if him telling me right now would make that much difference. I was all but dead on my feet. I might have enough strength to get me home, but anything else was beyond me.

I held up the knife. "What do you want me to do with this?"

He hesitated. "Technically, it's evidence, but I have no way of safely handling it. Take it with you, and keep it somewhere secure. If we need it, I'll let you know."

I swung off the pack and carefully tucked the knife away. "I took some photos of its position before I picked it up. I'll send them to you if that's helpful."

"It would be. Thanks." He hesitated. "Will you be all right getting back?"

"I think so." I wondered how he would have reacted if I'd said otherwise, and then decided it was better not to know. He probably would have just dragged one of his people out of bed, and there were already enough of us going without sleep. "Night, Aiden."

A smile briefly teased his lips. It only made me wish he'd put more effort into it.

"Given the time, good morning is more appropriate."

"A fact I have no desire to acknowledge." I hesitated, wanting to add something in order to simply remain in the presence of this frustrating, enigmatic man. But he had a job to do and I needed sleep. So I simply nodded and left.

But the night's twists hadn't yet ended. Maelle Defour was waiting for me at the café's door.

I stopped abruptly and gave her a somewhat tense smile. "To what do I owe this honor?"

"I have some information about your rogue vampire," she said, her tone mellow and friendly.

"Then you'd better come in and tell me." I dug the keys out of the backpack. "Because I have no intention of conversing with anyone in the damn cold night air."

She raised an immaculately groomed eyebrow. "You do realize that once you invite me over the threshold, you cannot subsequently forbid me from entering."

"Except that I'm a witch," I replied, swinging the door open. "And the magic that protected this place from the other vampire's assault this evening will also prevent you from entering if you intend either Belle or myself harm."

"That you can cast such a spell is yet another indication that you are not the lowly witch you claim."

She followed me into the café without hesitation. The remaining threads didn't even flicker, and the tension that had briefly risen disappeared just as quickly.

"Coffee or tea?" I asked. "Or don't you vampires partake of those sort of fluids?"

"It would be hard to keep our anonymity amongst the general public if we did not." She tugged off her gloves and perched somewhat regally on a chair. "A green tea would be lovely, if you have it."

I went behind the counter and pulled the kettle out. It was far easier than booting up the coffee machine. "I have seven varieties of green tea. The menu is on the table."

She briefly glanced at it and then said, "The pear one, thank you. Did the vampire cause that mess in his attack?"

"Yes. He brought backup in the form of a gun for hire."

I skimmed my hand over our remaining cups, eventually choosing a traditional rose-decorated one with a gold rim for her, and a plain white one for me. Cheery was beyond me right now. Once I made both pots of tea, I carried everything over and sat down opposite her.

"I thought you said earlier that you didn't know anything about our vampire."

"I didn't." She picked up her teapot and began to pour. The aroma of pear and jasmine teased the air. "But given his exploits endanger my position here, I contacted the registrar and enquired."

"Registrar? Who's that?"

Her cool gaze swept me. Judged me. "It's a what rather than who." She raised the cup and smiled. "I had a set similar to this when I lived in France back in the eighteen hundreds—a pleasant era in which to be a vampire. I suspect its selection was deliberate."

And I suspected she was even older than what she was admitting. "I do prefer to raise happy memories for our customers."

"That is a very good business practice." She took a sip of the tea. "The registrar is an organization that holds the records of every vampire created."

I blinked. "Is this a government initiative?"

Her smile didn't quite reach her eyes. "Hardly. Even in this day and age, the government can't be relied on to protect such explosive information. And in the wrong hands, it could be used to track down and kill every rebirth in Australia."

"So this organization not only records a vampire's existence, it keeps track of their movements?"

"All vampires must be registered, but it does not track their movements. It has no need."

I frowned. "Then why register them in the first place if not to keep track of their whereabouts?"

"Does not the witch council keep a register of all births, be they full or half-bloods?"

"Well, yes, but more because there are only six lines of witches and there's a need to keep track of lineage to ensure there's no chance of close kin marrying." I sipped my tea then added, "I wouldn't have thought that to be a problem vampires have."

"Indeed it is not. The registrar doesn't track their movements, simply because all vampires must report a location change to ensure there's no overlap of territory."

"I'm betting there're vampires out there who do not obey that rule." Ours was undoubtedly one of them, otherwise surely this registrar mob would have dealt with him.

"That has certainly happened, but it's also a situation that is quickly dealt with."

"How?"

She smiled. "Let's just say that the registrar has the means of finding every vampire in existence if they so desire—even those who have gone AWOL."

"Intriguing." And smart. Given the precarious position of vampires in the community, having a means of dealing with those vampires who went rogue was totally sensible—even if history suggested they weren't always dealt with in time to save lives.

"I take it, then, that it was this organization who gave you the information about our vampire?"

She nodded. "As I'm sure you're aware, it's very unusual for any vampire to hold such control of magic.

That gave them a good starting point, and it didn't take them too long to find his file."

I leaned forward and crossed my arms. "And?"

"His name before rebirth was Frederick Waverley. He was transported to Australia at the age of twenty for murdering his cousin in a duel of magic. He became a vampire thirty years later."

"So he *is* a witch." Even if one from the lower houses. "Is there any indication as to why he made the decision to become a vampire? Because that's a rare step for a witch to take."

"Why do men do so many things?" Her smile was one of cool amusement. "Of course, vampires by nature are loners *and* predators. Once he was in full control, he was released, as is our way."

"Was his maker also a blood witch or sorcerer? Because as a Waverley, he wouldn't have been born with the power he now has."

"She was not," Maelle said. "But it is not uncommon for those who must survive on blood to sometimes use it to enhance their powers in other areas."

Trepidation stirred. "Have you dabbled in such enhancement?"

Her smile was oddly predatory, even if it held no immediate threat. "I certainly have a small understanding of it, but no more than that. Such study is not without its risks, and I have no desire to fall down that particular rabbit hole."

"Would madness be one of those risks?"

"Not madness, not as such. But a singularity of thought and inability to think beyond their own wants and needs, yes."

Singularity of thought was certainly an apt description

for Frederick Waverley's current actions. "Have you any idea how long he was here the first time?"

"The records have it listed as five years, though he did not come into Castle Rock itself until the latter stages of that period."

"And he'd formed a pod by that time."

It was a statement more than a question, but she nodded in affirmation anyway. "And one of those women had a daughter by the name of Frieda. She had been gifted with blood."

Surprise rippled through me. Though I'd initially suspected the pod's abrupt departure from the reservation was indicative of that possibility, it made Waverley's current determination to avenge Frieda's death that much stranger.

"So she's alive?"

"No. Though her initiation and subsequent turning was indeed registered, the transfer wasn't fully successful, and she wasted away ten days later."

"I didn't even know it was possible for the blood sharing to fail."

"It always depends of the strength and mental stability of both the host and the turnee." She shrugged. "It is obvious that, in this case, neither were up to scratch."

It also meant Frieda could have taken her life so she could rise and take revenge on those who'd made her life hell—and that the note had been nothing more than subterfuge.

"Does this mean the registrar can pinpoint Frederick's location for us?"

"Within a certain radius, yes." She reached into her pocket then slid a piece of paper across the table to me.

On it was a coordinate range—and it seemed an overly large area in which to search to me. But I guessed it was better than nothing. "There's one other thing you need to be aware of."

I raised my eyebrows. "And that is?"

"The means of possible survival if indeed you find yourself caught in the trap of his magic."

Possible, not probable. But still, a slight chance was better than none at all. "I'm interested."

"As indeed you should be, given you are neither a fool nor weak." Her cool smile flashed again, but there was something in her tone, something that skirted the compliment and spoke instead of caginess. "Whatever else Frederick has become, whatever power he has drawn to him, he is in the end still a vampire—and one that has more than certainly fallen down the rabbit hole. Blood—human blood—will always distract him."

I stared at her, my heart suddenly racing in my chest. It said a lot for her self-control that there wasn't even a flicker of awareness in her eyes, nor any sign of hunger.

"Using myself as bait like that would be a very dangerous step to take." And one I might not survive.

"Indeed it would." She finished her tea and replaced the cup on the saucer. The normally cheery chime of china against china sounded more like a death knell. "But if he is magically stronger than you, or if he places you in a situation where you cannot access your own magic, then the blood rapture will perhaps be your one chance. If nothing else, it will give others the time to kill him."

I rose with her, my heart still racing rather uncomfortably. "If the registrar knew he was unstable, why wasn't he dealt with before now?"

"Because they were not aware of the situation until I

informed them. They also cannot move without proof of crime—which we now have, given he has been located in this reservation, and I am the only registered vampire in the area."

"So they're now on their way to deal with him?" Meaning neither Aiden nor I had to?

She hesitated. "Because we are within a reservation, the situation is a little trickier. They will certainly approach the council for permission to do so when they arrive here."

"And when is that likely to be?"

"They have not given me an exact time, but it will be sometime within the next twenty-four hours."

"That may not be quick enough." Not if the gnawing sensation in my gut was anything to go by.

"There is nothing I can do about that." She paused at the door and gave me a polite nod. "Until next we meet, young Elizabeth."

"Thanks for the information," I said. "I appreciate it."

"As you should." This time, amusement edged past the coolness in her pale eyes. "It is not every day I am so overly helpful."

"Then why have you been so now?"

"Because I have discovered over the long years of my life that when there are two powers within a given district, it is always better that they at least be respectful of one another. It is certainly preferable to a relationship based on animosity and distrust—that only ever ends badly."

Which was a warning, even if it was pleasantly said. "A sentiment I agree with."

"Good. I'm glad we understand each other."

With that, she left. I watched until she disappeared

around a distant corner, and then closed the door and went upstairs.

Sleep hit hard and fast, but so too did the dreams.

Aiden featured prominently, as did shoes.

Not just any shoes, but black-and-white wingtips.

Wingtips that were saturated in blood.

CHAPTER
eleven

It was nearly noon by the time I clattered down the stairs. The café was surprisingly full, so I swung into the kitchen to help Mike out. Once the lunch rush had eased, I sliced some ham from the bone to make sandwiches for both Belle and me, and then walked across to a corner table bathed in sunshine. She appeared a few minutes later and placed a tray holding a large teapot and a couple of cups on the table.

"You look like shit," she said, as she dropped down on the seat opposite.

I snorted softly. "Pot, meet kettle."

"Yeah, but my eye baggies couldn't hold a decent-size purse. I'd wager yours can." She reached across and snagged one of the sandwiches. "So where did the wisp lead you?"

I brought Belle up to speed and then said, "I don't suppose the gossip vine had an update on Anna's condition this morning?"

She shook her head. "They've been too busy ruminating on the reasons why someone might have shot at our door."

"Any interesting theories?"

"I think the best suggested Rosie was expressing her annoyance that we hadn't been able to find her diamond ring."

I blinked. "I can't remember meeting a Rosie, let alone being asked to find her diamond."

"You weren't. According to another of the gossips, Rosie has dementia and was referring to a past psychic rather than us."

"Oh. Good."

Belle reached for another sandwich half. "I *have* been giving the wisp's appearance here some thought, however."

"Why? It's more than likely Anna sent him."

"Given the state you found her in, it's doubtful she would have had the strength for *any* sort of magic, let alone be coherent enough to command a wisp."

"Agreed, but wisps aren't known for randomly deciding to help like that." Leading people astray, most certainly. But even then, it was generally only *after* they'd been called on for help.

"Which—when combined with the fact the wild magic interfered with your spell in the cemetery—suggests there is a greater force at work here."

"Meaning you think Anna's right? That the missing reservation witch is still here somewhere?"

"I think it's a possibility. There's an unusual sentience in the magic of this place."

I brushed the crumbs from my fingers. "I don't

suppose the spirits have anything to say about that possibility?"

"What do you think?"

"I think one of these days they're going to give us a direct answer and we're both going to keel over in shock." I leaned back. "I also think the vampire will make his final move tonight."

Concern flickered through her silver eyes. "You dreamed again?"

"Yes, but they weren't really clear and didn't make a whole lot of sense." I shrugged. "I just woke up with the sense that it would all soon end—but not before blood is spilled."

"Your dreams can be as unhelpful as the damn spirits."

Wasn't *that* the truth. I glanced past her as the door chime sounded and Aiden appeared. He spotted us immediately but the smile that tugged his lips failed to lift the weariness from his eyes.

"Afternoon, ladies." He sat between us, his knee lightly resting against mine. It said a lot about my state that my pulse could do little more than briefly flutter.

"You look as if you not only need a strong coffee," Belle said, as she pushed upright, "but a rather large energy jolt in the form of a chocolate brownie slab."

"Maybe not a slab," he said, expression amused. "The rest of your customers might complain if I devoured the lot."

"Most of our customers haven't got a full evening ahead of them."

Aiden's gaze shot to mine as she left. "I take from that comment you dreamed again last night?"

"I did. About shoes."

Surprise briefly flared across his expression. "I know shoe fetishes are common amongst women—my sisters included—but it's taking it a bit far to dream of them, isn't it?"

I couldn't help smiling, and had a vague feeling that was exactly what he'd intended. "I think most women would disagree with you on that."

"So what was so special about these shoes?"

"They were black-and-white wingtips, and covered in blood."

"The blood obviously signifies our vampire, but I can't see the connection with the wingtips."

"I saw them at the cabin that appeared in the first dream. I believe they're his."

"Even if they *are*, that's not really going to help find either the cabin or the vampire. And it's hardly practical to put an all-points out on a pair of shoes."

"I know that."

Belle brought over a mug of coffee and several pieces of the brownie, then left again. I drank my tea while he all but inhaled the rich slice.

"There is more if you want it," I said, amused.

His smile flashed, and this time it was full-blown and decidedly sexy. "Tempting, but even a werewolf's faster metabolic rate has its limits."

"The calories in chocolate don't count, and that's a fact."

"So Ciara insists."

"She sounds like a sensible woman."

"Sometimes," he murmured. "But mostly not."

The love he had for his sibling was very evident in his expression, and I couldn't help the slight twinge of envy. Despite the fact I'd nearly died trying to save my sister, I wouldn't have said any of us were that close.

"Did you manage to pull any information from last night's shooter?"

Aiden nodded. "He's not been overly helpful, though. He was hired a week ago, but can't tell us who by and wasn't called into action until last night."

"And do you believe he's telling the truth?"

He hesitated. "I'm inclined to. He did say he wasn't the only gun hired, but he wasn't sure what the others were up to. He was told to keep low until contacted."

"Was he able to give you the names and a description of the other men?"

"Again, no. But he was able to provide one for our vampire. We've put a reservation-wide alert out, so we'll be contacted if anyone stumbles into him."

If anyone stumbled into him, they'd be dead. I crossed my arms and said, "Tell me about Gabe."

All trace of amusement disappeared. He picked up his coffee and drank it—taking the time to carefully choose his words and cut the possibility of emotion spilling over, I knew.

"Gabe was assigned to us three years ago," he said eventually, "after the witch who'd been with the reservation for over fifty years decided to retire."

"Replacing a long-term incumbent would have been no easy task."

"Tarkan did indeed leave big shoes to fill. But Gabe was young, personable, and I don't think he was disliked by anyone in the reservation—even me."

"So what happened to change that?"

"It started when he and my youngest sister began dating—and, before you say it, I had no objections. Kate—Katie—might have been only nineteen, but she was well able to protect herself both physically and emotionally."

Might have… two words that spoke volumes.

"She'd been ill for months that same year—constant colds or fevers, weight loss, bruising easily." He hesitated. Grief ran through him, even if none of it reached his expression. "It took them a year to diagnose it as acute lymphocytic leukemia."

Which was a form of cancer… and if ever there was a single word that had the power to strike fear in even the strongest person, it was that one.

"Isn't that curable?"

"If it's caught in time, yes. It wasn't."

I reached out and placed a hand on his. Despite the fact I had all my shields up, his grief stormed my senses and had tears stinging my eyes. "I'm sorry, Aiden."

He shifted his hand, briefly gripping mine before releasing me.

"She began treatment immediately, but she just got sicker. We knew—" He paused and looked down at his hands. "When she approached my father wanting permission to marry Gabe, the pack made no objection, even though it went against tradition and rules."

I blinked. I hadn't been aware werewolves deliberately avoided anything more than a casual relationship with humans, but I guessed it *did* explain the very rare mention of half-breeds throughout the annals of history. And it was something both Belle and I had better keep in mind if either of us *did* start wanting something more than casual.

Not going to happen, Belle said. *It's all about the sex, remember. Hot, steamy, luscious sex.*

Idiot. To Aiden, I added, "Did they get the chance to

marry?"

"Yes. But that's when the problems started."

I frowned. "Marriage changed their relationship?"

"No. They were still besotted with each other. But Katie got sicker, and grew to hate all the drugs and the chemo and how they made her feel."

"I believe that's common—"

"Yes, but in *this* case, Gabe convinced her that he could do what science could not. She trusted him, ended her treatments, and died."

His bitterness and anger was so strong it broke through the barriers of his self-control and filled his voice.

My fingers twitched with the need to reach out and comfort him again, but I resisted. The force of his emotions was bad enough as it was—touching him might blow a circuit.

"As heart-wrenching as that must have been," I said, picking my words carefully, "it's hardly a crime. So why is there still a warrant out for his arrest?"

"Because she didn't just die. She was murdered. We found her body in the middle of a pentagram, a blade in her heart, and his fingerprints on the hilt."

"But he couldn't have—" I checked the rest of the sentence, but far too late.

"Don't tell me he couldn't when he very obviously *did*." Aiden's voice was quiet, but filled with an anger that lashed as sharply as any whip. "He killed her, and then he ran."

No, I wanted to repeat, *not possible*. Not if he loved her as fiercely as Aiden had implied.

But then, who was I to say the pain of watching his wife fade away hadn't somehow made him lose his mind?

"Where did you find her? Within pack grounds?"

"No. We might have been able to stop him if it had happened there."

I frowned. "Does that mean you had some warning?"

"Kate left us a note." Just for an instant, I saw the glimmer of tears. "She said she'd had enough of the pain, that if she was going to die anyway, she'd do it her own way, on her own terms. She said that Gabe had agreed to help her—that in doing this, she would be free and forever a part of the reservation."

Which was an odd statement to make. While ghosts certainly did exist, they were usually souls who had either died violently and unexpectedly, or those who—for whatever reason—refused to move on. His sister didn't seem to fit either description. "Where did you find her?"

"In the St. Erth forests, which is Marin territory."

"Why didn't they question her presence there? Didn't you say they—like the O'Connors—are rather restrictive about who can and can't enter their grounds?"

"When it comes to humans, yes, but it's not unusual for wolves to pass through the outskirts of each other's territories, and in this case, Gabe was accompanied by my sister. By the time they realized something was wrong, it was too late."

I think we need to see that place, Belle commented. *If Anna is right, if Gabe is here, then he's most likely to be in the area where her soul resides.*

Except that's impossible. The Marins would have found him by now.

Normally, yes, but if he's somehow managed to tap into the wild magic, then perhaps he's using it to hide his presence. Ask Aiden if he'll show you the area, she said. *See what he says.*

I hesitated, and then said, "Would it be possible for us to go there?"

He blinked and his gaze hardened. "Why?"

"Because if Gabe *is* still alive and here on the reservation, as Anna suggested, then he'll be in the place where his heart died."

"I don't believe for an instant he could avoid discovery for such a long period of time," Aiden all but growled. "But I won't say no to the chance of being proven wrong. Not if it results in this bastard being brought to justice."

He drained his coffee then thrust to his feet. "Let's go."

"What, now?" I said, caught by surprise.

"Have you got anything else you need to be doing right now?"

"Well no, but—"

"Then come. It'll only take an hour, and I'd rather sort it all out now than let it fester." He spun around and left.

Belle met me halfway to the door and handed me the ever-reliable backpack. Its weight told me she'd added a few extra additions to last night's contents.

"Thanks."

"Just be careful. There's something about this whole situation that isn't sitting right with me."

I frowned. "It's usually me who's afflicted with that sort of stuff, not you."

She rubbed her arms, her expression uneasy. "In all honesty, it's probably nothing more than a belated echo of the uneasiness you were feeling last night, but still—"

I squeezed her upper arm lightly. "I'll be fine."

She nodded. "Go, before our ranger changes his mind."

I swung the pack over my shoulder and hurried after

Aiden. He'd already climbed into his truck and was tapping his fingers against the steering wheel impatiently. I threw the pack into the foot well and then climbed in. "Sorry, but I wasn't about to go anywhere without some means of protection."

"Knives and potions aren't going to stop a bullet."

Again trepidation stirred. Whatever was coming, it involved bullets as much as magic. "Are guns even legal on the reservation?"

"For the general population, no, but there are some farmers on the outer edges who have been given special licenses. Snakes and other vermin can be a real problem around these parts."

Snakes were a problem Australia-wide, but surely other vermin—like foxes—would have more sense than to encroach on a werewolf reservation.

We'd just reached the outskirts of town when the incoming call sign flashed up on the truck's computer screen.

He flicked a button on the steering wheel and then said, voice carefully neutral, "What can I do for you, Blume?"

"Where are you?"

"Driving. And I'm not in the mood for games, so just spit out whatever it is you want."

"When I read Tala's report about the witch's dream, it said—"

"Ms. Grace is in the truck with me," Aiden said. "So if you have a question for her, ask it."

"Did you, or did you not," Blume said, "mention the presence of black-and-white wingtip shoes when describing that cabin your dream showed you?"

"I did." I shared an uneasy glance with Aiden.

"Why?"

"Because a parcel was just delivered to Hart, and inside is a wingtip shoe."

"You're staying at the Lodge, aren't you?" Aiden said.

"Yes."

"We'll be there in five." Aiden hit the accelerator, and then glanced at me. "The other business will have to wait."

I nodded and hung on as we hurtled through the streets, my knuckles white with the force of my grip against the door.

Five minutes later, he swung into the drive of what looked to be the grounds of an old school, and came to an abrupt halt at the building's entrance. I scrambled out of the truck and hurried after him as he strode up the steps to the door.

Blume was waiting for us in the foyer, and led us up a rather grand old staircase. A door at the far end of the wide hall was open. Hart was inside, perched on the arm of a well-padded chair. On the table in front of him was one of the two shoes I'd seen in my dream.

My steps faltered. I didn't have to get any closer to feel the foulness emanating from it.

"Is that the type of shoe you dreamed about?" Hart said, waving a hand at the wingtip on the table.

I swallowed to ease the sudden dryness in my throat. "It's not just the same type—it's actually his."

"And you're sure of that? I thought with psychometry that you had to touch it first or something?"

I gave him a smile that held little in the way of amusement. "It depends on the strength of the psychic and whether the object itself holds a strong enough connection to whoever—whatever—is being traced."

"So you *can* find him through it?" Blume asked.

"Probably." I crossed my arms, but it did little to ward off the encroaching chill. "There's one problem, however—that shoe is an invitation, gentlemen. We answer it, and we may well walk into a trap."

"Which is why we should make the attempt to track him *now*, when the sun has forced him to sleep," Hart said.

"He's got hired guns working for him, and they're not restricted by sunlight. I'm also betting he expects us to react immediately."

"All of which is undoubtedly true," Blume said. "But this may be our one chance to grab the bastard—we have no choice but to take it."

I glanced at Aiden, hoping he, at least, would see sense. "This really *isn't* a good idea."

"No, and it's therefore probably better if you remain here." He glanced down at the shoe, his expression giving little away. "We just need you to give us a general idea of location, and we'll—"

"What?" I cut in, tension giving my tone a harsh edge. "Detect and undo any spells he might have laid out?"

"Well, no—"

"I appreciate the concern, Aiden, but we both know I have no choice but to join the hunt."

"Agreed." Hart picked up the shoe and held it toward me. "So let's stop arguing and get this fucking show on the road."

Aiden pulled a pair of silicon gloves from the rear pocket of his jeans and handed them to me. I gave him a quick, tense smile and put them on.

Only then did I touch the shoe. The vibes that had poured from the bloodstone had been bad enough, but this… this was hell itself come to life. If there had *ever* been any good in our vampire, then it was long gone. His heart had died when Frieda had, and in its place a festering evil had slowly grown, until it had utterly consumed him.

The leather was so stained with his decay that even with the protection of the gloves, it burned my fingertips. It took every ounce of control I had not to throw it as far away from me as I could, and then scrub its touch from my skin. I took a deep, slow breath that failed to calm my nerves, and then cracked open the door to my psychic self.

Life beat within the cloud of foulness—a rhythm that spoke of slumber.

"Anything?" Blume asked.

I jumped slightly. "He's sleeping."

"You can tell that through just a touch?" Hart said.

"Yes. That doesn't mean there aren't traps, however."

"No, but again, it's a risk we'll have to take." Hart glanced across to his partner. "You remain here, just in case we need rescuing."

Blume nodded, though he didn't look all that happy to be missing out on the action. "Hang on while I check the tracker signal."

He walked across the room, picked up what looked to be a small remote, and fiddled with it. After a couple of seconds, it began to emit a soft beeping.

"Right," Hart said. "Let's go. You can drive, O'Connor."

Aiden didn't reply. He simply plucked the shoe from my fingertips then led the way out to his truck. After placing the wingtip on the console between the front seats, he said, "What direction?"

I hesitated as Blume settled into the rear seat, and then carefully brushed my gloved fingers across shoe's shiny toe. This time it wasn't just waves of decay that hit, but images—a dirt road, thick trees, an old cabin. One black-and-white wingtip shoe waiting patiently for the return of its brother.

I shivered and pulled my fingers away. "Head toward Argyle."

Aiden immediately swung the truck around and planted his foot. I touched the shoe again as we left Castle Rock and guided him. All too soon we left the main road and were once again driving along a dirt track heading deep in the heart of thick scrub.

It was the same dirt road the shoe had shown me.

When the road petered out and became little more than a goat track, Aiden stopped and leaned his arms on the steering wheel as he studied the ground ahead. "Rushdown Settlement is about two kilometers down that track, but it's a rather odd place for our vampire to be hiding out."

"Why?" Hart asked. "This area isn't exactly a major draw for tourists."

"No, but it *is* now an overnight stopping point for hikers. There's too big a risk of discovery if he bunked down here."

"Not if he's got daytime guards," Hart said, as he climbed out. "Or simply fed on the hikers and then chucked their bodies down one of the many mine shafts."

"I think even *we* would have noticed a sudden increase in the number of missing hikers." Aiden's quick glance at Hart verged on the edge of scathing, even if it wasn't evident in his voice.

I climbed out and joined the two men at the front of the truck. Though the eucalyptus-scented air was free of the trace of evil, trepidation pulsed through me nevertheless. The vampire might not be close, but something was.

Or some*one.*

Aiden waved a hand forward. "You've got the lead, Liz."

Though I was now holding the shoe at the very end of its laces, its heartbeat was stronger than ever. It led us down the path toward the old settlement—and I just had to hope that instinct was wrong, and that it wasn't also leading us into a trap.

The two men followed close on my heels—Aiden's steps inaudible over Hart's heavier tread—but I felt no safer for their closeness. Whatever I was sensing, whatever lay in wait up ahead, it was aimed at them more than me.

Which made no sense, given I was the one the vampire had sworn revenge on.

About three-quarters of a kilometer away from the truck, the shoe pulled us off the faint path and into the trees. I squeezed past several clumps of spiky gorse bushes and discovered another path. If the first one had been little more than a goat track, this could only be described as a mouse run.

I glanced briefly over my shoulder. "Is this a secondary track to the old settlement?"

"Not that I'm aware of, but there are a number of old mining shacks scattered throughout these hills." Aiden touched my shoulder, the contact light and all too brief. "Do you want me to take the lead? If the trap you fear is physical rather than magical, I'll have more chance of spotting it."

Images of the fishing line I'd almost stumbled into at the old mine flashed into my mind, and without hesitation, I stood to one side. But I felt no safer for his lead. Not given neither of us had seen the shaft trap before we'd fallen into it.

The trees soon began to thin out but the gorse did the opposite. I used the shoe to hold the worst of it away from my body as I edged past the various thickets, but with the stronger connection came the certainty that we were walking toward death and disaster. But again, it didn't feel aimed at me. It didn't really feel aimed at Aiden, either. Not yet, anyway.

Hart was its target. If he continued on, he would not see this day out.

I stopped so abruptly he all but plowed into my back. Only his quick reflexes saved us both from a tumble.

"Why the fuck did you stop?" he said.

"You need to go back." Urgency pulsed through my voice. "If you'll go on, you'll die."

"The shoe is telling you that?" He raised his eyebrows, disbelief evident.

"No, but—"

"Psychometry isn't clairvoyance," he continued. "So unless you're suddenly claiming that talent, let's all move on. It's pretty obvious even to me that there's no one other than us and the flies here in this goddamn shit of a place."

"You have to trust me—" I reached out and grabbed his forearm, trying to make him see. Trying to make him believe. "I may not have classic clairvoyance but I *do* dream, and that gives validity to what I'm feeling—"

"A mere *feeling* is not a good enough reason for me to depart, Ms. Grace." Hart's voice was edged with impatience. "I've known many a psychic over the years, and their predictions were wrong just as often as they were right."

"No psychic in existence has ever got it right one

hundred percent of the time, not even me," I said. "But I'm not wrong—not this time."

"We *are* dealing with a whole lot more than an ordinary criminal here," Aiden said. "I think it might be wise to listen—"

"I can't do my job in retreat," Hart said, annoyance deepening his tone. "And it certainly wouldn't be the first time I've faced the specter of death. So let's just move on."

I glanced at Aiden, who shrugged minutely and walked on. I followed. There wasn't much else I could do.

The ground began to rise more steeply, and as the trees continued to thin out, I got glimpses of what had to be the Rushdown Settlement below us. Smoke drifted from the chimney of a building on the outskirts of the small town, but even from here I could tell the cabin didn't match the one I'd seen in my dreams.

We finally reached the top of the ridge. Sitting in the middle of the rock-strewn clearing was the old shack made of stone and roughly split trees. Black plastic still covered what remained of the windows, but there was no smoke coming from the chimney, and the place looked and felt empty.

"This is it." I studied the clearing but couldn't see any indication of magic. "This is the cabin I saw in my dream."

Aiden's nostrils flared. After a moment, he said, "There's no one near. In fact, I doubt anyone has been here for some time."

"Even if he has now abandoned the place, we still have to go in," Hart said. "However unlikely, we might just find something that will at least tell us who he is."

"We already know that," I said, without really thinking. "He's Frederick Waverley, who was transported to Australia for murdering...."

My voice trailed off as I became aware that both men were staring at me—and then I remembered I hadn't actually passed on the information Maelle had given me.

I feigned innocence. "I told you that, I'm sure."

"No," Aiden growled. "You did not."

"Ah." I paused. "Sorry."

"Anything else you've conveniently forgotten to share?" Hart asked.

I hesitated and then told them everything else Maelle had said, omitting only the fact that she was my source and the bit about the registrar sending people here. The latter was not my information to pass on, especially given neither man appeared to be aware there was another vampire here.

"And how did you learn all this?" Hart asked.

I waved a hand airily. "The spirit world can be a rather helpful lot if they're so inclined."

As I'd hoped, neither man questioned me any further, although Aiden's expression suggested he, at least, didn't believe the information had come from spirits.

Six steps into the clearing, the pulsing in the shoe stopped. Fear surged and I froze, my gaze sweeping across the rubble-filled clearing yet again. It remained free of any taint of blood magic—there wasn't even a lingering echo to indicate it had ever been here.

So why was the shoe now dead?

What the hell was going on?

Suspecting I really *didn't* want an answer to that particular question, but knowing I had to seek it anyway, I forced my feet forward. The two men fanned out on either side of me, their guns drawn and expressions tense.

Nothing stirred; the clearing remained still and silent.

Even the buzz of insects seemed to have died.

I stopped again in front of the old door. Sitting in the woodbox nearby was the other wingtip shoe.

We were definitely in the right place.

I placed the shoe I was holding beside its mate and then pressed my right hand against the door. Once again I couldn't detect the residue of magic, and while that *should* have eased the tension pulsing through me, it did the exact opposite. No vampire would risk being caught unawares during the sunlit hours, so if Waverley wasn't using magic as a means of protection, what was he using?

I reached for the doorknob, but Aiden caught my hand and shook his head. He motioned me to one side, then glanced at Hart, who nodded and held his gun at the ready. Aiden gripped the handle and, after a pause, pushed the door wide open.

No one jumped out at us. No magic pounced.

"Anything?" Aiden said, with another quick look my way.

"No."

"Good." He edged around the corner and, after a minute, gave the all clear.

I followed him in. The light filtering in through the open doorway did little to lift the deeper shadows, but it was still enough to see that while the cabin might now be empty, someone had definitely been living here. An old camp bed had been set up in one corner and there was a table and a couple of chairs opposite this. To the right of the door was an old fireplace, with newspaper and twigs set up ready to be lit. To one side of the hearth was a rusting half drum filled with larger logs and a stack of newspapers.

Aiden walked over and picked up the latter. "The

latest date is last Tuesday, meaning it's more than possible our quarry hasn't been here since then."

"So why would he send us the shoe?" I said. "It doesn't make any sense—why lure us up here if not to either trap us or take us out?"

"Maybe he's so confident in his ability to escape us the shoe was nothing more than a dare—a 'find me if you can' message," Hart said.

"Which would be at odds with the methodic way he's gone about business so far," Aiden said.

"I don't think the term methodic could be applied to his attack on Ms. Grace last night."

"And yet, for all his fury, he had backup in the form of a hired gun, and also had an escape route planned out."

Hart grunted and glanced around again. "Well, this appears to be nothing more than a big, fat waste of time. Shall we head back?"

"I can't see that we have any other—" Aiden stopped, expression intent.

The fear that had been easing since we'd stepped into the cabin ratcheted up again. "What?"

The question came out slightly strangled, thanks to the fact my heart seemed to be pounding in the vicinity my throat.

"Movement, coming up the ridge," he said. "They're good, too. I can barely hear them."

"How close?" Hart asked softly. "And how many?"

"Two. Headed this way, but not taking our path." He paused, head slightly cocked to one side. "They've just split and are now approaching the clearing from the left and the right."

"What's the betting they're our vampire's hired guns?" Hart pulled his gun from its holster. "Shall we go

295

greet them?"

Aiden nodded and glanced at me. "Wait here."

"Please, both of you—be careful. This could be the trap I was sensing."

Neither man answered. They simply slipped out the door and disappeared into the scrub to the right and left of the cabin. I closed the door and then slid the bolt across. It probably wouldn't hold up if any great force was applied to it, but it nevertheless made me feel a little safer.

I stepped to one side and leaned back against the cool stone, my eyes closed but every other sense I had open. It didn't tell me what was happening. Aside from the gnawing certainty that the shit was about to hit the fan, my "other" senses were giving me little in the way of information.

I crossed my arms and clenched my fists against the need to unbolt the door and race out after the two men. At best, I'd only get in their way. And worst, I could end up a hostage and turn a dangerous situation into a deadly one.

But the silence ran on, eating at my nerves.

I pushed away from the wall and began to pace. It didn't help.

Then a sound not unlike the backfire of a car shattered the silence. I froze, my pulse racing and fear heavy in my heart.

That sound could only have been a gunshot.

I had no idea who had fired, but I desperately wanted to believe it had been either Aiden or Hart. Desperately wanted to believe that they were safe and unhurt—that the death and darkness I'd feared hadn't just landed.

I bit my lip against the instinctive need to call out, and resumed pacing.

Two minutes later, another shot echoed.

But again, it was followed by silence. Far too many minutes of silence.

Then footsteps approached—two sets, one quieter than the other. Tears of relief stung my eyes and I all but ran to the door. But just as I was about to throw back the bolt, caution stirred.

If it was Aiden and Hart approaching, why hadn't either of them called out?

I rose on my tiptoes and peered through one of the many cracks in the door.

It wasn't Aiden or Hart. It was two complete strangers.

And they both had their weapons aimed at the door.

CHAPTER
twelve

I threw myself sideways and covered my head with my hands, even as the door exploded under a fierce storm of gunfire. Splinters, dust, and even stone chips flew everywhere, small but dangerous missiles that bit into my skin as easily as the air.

I swore and scrambled away on hands and knees, heading for the corner near the fireplace, as far away from the door as was practical in this tiny, one-room cottage.

Belle? I screamed. *I need you to contact the rangers and Blume, and get them up here ASAP. Tell them to bring medics.*

Fuck, Lizzie, what's going on?

Gunfire. Lots of gunfire. I have no idea where Aiden and Hart are. No idea if they're injured or dead.

On it, Belle said. *Keep your head down.*

That's one thing you can be sure of.

As the buzz of her thoughts left mine, I raised a hand and began weaving a spell into the shadows, using them create a shield thick enough to disappear behind, but not heavy enough to draw attention.

The gunfire ceased and silence fell. The door was decimated, but the bolt and hinges had somehow survived the onslaught, and kept the remnants upright. Dust danced in the sunlight now flooding the middle portion of the cabin, but thankfully, shadows still claimed the corners.

Stones crunched, an indication that at least one of the men approached. My breath caught in my throat and I watched the door with a sense of dread, not daring to move lest the sound carry and tell them I was there.

Several beams of sunlight cut out—someone was now standing in front of the door. Listening, I suspected. Another step, then the black plastic of the nearest window rattled. Sweat trickled down my back, and it took every ounce of control I had to remain still and quiet.

The door crashed back on its hinges and two men flowed into the room. Wood dust spun through the air, causing a cloud thick enough to catch in my throat. I bit down hard on my lip, drawing blood as I fought the need to cough.

The taller of the two spun around, his dark gaze sweeping across the fireplace before coming to a rest on the shadows that concealed me. Just for an instant, I feared he'd either smelled the sweaty scent of fear or had sensed the presence of magic. He took a step forward, his gun still raised and eyes narrowed. My heart was now pounding so fast I was beginning to feel dizzy. There were no spells that could protect against bullets—if he decided to fire just to be sure the shadows were as empty as they seemed, I was dead.

"Nothing," his partner said, frustration evident in his tone. "She must have slipped out when we were taking care of the ranger and the other bloke."

His words had my heart stuttering to an uneven halt. No, I thought. Not possible. Aiden was a wolf, for fuck's sake. History had showed time and again that they weren't so easy to dispose of. "Taking care of" could have meant a thousand things. It didn't mean they were dead. It couldn't.

And yet the bit of me that had foreseen death whispered otherwise, and I bit down harder against the scream of denial.

God help me, I barely even knew the man, let alone had any confirmation of his death, and yet some part of me was already grieving the loss of possibilities.

The taller man grunted and put his gun away. It didn't ease the tension pounding through me. These two were pros—they could no doubt draw and fire quicker than I could ever cast a spell.

"We can't take long. All that gunfire is going to attract attention." He spun on one heel and strode out the door. "We should have fucking used silencers, even if it was against the freak's orders."

I frowned. Why would Waverley have ordered the two men *not* to use silencers? That made absolutely no sense—unless, of course, his wanted to not only attract attention, but to draw Aiden's forces away from the Redferns.

Thwarting his actions might have put me on his hit list, but Morris Redfern had been there since the death of the child Waverley obviously viewed as a daughter.

"You were more than welcome to." The smaller man cast a final look around the cabin, his gaze skimming across my corner with no sign of suspicion. "Me, I like my life too much."

Their footsteps faded, but I remained exactly where I was. I didn't even dare unravel the shadows. For all I knew, their retreat might be nothing more than a means of drawing me out of hiding.

The dust settled and time once again stretched on. I shifted slightly and glanced at my watch. Twenty minutes had passed—it seemed an eternity longer.

Then a feminine and all-too-familiar voice said, "Aiden? You there?"

Tala, Aiden's second. I let Belle know I'd been found and was now safe, then cast aside the shadows and scrambled upright. "No," I said. "He's not. Nor is Hart. I'm coming out."

I raised a hand to shield my eyes against the fading rays of sunlight. The clearing was empty and there was no immediate sign of Tala. Then the gorse at the left edge of the clearing moved and she stepped out, gun only partially lowered.

"Where's Aiden?"

"I don't know." I waved a hand toward the scrub and wished with all my being it were otherwise. Wished that for once in my goddamn life my psychic soul would give me a definitive answer rather than mere possibilities. "Someone tried sneaking up on us, and he and Hart left to investigate. There were two shots, and then the cabin was attacked."

Tala's gaze went past me. "How many men?"

"Two that I know of. There could have been more."

Bushes rustled to my left. Though I knew given Tala's lack of reaction it had to be someone she knew, fear still had my pulse rate climbing again. But as I glanced around, Blume and another man in a ranger's uniform stepped into the clearing. Neither looked happy. In fact,

Blume's body was practically humming with tension and anger.

"We found Hart," he said, voice curt. "He's dead. Shot in the head."

Tala asked the question I couldn't. "And Aiden?"

"No sign of him," the ranger said. "But we found his scent and Mac's tracing it right now. He'll update us if he finds anything."

Meaning it was still possible Aiden was alive. But even as part of me rejoiced that glimmer of hope, another whispered that there was no guarantee he would remain so. No guarantee that he was even moving under his own steam. This was all part of a larger plan—one that had yet to be fully revealed.

But it would be, instinct whispered, and all too soon.

"Right," Tala said. "I'll take Ms. Grace's statement and start investigations here. Byron, call in additional people and then go assist Mac. I want this entire mountain searched."

It won't do any good, I thought, as Byron slipped back into the scrub. Waverley was now intent on not only taking revenge on the Redferns, but on those of us who kept interfering.

"If all your people are now here," I asked. "Who's minding the Redferns?"

Tala frowned. "Maggie—"

"The receptionist I met at the station? She's also a ranger?"

"In training, but more than capable." Tala's tone was clipped.

"I'm not questioning her competence, but whatever else Waverley now has planned, they remain at the core of it all. One lone ranger might not be enough."

"One lone ranger is all we have at the moment." She frowned. "Waverley?"

"That's the vampire's name—Frederick Waverley."

"And when the fuck did you learn *that*?" Blume cut in.

I glanced at him. "Earlier today, but it won't help as it's his birth name and he changed it long ago."

"His birth name would have allowed us to contract the registrar and perhaps even gotten us help." Blume's voice was devoid of emotion, but his anger was so fierce his aura was little more than a black haze.

But the fact he knew about the registrar was interesting, as was Tala's confusion. Obviously, the rangers—and perhaps even werewolves as a whole—weren't aware of its existence.

Blume must have realized this, because he glanced at her and waved a hand. "Later."

"It would seem our psychic isn't the only one keeping secrets. But you guys never were the caring, sharing types." Her gaze returned to me. "I'll arrange to get extra people allocated to the Redferns. In the meantime, tell me what happened here."

By the time I had, the shadows of dusk were closing in, mirroring the trepidation that was settling deeper into my soul.

"If we bring something of Aiden's to you, do you think you can find him?" she asked.

"Maybe. If he isn't dead." I paused, and shrugged. "But Waverley is obviously aware of my psychometry skills, and will have countermeasures in place."

She raised her eyebrows. "How can magic counter a psychic skill?"

"A witch can counter just about anything as long as

303

they have the skill and knowledge."

Anything except bullets and death. And *that* possibility still haunted my inner corridors, and would only grow stronger with the onset of night.

"Have you picked up the wingtip since you arrived here?" Blume asked.

I crossed my arms and tried to ignore the chill that rose at the thought of going anywhere near that shoe again. "Sorry, but I was too busy trying to stay alive to give the damn shoe a second thought."

He frowned. "But you should still be able to trace him through it, shouldn't you?"

"That shoe led us into a trap, just as I'd warned. If it were possible to trace him through it, we wouldn't now be standing in this damn clearing."

"I still think you should try." He strode over to the woodbox and grabbed one of the shoes. "Here."

He tossed it toward me. I caught it instinctively and quickly switched it to my gloved hand. A vague sense of hunger stirred across my senses and then died. Whatever spell had been crafted onto this shoe to deceive my psychic senses had long faded—as had whatever connection Waverley had to these shoes.

"Nothing." I tossed the shoe back. "He's awake, but that's all I'm getting."

"Damn." He put the shoe back and thrust a hand through his short hair. "If Waverley *has* snatched O'Connor rather than kill him, we'll undoubtedly hear from him."

"You won't," I countered. "But I will."

"Then perhaps we'd better get back to your café. If he *does* attempt contact, that's where it'll happen."

He was the last person I wanted to go anywhere with,

but I didn't particularly want to walk anywhere alone, either. His company was better than nothing.

I glanced at Tala. "Can I leave?"

She nodded and looked at Blume. "If Waverley does make contact, you're to let us know immediately. That clear?"

He gave her a noncommittal sort of smile and motioned me to follow him.

True night had settled in by the time we made it back to the café. Belle's welcoming smile faded when she saw Blume behind me rather than Aiden.

"You haven't found him?" she asked.

"Not yet."

"Ah." Her gaze flicked to Blume. "And you're here to protect us or something?"

"Or something." He got out his phone and then dropped down onto a chair. "I'd appreciate a coffee—black—if that's possible."

Belle glanced at me. "You?"

I shook my head. "I'm heading upstairs for a shower."

She came up about half an hour later and dropped onto the couch beside me. "Blume has reported in to his bosses and requested more help."

"It'll all be over by the time they get here."

"Yeah." She paused. "It's a shame about Hart. He was a pompous ass, but he didn't deserve to die like that."

"At least it was quick—that's more than Waverley gave his other victims."

"I guess." She wrinkled her nose. "He had a kid."

I didn't say anything. No kid deserved to grow up without their dad, but nothing I could say—no utterance of regret or sorrow—would change what had happened.

Belle reached for the remote and turned the TV on. We sat there in silence, watching the news and the programs that followed. It didn't relax either of us.

Downstairs, the chime above the café's door sounded, a merry tune so at odds with the apprehension hanging like a pall over the café. I waited, body tense, for another attack, but nothing else happened. After several seconds, footsteps echoed as Blume moved cautiously toward the door. I glanced at Belle; we rose as one and bolted for the stairs.

"Someone slipped a note under the door," Blume said, without looking at us. "Are either of you sensing the presence of anyone nearby?"

"No," Belle said. "But given Waverley has shown a penchant for using gunmen, it wasn't all that wise to be standing in front of the door before you discovered that."

"I'm not in front, I'm to one side, as is standard." His gaze flicked to me. "If there's no one near, how did the note get here? Magic?"

"Possibly, given that chime only sounds when someone is entering the café."

I stopped next to Blume and placed a hand against the door. A trace of foul energy lingered around the chime, but the threads of our spells had neither been challenged nor activated. The latter wasn't really a surprise—while the note undoubtedly held a threat, neither its delivery nor the ringing of the bell posed any danger.

Blume picked up the folded note and read it. "I have the ranger. If you wish to see him alive, bring Morris Redfern to the clearing you found Karen in at midnight. Do not involve the IIT or the rangers. If I sense either, he dies. Disobey me in any way, and he dies."

"Obey," Belle murmured, "and everyone dies—you, Aiden, and Redfern."

I glanced at her. "What other choice have we got though?"

"He's going to have measures in place to counter your magic, Lizzie. You can't do it. Not alone."

"I agree," Blume said. "Even if he *wasn't* planning to kill all three of you, it's simply unacceptable to trade one life for another."

"So we do nothing and just let Aiden die?" I bit back. "That's just as unacceptable in my opinion."

Not to mention the fact that it would make life here pretty near untenable.

"Reinforcements *are* on their way," Blume said. "We *will* stop this bastard."

"Are those reinforcements going to be here by midnight?"

"Well, no, but—"

"Then the statement is meaningless. I won't sit back and do nothing. I can't."

"And I won't let either you or Redfern anywhere near that madman."

I stared at him for a moment. "You're welcome to try and stop me, Blume, but you won't succeed."

He studied me for several seconds, then nodded, as if in acceptance. "But *that* doesn't alter the fact I will not put Redfern into the path of that madman."

Which left us at an impasse.

"Maybe not," Belle said slowly. "He's familiar enough with the feel of your magic after his attack on us here, but I'm thinking he's not so familiar with mine."

"No," I said automatically. "There's no way known you're taking my place."

"Not your place—Redfern's."

"Forgive me from pointing out the obvious," Blume said, "but you will never, ever be mistaken for Redfern. Not under any light."

"I might if I'm using a glamour."

"Can a glamour counter the fact that you're a six-foot-tall, strongly built woman, and Redfern is at best five-ten and a weed to boot?"

Belle grinned. "If it's built as divinely as me, yes."

"He's going to be layering that clearing with all manner of protection spells," I said. "Even if the glamour *does* hold, he'll sense the presence of magic around you."

"Yes, but he'll expect at least some sort of protection around Redfern. He knows you're not a fool."

"Neither is he. He might be from the Waverley line of witches, but his use of blood magic has increased the overall potency of his spells," I said. "It's likely my magic will be restricted the moment we enter his circle."

"Yours will be, but there's a good chance mine won't—"

"Even if that *were* the case, your magic alone won't defeat him—"

"Then we don't rely on just my magic to defeat him."

I stared at her for several altogether too-fast heartbeats. "That's a fucking dangerous step, Belle—"

"I know." She placed a hand on my arm, a light touch that was meant to be reassuring but failed miserably in its task. "But I also know it could be the only way any of us walk away alive."

So say the spirits?

Yes. Her mental tone was grim. *You're right—even if our spells did hold up against his assault here, they won't in that clearing. He's had time to plan and we're doing this on the fly. But we have little other choice if we want to save Aiden and defeat this bastard.*

I'm betting the spirits are not guaranteeing success.

They never do. But a small chance is better than none.

"I get the distinct feeling I'm missing out on a major part of this conversation." Blume's comment was edged with annoyance. "What step is dangerous?"

I glanced at him. "Using the wild magic. Carrying it with me into Waverley's protection circle."

Blume blinked. "Is something like that even possible? I thought that stuff could only be controlled and guided, but not ever used."

"In theory, a strong enough witch—be they of the light or of darkness—can call upon it to boost the strength of their spellwork, but I don't know of any who have tried and survived."

And given that, how much more dangerous was calling it into my body going to be? Could human flesh and bone even withstand such a force?

Blume frowned. "Why not? Don't witches draw from the energy of the world as a matter of course?"

"Yes, but the source of the wild magic is the deeper recesses of the earth. Its volatility is what makes it impractical for spells." As demonstrated by what had happened to my spell in the cemetery. The presence of wild magic had turned a simple diversion into something far more dangerous.

I rubbed my arms against the chill seeping deep into my bones. That chill wasn't only fear, but the suspicion that even if I did survive the next few hours, things were never going to be the same for me, magic-wise.

"But why? The source is ultimately the same—the earth and all that lives on and within it."

"Think of magic as electricity," Belle said. "If you

touch your tongue to a battery, it will at best give you a mild shock. Do the same to a live wire, and it will kill you."

"And wild magic is the live wire?"

She nodded. "The stuff here is also without the protection of an authorized witch, and that makes it even more dangerous."

His frown grew. "Why?"

"Because it seems to hold an odd sort of sentience," I cut in. "We have no idea why, but I suspect it has something to do with Gabe."

"Impossible. Gabe has a warrant out for his arrest. He wouldn't be stupid enough to remain within the reservation."

"That might be true," Belle said. "But it doesn't alter the fact that something—or someone—is influencing the magic here, and an authorized witch such as Gabe is the only person who could."

He shrugged and glanced at his watch. "We've under two hours to make arrangements and meet Waverley's deadline. What do you need from me?"

"Given you won't bring Redfern out of hiding, we need a photo of him," I said. "And a set of his clothes."

Blume nodded. "Anything else?"

"No, but we do need to ensure there's no one watching this place. If there is, our plan could fail before it even starts."

"I can take care of any followers." Blume glanced at Belle. "Although I thought you said there was no one near."

"There isn't, but telepathy does have range limits."

"Then you'll need to become Redfern out in the forest rather than here, just to be certain no one suspects."

He glanced at his watch again. "I'll be back in fifteen with the stuff you need."

Which gave us enough time to make a pot of herbal tea designed to boost strength and clarity, and grab something to eat.

He returned with not only the items we'd requested, but also a black carryall. He didn't explain the latter and neither of us asked. We simply went into the reading room, locked the door, and then got down to business of not only creating some serious magic, but also some very *un*magical vampire impediments.

They might be a last resort, but—if instinct was to be believed—they could also be the difference between surviving and not.

Blume rose as we walked out forty-five minutes later. "I called the rangers while you were in there doing your thing. Tala has assigned two extra people to watch the Redferns, just in case this is a diversion. She and Mac have done a run around the immediate area—there's no one watching the café."

"Good." I glanced at my watch. We were beginning to push it timewise—there was now just under an hour left, and we not only had to get into the forest, but alter Belle's form and call the wild magic.

And if it *didn't* respond, we were going to be well and truly up that well-known creek without a paddle.

"There's one more thing you both need before you can leave." Blume reached into the black carryall and pulled out a cell phone, a small black box, and a gun. The latter he held up. "Do either of you know how to use one of these?"

"No."

"Then we'll skip that idea." He placed the gun down then handed Belle the cell phone. "I'll remotely activate this once you get into the forest. Waverley might ask you both to empty your pockets, but I doubt he'll think anything of a regular-looking phone."

"I'm gathering it's anything but that, then." She studied it briefly before tucking it into the pack she carried.

"Oh, it is a phone, but it's one we can remotely access. Through it, we'll be able to track your location, and hear everything that's said." He opened the box and pulled out a rather plain-looking ladies' watch. "And this is for you, Ms. Grace. It'll record both video and audio. You just have to activate it by pushing this button here."

He pointed at the largest of the three buttons on the watch. I undid my own watch and then strapped his on. While it was larger than the one I usually wore, it didn't look too out of place on my wrist.

I glanced across to Belle. "Ready?"

Her tension echoed through me, but all she said was "Yes."

We headed out. After I'd locked the door again, Blume headed left while we went right. The night was still and quiet, but the air held an odd note of expectation. Whether Waverley was so positive of victory this time around that his certainty was breaching the distance between us, or it was simply a product of both my fear and imagination, I couldn't say.

We quickly left Castle Rock's well-lit streets for the deeper shadows of Kalimna Park. There was little indication of life in the immediate area—even the crickets were silent.

Once past the outskirts of the park and completely alone, we stopped and swung our packs off. Belle pulled out Redfern's clothes and quickly changed, while I carefully retrieved the small gemstone we'd attached the glamour spell to from its secure canister and examined it. Belle's spell formation was seamless, with no faults or fissures that I could see. But the true test would come not on the spell's activation, but whether it held up against Waverley's magic.

Belle stuffed her clothes into the pack, tucked it between the exposed roots of an old gum tree, and cast a quick spell so she could find it again later. She pulled off one of her boots—the style of which was basic enough to pass as men's footwear rather than women's—and then her sock. I handed her the stone. She placed it underneath a couple of toes and put her footwear back on.

She adjusted her boot a little and then raised a hand and began the activation incantation. As the power of the trees and the earth stirred in response and began to weave through the spell, strengthening it, her form flickered—an effect that reminded me somewhat of a television not quite tuned right. As the spell neared its peak, the glamour rolled up her body, concealing her form under the portrait of another. When it reached the top of her head, the force of the spell faded, becoming little more than a barely noticeable background buzz.

The person who stood in front of me now was a thinly built man with a pockmarked face, sallow cheeks, and receding gray hair. Morris Redfern, exactly as he'd appeared in the photograph Blume had given us.

"Move around," I instructed.

She turned and walked away several steps. A tree

branch tugged at her borrowed shirt, but the glamour didn't react to either the branch's encroachment or to her movement. There wasn't even the slightest shimmer.

"I think this glamour might be one of your best spells ever, Belle."

"It needs to be to fool Waverley."

Her voice remained the same—a glamour could only change the *perception* of appearance, which meant Belle wouldn't be able to speak once we got into that clearing.

"Your turn now," she added. "Call the wild magic."

"Not until we get closer."

And not *just* because the less time I had to contain it within me, the better it would be for my survival rate, but because we had no real idea what was going to happen when I *did* call to it. We really were stepping into uncharted waters in even attempting this.

I pulled the sharpened stakes from the backpack and handed two to Belle. While ash, rowan, oak, or hawthorn were generally accepted as the best woods to use for staking vampires—at least according to wisdom in the book of vampires Belle's granny had left her—all we'd had on hand was birch. It was generally used in cleansing rituals or to calm emotions, but in the past it had also been ascribed the ability to expel evil spirits.

And evil was certainly an apt description for our vampire.

Belle placed her two under her loose shirtsleeves, holding them in place with the help of two thin rubber bands. I did the same, and then tucked a third one—pointy end up—into the waist of my jeans behind my back.

Which left only a couple of charms, and two warding potions contained in fragile glass. I shoved the charms in my pockets and then carefully slung the pack over my shoulder and continued up the road.

Where it quickly became evident there would be no need to call the wild magic. It was coming to us.

And it was—yet again—very, *very* angry.

"Fucking hell," Belle whispered. "It really *is* aware."

"Yeah." I flexed my fingers, trying to ease not only tension but also the odd and unexpected tingle heating their tips. It was almost as if the wild forces were already gathering around them. "The question is, is that sentience coming from the wild magic itself, or from whatever Gabe has done to it?"

She hesitated. "There's definitely some sort of outside force woven into its fibers, but I'm not sensing it's specifically male. And surely we would, given wild magic is inherently ascribed as a feminine force."

"Except that what we're dealing with here is a rather large and well-developed wellspring," I said. "So if Gabe *did* weave some sort of spell into or around it, its presence will be muted by the sheer force that surrounds it."

"Maybe." She frowned. "Let's just hope that whatever the reason, it doesn't interfere with our plans."

And if it did…. I firmly thrust the rest of that thought away. I really didn't want to think of the possible consequences in any way, shape, or form right now.

The darkness grew heavier as the trees closed in on the road, their arching branches inhibiting the moon's light but not its power. Like the wild magic, it sang through my veins, but it was a power that wouldn't help us when it came to our confrontation with Waverley. Given he was a witch as much as a vampire, he'd be feeling the moon's strength as keenly as either of us.

We followed the road for another half a mile or so

before instinct stirred and I slowed, looking for the path I'd taken the last two times I'd journeyed up to that clearing. After a few seconds, I spotted it, and headed in. As the shadows deepened to ink, I once again stopped.

The time had come.

I pulled off my footwear, shoved my socks into my boots, and then tied them to my backpack. After digging my toes into the soft soil to both ground myself and to provide a deeper connection with the force I was about to call up, I took a deep breath and simply said, *Come to me.*

For several seconds, nothing happened. My fingertips continued to burn, but the sentient force that had been trailing us since we'd entered this place neither responded nor retreated.

I flung my arms out and repeated the plea.

It came.

And with such force that I staggered back several steps. All I felt, all I could see, was the energy that poured into me. It stretched the very fibers of my being to the point of unviability, until it seemed inevitable that I would shatter into a thousand different pieces, becoming just a soul locked within the force I had called.

But just as the point of no return loomed, the magic snapped away and I returned to myself. My entire body trembled with physical weakness, but there was nothing weak about the force now residing within me. The sheer weight of it—the sheer *power* of it—was frightening. It was the fiercest storm ever created, a volcano on the verge of eruption, the heat of the ground under my feet and strength of the forest around us. No human was ever meant to contain this sort of power. No human was ever meant to control it.

And it was in me.

A part of me.

And as angry as all fuck.

At Waverly. At what he had done. At what he was *now* doing.

I had control, but I had to wonder for how long. The wild magic—or whatever was causing the cognizance we were sensing within it—wanted to erase his presence from not just this reservation, but from the world itself.

But the wellspring could be irrevocably stained by such an action—and that was the one thing we desperately needed to avoid.

I took a deep breath that did little to ease the growing fear and trepidation, and glanced around at Belle.

Her face was pale and her expression filled with a mix of awe and fear. "Your eyes... they're glowing silver."

"It shouldn't be a problem, given I've the coloring of a blueblood and he hasn't seen me. I'm only surprised the rest of me isn't glowing." The words came out scratchy— harsh. My throat was raw and burned, and I had a very bad feeling the rest of me would soon be in a similar state if I didn't quickly release the wild magic. "We'd better go."

She nodded. I turned and led the way. Despite the utter darkness, I could see as clearly as if it were day. Our progress was faster than any other time I'd come through here, simply because no trees or shrubs snagged at us—the branches simply drew back as we approached, giving us an unhindered path to follow.

The wild magic was ensuring we reached the clearing as quickly as possible.

The ground once again began to slope upwards and up ahead, flickering through the trees, was a warm, golden light. The teasing hint of smoke on the air told me it was from a fire rather than from a wisp or even magic. *That* suggested he was concentrating all his endeavors on containment and whatever other spells he might have waiting for us.

Ready? I asked silently.

As I'll ever be. Her mental tone was flat, but I could feel both her fear and determination. *If I don't survive this… it has been an honor to be both your friend and your familiar. May the next life grant us a continuation of both.*

Tears stung my eyes and I silently—but fiercely—hugged her. She wasn't just my friend and familiar, she was my soul sister, and the only reason I was standing here today. The thought of losing her—of going on without her—tore me apart. It simply wasn't possible.

After several seconds, she gently pulled away and motioned me to go on. I brushed the tears from my eyes and did so.

The golden light grew brighter, but there was darkness in this place now, a darkness that had nothing to do with the night. It wasn't just coming from the man who waited for us up ahead, but also from the spells he'd woven around the clearing. Those threads were thick and ugly, and clung with tiny tendrils to the trees that lined the clearing, as if unable to support their own weight.

Holy fuck, dark doesn't even begin to describe the feel of that stuff, Belle said. *If I didn't know better, I'd think hell itself had been exhumed.*

I once read that the more blood used in spellwork, the deeper the connection to hell. It is, after all, what awaits them on death. I stopped just short of the spell threads and scanned the clearing. I couldn't immediately see either Waverley or Aiden, which suggested they were standing on the other side of the huge bonfire burning in the center of the clearing. *Are you sensing anyone else in the immediate vicinity?*

No. She paused. *Aiden's in a whole world of pain. He's barely conscious.*

At least he was still alive. I'd half expected it to be otherwise. Of course, just because he was alive didn't mean he would remain that way for long.

"Let's get this show on the road." I pressed the button on Blume's watch to start recording, saw Belle do the same with the phone, and then as one we strode forward.

Straight into the heart of Waverley's magic.

Straight into his trap.

CHAPTER
thirteen

We might have done everything we could to brace ourselves against his magic, might have done everything we could to counter his spells, but there was no way we could ever have understood or appreciated the sheer depths of depravity and power of it. Not until we'd stepped into it.

It was unlike anything I'd ever felt before—a living thing that tore at every part of me. It was hundreds of needle-sharp claws ripping into my skin and burrowing into my body. Pinpricks of blood began to dot my skin and stain my clothes as the invading threads dug deeper and deeper, as if trying to reach the very heart of me.

Fear surged, overwhelming the pain as realization hit. This spell *wasn't* trying to kill me. It was attempting to do something far worse.

It was trying to tear my magic away from my soul.

A single wave of power broke away from the force

that resided within me and washed through the layers of my being. It wrapped around each of those tiny claws and stilled them in an instant. Then—slowly, and almost lovingly—it crushed them, until there was nothing left but the ashes of ill intent.

While Waverley's magic might have failed in its ultimate task, the remaining threads of it still spun all around me. It was a foul and suppressive weight that had my body trembling and my knees buckling under its force. I somehow managed to lock them and remain upright, but between the wild magic within me and the dark threads pressing down on me, I wasn't sure how much longer that was going to be the case.

I shook my head, trying to clear it, and tried a simple healing incantation—one of the very first spells taught in witch schools. Nothing happened. My magic was still within me—I could feel it stirring, trying to respond—but a barrier had now been placed between us.

I swore and swiped at the sweat dribbling down the side of my face. The claws might have been contained, but it still felt as if a thousand tiny ants were biting at my skin. Only this time it wasn't the blood magic but rather the wild. It wanted out.

Desperately.

A sharp hiss had my head snapping sideways. The glamour was still in place, but Belle's fists were clenched and her thoughts were ablaze with pain.

I wanted to reach out, to offer both comfort and strength, but I didn't have enough of the latter and I certainly didn't dare touch her. The glamour might be holding against whatever exclusions Waverly had woven into his spells, but something as simple as a light touch might just shatter it.

I'm okay. Her gaze met mine; determination and fury gleamed in the silver depths. *We can beat this bastard. He may be magically stronger than us, but he's also overconfident. That will be his downfall.*

You're reading him?

In bits and bobs. Not enough to attempt any sort of mental control.

Damn. *And your magic?*

Unhampered. But I didn't throw up a mental wall fast enough, and got caught in the backwash that was hitting you.

Fuck, I didn't even think to—

Like you had the time. But you were right—my magic alone will not counter his.

It might be enough to help Aiden, though. And right now, that was all I was worried about. *Keep your eyes down, Belle. The glamour isn't quite reaching them.*

Well, fuck. She instantly looked at the ground. *Is it failing anywhere else?*

No.

"So nice of you to join us, Lizzie," Waverley said, so unexpectedly I jumped. "I can call you Lizzie, can't I?"

He was, as I'd presumed, standing on the far side of the fire. Sitting on the ground beside him, his hands tied securely around a tree with a thick piece of wire, was Aiden.

He looked like death warmed over. His skin was gray, and sweat poured down his face and soaked his shirt. I couldn't immediately see the reason, as he didn't appear to be wounded, and other than the gash that stretched across his forehead from his right temple, there was little blood.

And then I spotted something sticking out of his shoulder—something that looked a lot like a small letter opener. One that gleamed brightly in the firelight.

Silver. It was made of silver.

No wonder there wasn't any blood. The silver blade would have cauterized the wound even as it slid into his flesh. He was in no danger of dying from blood loss, but he certainly *could* die from silver poisoning.

And very quickly.

The wild magic was roiling within me, eager for release—to rend and tear. Something very strange was going on here—something that was more than mere sentience. The emotions I sensed were *human*, even if they were wrapped within the wilder energy of this world.

And *that* was not only dangerous, but there was a very real risk of staining.

I clenched my fists and silently explained to the awareness within the wild magic why its goal had to be containment rather than killing. I had no idea whether it could—or would—listen to me, but I had to at least try. The angry stirring within me didn't ease, but it didn't pour out and attack Waverley, either.

"You can call me Lizzie, as long as you don't mind me calling you Waverley. Or would you prefer Frederick?"

Surprise briefly broke through the smugness. "It would appear someone has been in contact with the registrar. That does make things a little more awkward."

"Indeed," I said. "Especially given they aren't exactly pleased about your exploits here."

Aiden raised his head as I spoke. Though his expression was tight with pain, there was nothing but fury in the blue depths of his eyes.

"Fuck, Liz," he growled. "What the hell are you doing here?"

"Saving your life." I dug my nails deeper into my palms as the wild magic twisted and churned inside. Those ants weren't just biting now, they were burning. Any fiercer and I'd start melting.

"Not at the cost of another, for fuck's sake."

Waverley kicked him hard enough to draw a hiss of pain. "Shut the hell up, my dear ranger. This conversation doesn't involve you. Though I will admit that I am, like you, somewhat surprised at Redfern's presence here this evening."

Sweat glinted off Aiden's lashes as he continued to glare at me, but a heartbeat later his eyes went wide. Belle had just told him to shut up and play along.

I stopped several feet short of the bonfire. Its heat rolled over me, a warm caress that did little to ease the growing chill in my body—a chill not even the violent presence of the wild magic could erase.

"Why? Isn't that what you asked me to do?"

"Indeed. I just didn't think you'd give in so easily." His gaze narrowed as it flicked to Belle. "There is magic around him."

I smiled, though it held little in the way of satisfaction. He might not have sensed the reason for that magic, but there was no guarantee it would remain that way. "You surely didn't think I was going to make it *that* easy on you, did you?"

"Indeed, but I have measures in place—"

"Indeed," I echoed. "But such measures were designed to render any attempt of spellwork *within* its boundaries inert. It wasn't designed to counter spells created outside of it, was it now?"

A delighted smile creased his features. "Bravo, Lizzie. I'm almost saddened by the thought of having to kill you."

"If I die, Redfern dies," I said evenly. "And you forgo your chance of revenge."

His amusement deepened. "What makes you think I'd care? All I want in the end is his death."

"If that were true, you could have killed them all months ago, rather than concocting such elaborate plans to make them all suffer *before* you murdered them."

"That is also true."

He took a step toward me, and that was when I saw the fishing wire that was looped around Aiden's neck. It had snapped taut when Waverley moved, and though it wasn't cutting deep enough yet to cause major damage, blood was beginning to trickle down Aiden's neck.

But that wire wasn't the only thing connecting the two men. Twining around the fishing line was a needle-fine black thread—something I shouldn't have seen in the darkness. I narrowed my gaze and, after a heartbeat, I realized what it was—a rebound spell.

Any attack we made on Waverley would be felt by Aiden—and *that* meant it was even more imperative we got him out of harm's way before we tried anything against Waverley.

"If you want Redfern, then release Aiden." My voice was surprisingly even considering the turmoil in my body and the toll it was beginning to take. It wasn't just the ants now—my muscles trembled and even my bones began to ache. Everything felt like it was turning to mush. Perhaps I was *actually* melting. "Once he's free of this clearing, we'll deal."

Waverley laughed. "You, my dear witch, are in no position to barter right now."

There's someone sneaking up behind us, Belle said. *He's armed.*

I reached into my left pocket and wrapped my fingers around the charm. *Location?*

If Waverley is standing one o'clock, then our sneaky thug is at seven.

"Oh, but I am," I said to Waverley. "And will be for as long as I hold the strings of Redfern's life in my hands."

With that, I turned and threw the charm into the forest. There was a brief retort and then someone started screaming—it was a high-pitched sound that was both fear and confusion.

But then, suddenly seeing a dozen or more hairy huntsman spiders crawling all over you often had that sort of effect.

Waverley's moving, Belle warned.

I immediately swung back around. Waverley had taken several steps closer and the garrote had again tightened. Blood ringed Aiden's neck and stained his shirt collar.

"Release the ranger, and you get what you want," I said bluntly. "It's as simple as that."

"I will not fucking leave you to face this madman alone." Aiden's voice was raw—harsh—but the anger pulsing from him wasn't aimed at me. It was aimed at the situation, and at his own helplessness.

"You, Ranger, will do precisely as ordered. This fight is *not* yours. It was *never* yours." My words were almost as harsh and as pain-filled as his. I needed this ended and quickly, otherwise our small chance of surviving would melt away as quickly as my strength was beginning to.

Waverley studied me for several seconds before his gaze flicked to Belle. His eyes narrowed and, for one terrifying moment, I thought he'd seen through our ruse. My heart was racing so hard now it felt ready to tear out of my chest—and maybe that played to our favor. As a vampire, he'd hear the siren call of it, even from where he was standing, and it would suggest fear rather than confidence. Artlessness rather than scheming.

"Fine," he said abruptly. "We'll play it your way for the time being."

He pulled a knife from his pocket and moved back to Aiden, first cutting the ropes that bound him to the tree, and then the wire. It remained embedded in his neck, as Aiden made no move to remove it. He was too busy fighting unconsciousness after the sudden release of his wounded arm had jarred the silver letter opener in his shoulder.

My psychic senses were at least in working order. It was a shame one of us didn't have telekinesis—it would have been a useful skill in a situation like this.

He shoved the knife away then grabbed Aiden by his good arm and roughly hauled him upright. Aiden hissed and his face went grayer. He was barely holding on. I crossed mental fingers that he had enough strength to get out of the clearing—out of harm's way.

Except for one thing—Waverley's rebound spell hadn't been severed along with the wire.

Fuck, fuck, *fuck*....

"You may leave, Ranger."

"Except that he can't," I said. "I may not be able to create magic, but I can still see it, vampire. Kill the rebound spell that holds the ranger in your power, or I'll follow through with my threat."

He studied me for several too-long seconds, and then murmured an incantation. Power surged, a dark sensation that had my skin crawling, and the black thread connecting him to Aiden disintegrated. Relief stirred, but it wasn't as if he was actually safe yet.

"Go," Waverly said, and pushed Aiden forward so

hard he stumbled for several steps before he caught his balance.

Just for an instant, our gazes locked.

He had *no* intention of leaving.

Belle—

On it.

But even as she reached for Aiden's thoughts, Waverly made his move. There was a flick of power, and then flames erupted from the bonfire, a huge wall of heat that reached for the treetops and cut the two men from sight. Belle and I jumped back to avoid getting burned, but the fire snagged the edge of her jacket and it went up in a huge whoosh. She cursed and quickly stripped it off and threw it to the ground... and then looked at me in horror.

From the other side of the fire, there was a roar of fury. Waverley had heard her. He knew.

The wild magic poured from me, a violent wash of energy against which even fire gave way. I caught its tail, demanding restraint rather than death, but I had no idea if it was in any way paying attention to me now.

A shot rang out and I froze, my heart beating somewhere in my throat as I waited for the thump of body hitting the ground.

There was nothing to be heard other than the roar of the fire.

Nothing to see except movement to our right.

Waverley, coming at us so fast he was little more than a blur.

I shoved Belle sideways, reached for the stake behind my back, and lunged forward to meet him. He saw it at the last possible moment and threw himself sideways. The stake stabbed through his side rather than his black heart. He rolled to his feet and staggered away, the smell of burning flesh stinging the air even as he ripped the birch free and threw it on the ground.

I grabbed another one. *Belle, get Aiden and get out of here.*

I won't fucking leave you here with—

It's an order, Belle. Go.

I didn't often give her orders—in fact, I couldn't even remember the last time I *had*—but she had no choice in the matter when I did. Her fury and frustration hit me but I slammed my mental barriers down hard and swung the backpack off my shoulder.

At that moment, Waverley turned and raised a gun.

Without thought, I dropped the pack, threw myself at Belle, and knocked her away. The bullet aimed at her spine punched through my upper arm, and sent me spinning. I hit the ground hard, and so damn close to the fire that my clothes and hair began to singe.

Before I could move, a hand twisted around my hair and hauled me upright. I yelled in pain and fury, and lashed backward with the stake. He dodged the blow without releasing me, then caught my hand in his and ripped the birch from my grip.

Then he pulled me close, his grip viselike. I couldn't move. I could barely even breathe. Blood was dripping from my fingertips, pain was white-hot heat pounding through me, and my vision was fading in and out.

"Using the wild magic was a clever move." Waverley's teeth grazed my neck as he spoke. "But it perhaps would have been wise to order it to protect you rather than the wolf and your friend."

And with that, he tore at my neck and began to feed. I screamed and, with every ounce of metaphysical strength I had left, reached for the wild magic.

It came.

Not from the force I'd carried into the clearing, but rather from the trees and the ground and the air itself. There was no sense of sentience within it this time; there was simply power. Mind-blowing, incredible power.

Waverley gave no indication that he sensed its rise, not even when energy wound around the two of us. He was too far down the path of blood rapture, just as Maelle had said.

When the wild force had totally surrounded us, it grabbed Waverley, pulled his teeth from my flesh, and then flung him across the clearing. Wisps of power touched both the bite and the wound on my shoulder, and the blood flow instantly stemmed. I was still shaking with weakness and pain, and there was an odd disconnect gathering speed in my brain, but I was alive and upright.

And I still had a vampire to kill.

I pulled the last stake from underneath my sleeve and slowly, but carefully, turned around.

Waverley was suspended in the air, three feet off the ground. The wild magic pulsed around him, a cage that rippled with all the colors of creation. Anger contorted his features and the black threads of his magic began to twist and tear at his prison. They had little effect.

He'd obviously used most of his strength on the spells that guarded this place; otherwise, he would not have used a gun against us rather than magic. And even though he'd fed from me, it had not been enough to boost his strength for long.

As the black threads faded and his spelling stopped, I took a step. But my legs felt like jelly and simply gave out. Pain reverberated through me as my knees hit the ground, and I sucked in air, fighting the deepening call of unconsciousness.

If I couldn't get to Waverley, then he'd have to come to me.

"Loop the fishing wire around his neck and his feet," I ordered. "Then bring him to me."

Again the wild magic obeyed. Waverley was brought forward and then forced into a sitting position in front of me. The fishing wire appeared, and was quickly wound around his neck and his feet.

He didn't say anything. He simply glared at me as the wire got tighter and tighter, until a gaping wound appeared and blood washed down his neck.

"Tie the wire off then release your hold on him," I continued. The wild magic could not be involved in his death in *any* way. I had no idea if it could be stained by something as simple as holding evil still while I erased its presence from this place, but I sure as hell wasn't going to take the chance

As the powerful rainbow somewhat reluctantly pulled away, I pressed the stake against Waverley's heart. Though his shirt lay between the birch and his skin, it didn't remain that way for long. As the material smoldered away to reveal his flesh to the sharp point, I said, "This is for Karen, Mason, Marjorie, and Anna. May you rot in hell for all eternity for the pain and the suffering you inflicted on them."

And with every ounce of strength I had left, I shoved the stake deep into his heart.

He didn't scream. He didn't get the chance. His body simply burst into flame and consumed him.

But even as hell reached for his soul with eager fingers, the unconsciousness I'd been fighting finally overcame me, and I knew no more.

Epilogue

They kept me in hospital under observation for five long days. It wasn't my arm they were worried about—even though the bullet had gouged out a good chunk of flesh that would result in a decent scar, it was still just a flesh wound.

They weren't even worried about the blood loss—a transfusion had fixed that easily enough.

It was the damn vampire bite that concerned them—or, more precisely, the possibility of serious infection. Apparently, more than half of the people who actually survived vampire attacks subsequently wasted away within a couple of days.

Happily, I wasn't one of those people, though I suspected the wild magic had a whole lot to do with that. Aside from being so damn tired I could barely move without needing several hours of sleep to recover, there'd been no lasting side effects from carrying the wild magic within my body. There had, however, been at least one physical change—my green eyes were now ringed by silver. A silver that ran with the colors of all creation.

If that was the only price I paid, then I'd gotten out

of the whole experience very lightly. And if it wasn't, well, I'd worry about that when the time came. Right now, I was simply glad to be alive.

As the sixth morning rolled around, they finally cleared me to leave, though they gave me a bucketload of antibiotics and orders to take it easy for another couple of weeks. I rang Belle to let her know, and then carefully climbed out of bed and got dressed. After which I sat back down and tried to curb my impatience.

Footsteps finally approached the room. I grabbed my bag and headed for the door. "About bloody time—"

The rest of the comment died on my lips. It wasn't Belle who'd come to pick me up. It was Aiden.

"You," I all but blurted, even as I came to an abrupt halt. His right arm was in a sling, but he otherwise looked as fit and healthy as ever.

A smile touched the corners of his eyes, warming both them and me. "Alive and in person, thanks to you."

"Hardly just me." My gaze dropped briefly to the sling. His arm didn't appear to be bandaged, but that didn't really mean anything given silver ate away at a werewolf's flesh and muscle even as it poisoned their blood. "How bad is it?"

"They're saying that if I keep doing the physical therapy, I'll regain full use." His mouth twisted. "I have, unfortunately, been placed on damn sick leave until that happens."

I frowned. "Then why are you here?"

That eyebrow rose once again, but this time, there was only amusement evident. "You need a lift home, do you not?"

"I do, but Belle—"

"Asked me to do the honors," he said. "I was

indulging in a cup of coffee and several of those addictive brownies when she got your call. You'll be pleased to hear the place is packed."

"No doubt the gossip brigade is trying to figure out what exactly happened last week."

"We're on a total news lockdown, so I wish them luck." He turned and offered me his good arm. "Shall we?"

I hesitated briefly, and then hooked my arm through his. His scent spun around me, warm, musky, and enticing, and I had to clamp down on the stirrings of desire. But the smile that teased the corners of his lips told me he'd caught it.

He didn't say anything, however, and simply escorted me out of the hospital. At least the silence was a companionable one, with little evidence of the enmity that had accompanied our first meeting. Granted, *that* had been under extenuating circumstances, but still… it was a nice development.

He led me toward an old Ford wagon rather than his truck. He must have caught my surprise, because he opened the door and said, "I borrowed it from a friend— it's automatic, and easier to manage when you only have one good arm."

"Sensible."

"I can be on rare occasions." He helped me in, put my overnight bag in the rear, and then climbed into the driver seat.

"Have you heard how Anna is?" I asked.

"They transferred her down to Melbourne." He carefully reversed out of the parking space. "But they're saying the burns aren't as bad as they initially appeared— she only required a minor skin graft."

"I'm so glad," I said, even as I wondered if the holy water had been behind that miraculous recovery. "What about Blume?"

"He left the day after he took your statement." He hesitated. "Hart's funeral was yesterday. Two council elders attended."

"I thought the elders hated the IIT?"

"They do, but Hart died in the course of doing his duty here on the reservation. It would be unjust to both his memory and to the sacrifice he made not to attend."

I nodded and glanced at the window. It was odd, but now that the danger was over, I wasn't entirely sure how to act in his presence. He might appear relaxed, but there was still a deeper wariness in him.

We arrived at the café all too soon. I gripped the door handle as he came to a stop, and said, "You coming in for another coffee? My shout."

He hesitated. "I can't."

"Ah." Well then. "Thanks for the lift home—"

He reached across and placed his hand on my leg. A giveaway tremor raced through me, and once again a smile tugged at his lips. But the wariness sharpened in his eyes.

"I have an appointment I can't get out of, otherwise I would," he said. "But how about dinner when you're feeling stronger?"

My pulse stuttered for several seconds and then jumped into overdrive.

"If you're feeling the need to thank me, forget it." I forced a smile. "I was only doing what any witch would do in the same situation."

Any seriously insane witch, that was.

"I doubt most witches would quite go to the lengths you did—"

KERI ARTHUR

"Yeah, because they'd actually have the talent and skills to deal with Waverley without ever letting the situation get so out of control." My voice was dry. "Shout me a beer at Émigré next time we're all there."

"You're not going to make this easy, are you?" he muttered, and then took a deep breath. "Lizzie Grace, I very much would like to take you to dinner as soon as you're well enough."

I blinked. "But I'm a witch. You hate witches."

"Apparently," he said, voice dry and amusement glittering in his blue eyes, "not as much as I thought I did."

"So this is a date?" That edge of incredulousness remained in my voice. "You're actually asking me out on a date?"

"I am indeed." He lifted his hand from my leg and lightly brushed my cheek. "You might be a witch, but you're also a strong, stubborn, intriguing, beautiful, annoying woman I'd really like to know better."

I laughed. "With a statement like that, how can I resist? Ring me tomorrow, and we'll talk."

"I look forward to it."

So did I.

With a somewhat silly grin on my face, I got out, grabbed my overnight bag from the rear seat, and all but skipped into the café.

About the Author

Keri Arthur, author of the New York Times bestselling Riley Jenson Guardian series, has now written more than thirty-seven novels. She's received several nominations in the Best Contemporary Paranormal category of the Romantic Times Reviewers Choice Awards and has won RT's Career Achievement Award for urban fantasy. She lives with her daughter in Melbourne, Australia.

31086683R00200

Printed in Poland
by Amazon Fulfillment
Poland Sp. z o.o., Wrocław